Don't
Ask

MIROLAND IMPRINT 34

Guernica Editions Inc. acknowledges the support of the Canada Council
for the Arts and the Ontario Arts Council. The Ontario Arts Council
is an agency of the Government of Ontario.
We acknowledge the financial support of the Government of Canada.

Don't
Ask

Gina Roitman

MiroLand
p u b l i s h e r s

MIROLAND (GUERNICA)
TORONTO • CHICAGO • BUFFALO • LANCASTER (U.K.)
2022

Antonio D'Alfonso, Guernica Founder

Connie McParland, Michael Mirolla, series editors
Sonia Di Placido, editor
Cover design, Rafael Chimicatti
Interior design, David Moratto
Guernica Editions Inc.
287 Templemead Drive, Hamilton, ON L8W 2W4
2250 Military Road, Tonawanda, N.Y. 14150-6000 U.S.A.
www.guernicaeditions.com

Distributors:
Independent Publishers Group (IPG)
600 North Pulaski Road, Chicago IL 60624
University of Toronto Press Distribution (UTP)
5201 Dufferin Street, Toronto (ON), Canada M3H 5T8
Gazelle Book Services
White Cross Mills, High Town, Lancaster LA1 4XS U.K.

First edition.
Printed in Canada.

Legal Deposit—First Quarter
Library of Congress Catalog Card Number: 2021949330
Library and Archives Canada Cataloguing in Publication
Title: Don't ask / Gina Roitman.
Names: Roitman, Gina, 1948- author.
Description: First edition.
Identifiers: Canadiana (print) 20210357800 |
Canadiana (ebook) 20210357819 | ISBN 9781771837118 (softcover) |
ISBN 9781771837125 (EPUB)
Classification: LCC PS8635.O443 D66 2022 | DDC C813/.6—dc23

For Benjamin and Jacob,
and Axel for your abiding patience,
support, and love.

Give sorrow words;
the grief that does not speak knits up the o-er wrought
heart and bids it break.
   —**William Shakespeare**, *Macbeth*

Glossary

A

Aroise gevorfeneh gelt Wasted money

B

Bist du eine Yideneh? Are you a Jewish woman?
Bratkartoffeln Home fries
Bundesstrasse Federal highway

D

Der Todesengel Angel of Death
Du bist eine narish kindt You are a foolish child

F

Feigelach Gays
Ferd Horse
Fetter Uncle
Fit wie ein Turnschuh In fine form

G

Geschichteh Story
Gotteinu God in heaven

H

Aleva ha'shalom May she rest in peace
Hilfspolizei Auxiliary police

K

Kaffeefahrt Leisurely drive
Köln Cologne

M

Maidel Girl
Meine teireh tochter My dear daughter
Mein Gott My God
Minyan A quorum of ten Jewish men required for prayer

N

Nicht müglich Not possible
Nisht tzu gloiben Not to be believed
Nu? Well?

O

Oberstleutnant Lieutenant colonel

P

Paskudniak *Contemptible or nasty person*
Parshah *Weekly Torah portion*
Puchineh kohldreh *Feather comforter*

Q

Quatsch Nonsense
Qvelling Taking pleasure

R

Rotkohl Red cabbage
Rundes yahr Round year (birthday marking a new decade)

S

Sauber Clean
Schvantz Penis
Schvartze Blacks
Shprintzeh Leah Coddled woman
Shtickel Piece
Sympatiche Genteel, Empathic, Responsive

T

Tovarishchi Comrades

V

Vati Father
Vilde chayeh Wild animal

W

Weihnachtsmarkt Christmas market

Z

Zhid Jew

Introduction

An old Jewish joke goes something like this: Every weekday, month after month, year after year, two men stand waiting for the bus to go to work.

After many, many years, one man suddenly turns to the other and quietly says, "Excuse me but I don't understand something. More than twenty years now, we stand at this bus stop every day, waiting in silence for the bus, and not once did you ever look at me and speak. You've never said, 'Hello. How are you? Let me introduce myself. My name is …' More than twenty years! Not a word."

Surprised by the sudden confrontation and feeling a little guilty, the man says, "You're right, 110 per cent! I'm embarrassed. This is a shame. Twenty years and never one word between us. This minute, let us change that." And he stretches out his hand. "My name is Sam. Nice to make your acquaintance."

Taking the outstretched hand, the man says, "Bennie, my name is Bennie."

"Bennie. Wonderful, wonderful!" Sam exclaims. "So, how are you?"

"Ach," Bennie replies, "don't ask."

HANNAH
AUGUST 2000

CHAPTER ONE

She was running late. Punctuality was one of her mother's many obsessions but Hannah, afflicted by an elastic sense of time, had never mastered Rokhl's rule. She remembered well one of the first notes Rokhl had written in what eventually became their common mode of communication. It had read: *When there was roll call in Auschwitz, late one minute meant dead the next.*

Hannah shouldn't have taken that last phone call, but the client had said he needed to speak to her immediately. Her best friend, Marilyn, maintained that Hannah was incapable of saying no to anyone who claimed to need her. "You're a real estate agent, Hannah, a real estate agent, not a brain surgeon." Friends since childhood, Marilyn had an annoying way of repeating certain phrases for emphasis. "Nobody will die if you don't respond immediately, nobody."

If she hadn't taken the call maybe she wouldn't be stuck in the stifling August heat, chewing on her cuticles, and endlessly replaying the fight she and her mother had had the night before. It had left Hannah deeply shaken. Open disagreement between them was as rare as motherly hugs. Long ago, Hannah had recognized that her mother wore silence as protective gear against the world. Sometimes that silence was a body shield, sometimes a sound barrier to force Hannah into silence as well. Last night, however, Rokhl had raised her voice for the first time in Hannah's memory. The transformation in the woman who did nothing out of character for all of her 45 years had left Hannah shaken.

When she was a child, Hannah had believed that Rokhl's voice was impaired, that it was physically unable to project above a certain soft range, and that using it too often was painful for Rokhl. But last night, her mother gave lie to that with a keening wail not heard even upon the death of Hannah's father, Barak. It grew like a siren gathering strength and turned into a shrill, high-pitched harangue. It demanded that Hannah must not, under any circumstances, ever travel to Germany. Stunned by her mother's new faculty for making herself heard, Hannah hastily made a promise. This morning, however, she was uncertain whether she could keep it. On her way to pick-up Rokhl for a doctor's appointment, traffic had crept at a maddeningly slow pace. It was almost as if unseen forces were aware of Hannah's reluctance to face her mother.

In an effort to drown out a replay of the previous night's scene, Hannah had turned on the radio and was not surprised that there'd been an accident. Likely, everyone was taking their turn gawking at the disaster. What was this human compulsion, Hannah wondered, not for the first time, to bear witness to the misfortune of others? It was as if by surveying a calamity people imagined they could protect themselves from it. For her, it was a point of honour never to look.

Finally able to head off the expressway, Hannah accelerated down Barclay imagining Rokhl sitting in the front hall, twisting a tissue and staring balefully at the door. She pulled into the driveway of what she still thought of as her father's house although Barak had been dead for two years. The stop was so abrupt her tires squealed—the screech tracing a shiver down Hannah's sweaty spine, but when she opened the car door a blast of August heat momentarily knocked her back into the cool interior.

Recovering her nerve, she hurried up the crumbling concrete steps of the duplex—her spike heel catching in a crack as it had done so many times before. Nanoseconds before her knee made contact with the cement, she managed to regain her balance. Saved, she thought, although a battered knee was preferable to the bruised look she knew was on her mother's face when she walked into the house. Hannah peered through the curtained window of the door then fumbled the key into the lock. *Click.* Click? That was the sound the bolt made when sliding shut—the door was open! Hannah's brain was working hard to compute the information. Rokhl's door was always locked. The August heat pressed against Hannah's back, her blouse clinging to her like a frightened child. She leaned her forehead on the wood for a moment, turned the key again and pushed the door open entering the cool of the tiny vestibule. The old, flowered wallpaper exhaled its familiar dusty odour with a slight hint of mould. Since her father's death, her parents' home seemed to be decaying more rapidly.

"Ma?" she called out, entering the damp gloom. "Rokhl?" Her voice rustled through the flat like a broom on a linoleum floor. Sweat mushroomed on Hannah's upper lip as her eyes darted into the dim hallway.

"Ma?" she called again, heading for the kitchen.

If Rokhl had left in a fury without her, there would be a note. But after checking all the familiar places: the front of the fridge, the tray under Rokhl's myriad of medications, the utility drawer with the carefully separated rubber bands, twist ties, and ball of string, each time, Hannah came up empty. *What is the matter with you?* Her father's words echoed in the still air of the hallway. *You are our only child; the only family your mother has left. You are supposed to watch over and care for her. What she lived through in her life you'll never know. Don't ask. But know you are all she has. Promise me you will watch over Rokhl when I'm gone. Promise me!*

How many times had Barak hammered those words into her head, especially in the final stages of his cancer? Hannah reasoned that Rokhl must have left in a panic over being late for her appointment. If anything happened to her mother, it was Hannah's fault. She should have been on time. But where is the note? Hannah took a tissue from her purse and dabbed at her brow and upper lip. The house was stifling hot despite the semi-gloom, but she forced herself to calm down and think. If Rokhl had taken the bus to get to the doctor's appointment (a taxi being reserved strictly for life-or-death matters), she would still have left a note. There was *always* a note.

Hannah went back into the hall. Uncertain, she stood a moment scanning the uniformly beige walls for some inspiration. The decor in the duplex was sparse; a few cast off prints from Hannah's first apartment were a sad attempt to introduce some colour but what still dominated was a family photo. It had been taken in a studio on Park Avenue when she was four. In it, Barak stands relaxed in an impeccable pinstripe suit; Hannah in a white blouse, a box-pleat skirt and a white satin bow almost lost in the sea of her dense, copper curls and Rokhl also in a white blouse buttoned to the neck in a dark, fitted jacket that shows off her tiny waist. Although facing forward, Rokhl isn't looking into the camera. Instead, her eyes are locked on her husband with an expression Hannah was never able to interpret. Positioned between the two of them, Hannah had been made to sit on a stool but appeared to be straining forward as if ready to bolt. She had refused a smile despite the photographer's best efforts to cajole one out of her. To this day, she still hated having her picture taken.

Frustrated, Hannah sat down at the wrought iron telephone table with its old black, rotary dial phone. Rokhl would not hear of replacing it saying that it was still perfectly good. Eventually, Hanna had stopped trying to get her to change her mind. She lifted the receiver and called the doctor's office, waiting impatiently for each turn of the rotary dial to be completed.

"Hi Betty," Hannah said when Dr. Rubin's nurse finally answered. "I'm sorry to trouble you but is my mother there?"

"No, and I was getting concerned," Betty said. "You guys are always so punctual. Is anything wrong?"

"No, no … of course not. I got caught at the office and I think my mother lost patience waiting for me. She'll probably show up any minute. Would you mind having her call me when she does?"

"Sure, sure …" Betty said, already onto another task. "OK. Bye."

"Bye," Hannah said to the dial tone.

She raked her nails through her thick hair and examined the copper strands that came back laced between her fingers. When she was young, Rokhl used to whistle a high, bird-like trill as she brushed her daughter's hair until it shone like a bright penny. As if mesmerized,

Hannah would watch the arc of her mother's arm complete a slow, downward stroke, the movement carried out in the same precise way each time. Rokhl's pale skin was so delicate except for the scar on her forearm—a lumpy welt of red and blue like the tiny tableau of a mountain range. Rokhl's whistling as she gently ministered to her daughter's tangled mass—a silken thread of intimacy binding their daily lives in a way that comforted young Hannah.

Balefully stuffing the loose strands of hair into her pocket, Hannah absentmindedly opened the hall closet and was momentarily confused when she spied Rokhl's purse. She reached in and turned it over slowly as if to reassure herself she wasn't mistaken. It was a bag she knew well with all its little zippered compartments because it had once belonged to her, earmarked for the Pioneer Women's annual bazaar until Rokhl snatched it from the pile. Her mother could not bear to throw anything out, a habit that she had transmitted to her daughter. In a corner of Hannah's cedar closet, four shoeboxes—one for each decade and a fresh one marked 2000, printed in heavy black marker on the end of each box—contained Rokhl's notes neatly stacked. Like the dream logs she had been keeping since her teens, Hannah planned to one day read them all at once. When she had to.

Ignoring the hammering of her heart, Hannah unzipped the main compartment. Her mother's wallet which had also once been hers lay next to a crumpled cotton handkerchief with a faded embroidered rose on the edge and an old black comb. In the front compartment, Hanna found a scrap of paper. On it was Rokhl's meticulous script. Her hands suddenly trembling, she pulled the note out of the bag and laid it in her lap. On the day her mother disappeared, Hannah read the last note Rokhl would leave her.

I am not her, it said.

CHAPTER TWO

Hannah waited 24 hours before calling the police, knowing Rokhl would have been mortified: *O mein Gott! The police!* To bring yourself to the notice of the authorities was something to be avoided at all costs. It was one of Rokhl's many unspoken rules. If she was in the car with Hannah and a siren wailed, no matter how far away, no matter what kind of siren it was—ambulance, fire truck or police—Hannah had to immediately pull over to the side of the road and stop the car. And no one was allowed to move until the sound had died away. "You never know ..." was all the explanation Hannah ever got and for Rokhl, that was saying a lot.

I am not her.

On the day Rokhl disappeared, in the gloom of the beige hallway, on the edge of the wrought iron seat next to a phone that rarely rang, Hannah sat folding and unfolding the note, as if by some magic its meaning would be revealed. What did Rokhl mean by *'her'?* Was it a mistake? Didn't Rokhl mean 'I am not here?' Not that it made any more sense. And if she could decipher it, what could it tell her except what was obvious? Rokhl had left home without her purse, no wallet so no means of identification and with no known destination in mind. Deep in Hannah's belly a larva of worry was growing.

Hannah slid into the sweltering car. Almost instantly, sweat filmed her face and trickled down the curve of her clenched jaw. She stared out of the windshield at the front door of the duplex as if half expecting that by some miracle her mother would suddenly appear. For almost all of her 45 years, Hannah could predict Rokhl's every move, although never her motives, never the why. Now this. Nothing had prepared her for this. Not even the shocking exchange she and Rokhl had had the night before. Like an anxious child, Hannah brought her thumb to her mouth and started chewing on the cuticle.

"You're eating yourself up alive," Marilyn would say, "… a classic case of self-cannibalization."

Marilyn had a theory for and an opinion on everything. For a moment, phone in hand, Hannah thought about calling her best friend but hesitated. To call would be to admit that something serious had happened. There was no real proof of that, not yet. A thin line of blood trickled from Hannah's thumb. Cause and effect. The sharp pain came as welcome relief. She began to coast up one block and down another, trolling through the streets of the area she knew like the contours of her mother's face. She drove half-believing that she might spot Rokhl, or by some fluke, maybe someone familiar. But after so many years in Montreal, her mother's smattering of acquaintances, those who hadn't died, were living far away in Israel or Miami. Slowly rolling past rundown apartment buildings, Hannah worked on recalling anyone she might contact about Rokhl. No one came to mind.

⌇ Since her father's death, Hannah had avoided thinking about how bereft of human contact her mother's life had become. She did not want to consider how much Rokhl needed her every day. It was easier just to perform her duties: make the daily calls, take her mother food shopping for a large order once a week, chauffeur her to medical appointments, and share a Friday night dinner together at the duplex on Barclay. Hannah had tried to get Rokhl to do more but her mother didn't want to leave her home, not even to have dinner at Hannah's just for a change. It finally became clear, Hannah confided to Marilyn one day, that after Barak's death Rokhl had closed herself up in a ghetto of her own making.

First, Hannah covered a ten-block radius by car then struck out on foot, crisscrossing the back lanes she had roamed as a child. Much had changed since those summers, decades ago, when she had played with her friends on shimmering asphalt driveways and in back alleys. As playgrounds, they were so much more welcoming back then, cleaner and with metal garbage cans neatly lined up against new building walls. Now, it shocked her to see so many condoms; the way garbage spilled from torn green bags; and orphaned plastic stirred by half-hearted breezes floating low to the ground like deflated ghosts. The alleys reeked of cumin, curry, and jerk seasoning, smells she adored when they were cooking, not rotting.

Most of the immigrant Jews, Holocaust survivors like her parents who had once filled these apartment buildings, had long since moved away. Either they followed their children to Toronto or clustering like flocks of seagulls in the high-rise condos around the Cavendish Mall from which each December, if ambulatory, they headed south to Florida. Her father had refused to go that route, refused to sell the duplex he had worked so hard for decades in 'that *fahrkakteh shmateh* factory' to pay off the mortgage. A lifelong unionist, Barak labelled those who had fled to the middle class and better addresses to be poseurs.

"What for would I move? I'm comfortable, no one bothers us as much as we bother each other, right Rokhl?" He never waited for a reply.

"When we die, you will sell it. It's your inheritance, Hannah. If we sell it, the money we make will be thrown away on moving, painting, condo fees. Feh! Fees, shmees ... who needs it? *Aroise gevorfeneh gelt ...*"

It's not thrown out money, Hannah had protested; it was a good investment, but Barak would have none of his daughter's advice. Eventually, it grew too dark to keep going. Hannah returned to the empty duplex to wait although she wasn't sure for what. "Maybe I'm waiting for the realization to sink in," she said aloud, startling herself. She examined the blisters on her feet, prodding the swollen skin, anticipating pain but unsurprised by the lack of it. Exhausted, she lay down on the narrow bed where she had collected the dreams of her childhood and tried not to think about how much Rokhl feared the dark. She got up and lit candles as Rokhl used to do when Hannah was out on a date. She placed them in the kitchen and the front hall so that when her mother returned, it would not be to a pitch-black house.

As Hannah lay in the gloom, an army of fears marched across her chest and made camp until she could barely breathe. The last fear was the heaviest. What if, it asked with an evil gleam, this disappearing act was related to the altercation they had the night before? Hannah had been wilfully suppressing the disturbing image of Rokhl out of control—her face contorted, her arm raised in a fist. It was a vision that had been flickering in the back of Hannah's mind all through the search. The last time Hannah had seen her mother, the passive face she had known was twisted beyond recognition. Rokhl had been shouting. Shouting! Never in her memory did she recall her mother raising her voice. Hannah might have been less surprised if she had witnessed the Sphinx get up and stretch.

In a half dream, Hannah envisioned her mother like a cat lying across a barren expanse of sand, her face impassive and her eyes lustrous as sapphires. Beneath their glow, Hannah felt small, helpless. She floated in a soupy, thin sleep, half waking every time a car drove by, its headlights flashing light past her window.

By 6 a.m., bright sunlight broke through the half-open Venetian blinds and took up a relentless assault on Hannah's eyelids. She sat up and for a moment, couldn't remember where she was or why she was there. When she got her bearings, she marvelled at how the house had a hollow feel. Without deciding to do so, Hannah picked-up the phone and dialled 911. An hour later, washed but in yesterday's clothes, she watched the police cruiser pull up. Inside were two young officers; the taller one came to the door and introduced himself as Constable Pierre Langlois and suggested that he follow her inside while his partner looked around outside. In the kitchen, Hannah gestured to the officer to have a seat on one of the aqua vinyl chairs, shiny with age and a million coatings of Pledge. The metal legs scraped on the linoleum as the officer pulled closer to the old Formica table edged in chrome. Const. Langlois was sitting in the chair that Barak had always occupied at the head of the table. From there, he asked his questions with more gentleness than her father could ever manage and took notes as Hannah described her mother, what she had likely been wearing, and when she had been seen last.

"How old is your mother?"

"Seventy-two."

"Does she live alone?"

"Yes."

"When did you last have contact with her?"

"Two nights ago."

There were a dozen questions. Cautiously, Hannah answered them without offering up any extraneous information, so afraid was she to taint the process by her blossoming fear. The officer turned and looked around the room and spotted the tray of medications on the counter. He walked over to the collection, lifting, and scrutinizing each container, noting the prescription, then turned to Hannah, "Did your mother ever show any signs of senility, dementia, or the early stages of Alzheimer's?" he asked.

"No."

"No loss of memory, maybe erratic or childish behaviour?"

"No ... no, not at all."

Did Hannah know what those signs were, he had asked. At another time, Hannah might have been annoyed by such a line of questioning. Like Barak, she did not like to be challenged. But that morning, she was grateful for the orderly way in which she was being forced to think.

"No, she didn't display any of those signs," she responded. "My mother was of relatively sound mind and body."

He nodded and wrote something on his pad. Hannah waited like a pedestrian at a crosswalk impatient to move on.

"Can I look around the house, please?" he asked.

Hannah nodded and they both stood up at once. The constable was tall, maybe six-two. She smiled up at him, suddenly weary, feeling exposed as if she unexpectedly found herself in a strange city wandering about without a map. At that moment, she wished she had called Marilyn.

"Please ..." Const. Langlois said. "Can we look?"

She almost suggested that he could see everything he needed right there from the kitchen table, the house was that small. Instead, she led him through the hall and to the door of each of the other four rooms.

"Is anything missing?" he asked as he checked the surfaces of dressers and desks and bathroom counters. Hannah bit back the words bubbling up in her throat: *Yes, MY MOTHER! My mother is missing, and I don't care about anything else.* Instead, she quietly described finding the door unlocked.

"But there was nothing else unusual," she said. "Nothing was missing or disturbed."

Nothing missing, she thought but something—an aching, throbbing hollowness—had been added. It filled the house. Wherever it came from, it was slowly consuming all the unoccupied space and available oxygen. She was certain there was barely enough to sustain her and the officer.

"Did your mother sometimes forget to lock the door?"

"Never ..." Hannah replied, "... or at least, not that I can ever recall. Locking the door was something she was very careful about. Lately, her short-term memory has not been that good, she's just turned 72 and she's grown a bit forgetful since my father died a few years ago. She'll leave the house then turn around and return just to check the door because she can't remember locking it. But I don't think that's so unusual. On the whole, my mother is a very careful person."

A careful person. Could there be a more euphemistic phrase? Careful as in private, guarded, concealed, isolated, non-communicative, removed, secluded, secretive, separate, sequestered, solitary, withdrawn. Yes, Rokhl had always locked the door. The constable made a note and moved towards the entrance. He checked the door jamb and opened the door letting in a wave of warm air as he examined the lock from all sides. Hannah tried some deep breathing. Once done, the constable with Hannah trailing behind, revisited each room to examine the windows. When he was finally finished, they returned to the kitchen. Const. Langlois indicated that he was going to sit down again. He reviewed the details he had noted and then asked Hannah for a photo. She had one in her wallet, taken of Rokhl before Barak's cancer diagnosis. She asked if she would get the photo back. It was precious, she said and as she spoke, Hannah had the feeling she had seen this episode before. Was it on *Law and Order*, or *Missing*?

☞ As the cruiser drove away, Mrs. Orenstein, Rokhl's neighbour, came marching up the walk. Now that the coast was clear, Hannah could tell Mrs. Orenstein was on a fact-finding mission of her own. She was the block's self-appointed guardian, keeping a relentless watch from behind her living room curtains. Hannah realized guiltily that she had not even thought to check with Mrs. Orenstein.

"Did you see anything?" she asked hopefully after explaining the situation. But Mrs. Orenstein had been at a doctor's appointment all afternoon.

"You could die sitting in the waiting room and that *fahrkakteh* secretary would still make you wait your turn. Oy! Don't get old, Hannaleh darling, don't get old. It's no fun and you're treated like yesterday's garbage."

Hannah had patiently listened to all of this before but today she was in no mood for Mrs. Orenstein's litany of woes. Hannah began to edge away, making her way down the front steps towards the Subaru. At that moment Mrs. Orenstein lobbed her best shot.

"So, when did you speak to your mother last? You know, you should call her every day?

"Yes, I know, I do call ..."

"You know, Hannah," she said, moving to narrow the distance between them, "I try many times to invite her for tea but you know your mother, she was always a little bit too much to herself, what people sometimes call a private person, right?"

"Well, she just ..."

"... I try many times to make conversation with her but she only smiles at me and looks over my shoulder like maybe there's someone standing there behind me, you know? After so many years, a person stops trying."

Hannah bit her tongue as she had been taught to do and turned away with a nod.

"Let's hope for the best ..." Mrs. Orenstein called out, "and you'll let me know, won't you, Hannah, as soon as you hear something, eh?"

There was nothing but silence for the next two days except for a single phone call from a Det.-Sgt. Desjardins who said he was now in charge of the case. And then, nothing, not even a word that there *was* no news, despite the six messages she left on Desjardins' voicemail. Wednesday morning, Hannah sat in her car unable to determine where she should go. She pulled out her cell phone and called her assistant, Danielle. It had been 24 hours since she had spoken at length to anyone. Without too much preamble, Hannah explained her absence and a little about the situation. Danielle said she'd take care of everything. She would clear Hannah's calendar for the rest of the week with the explanation that there was a family emergency, but nothing more.

"Is there someone I should call? Do you need to speak to or be with someone?" she asked. Danielle was the best, the one who would jump in to fill any vacuum, take up any task.

"There's no one but me, honey," Hannah said, "And Marilyn. I'm calling her next."

She was finally ready for Marilyn to help sort out the jumble of emotions that were crawling around inside her head like blind mice. Marilyn would cook something for her, even though she wasn't hungry. Hannah suddenly realized that she had not had a meal in almost two days. If anything, what she had been consuming was her own flesh.

CHAPTER THREE

"**I**t's all right. I'm here," Marilyn said, rushing to Hannah, wrapping her friend in a tight embrace. "Why didn't you call me sooner? You should have called me right away as soon as you knew something was wrong. What made you think you should go through this, this ... thing ... on your own?" Pressed against Marilyn's voluminous chest, Hannah remained quiet until Marilyn stepped back and looked her over.

"Your composure is unnatural," she said with her usual bluntness. Marilyn didn't expect a response. She knew better.

"I would drop everything in a heartbeat to be here for you. You know after my girls and Bram you are the closest to my heart." She pushed a long lock of salt-and-pepper hair from her temple, her eyes brimming as she reached out and gathered Hannah once again into a gentle hug. Hugs were Marilyn's specialty, almost a trademark, and she was never the first to let go. It had always been that way.

"Go ahead," Marilyn whispered into Hannah's hair. "You have the right to cry. It's all right to let go."

But Hannah couldn't.

"It's OK, Marilyn. Really, I'm OK," she said pulling away, raising her chin.

Marilyn shrugged, knowing she was up against a long, complicated history. She had once observed Hannah and Rokhl in a scene she had never experienced in her young life. They were about nine years old when Hannah had fallen and badly scraped her leg. She ran to Rokhl in tears, her leg raw and torn. But Rokhl did not reach out and embrace her crying child nor did she immediately tend the wound. Instead, she stood with her arms by her side, waiting silently for her daughter's tears to stop. Distraught, Hannah hugged her mother's knees but still Rokhl withheld any comfort. Marilyn had stood wide-eyed. Only when the sobbing stopped did Hannah receive her re-ward—a brief hug and a gentle hand that came down to caress her tangle of hair. Rokhl cleaned the wound and there was not a sound from Hannah when her mother applied the iodine on the raw skin. If she couldn't comfort her friend, Marilyn reasoned, the next best thing was to feed her and take charge of organizing a concerted effort to get Hannah and Danielle and herself on the phone calling the various Montreal hospitals every few hours.

"It's the only thing to do," Marilyn had said. "Between the chronic shortage of staff and the mountains of paperwork, it could take days before news might filter through the hospital to the police. Besides, it's something you can do to keep from going crazy." Her hand gently rubbed Hannah's shoulder.

Hannah hated to admit it, but Marilyn was right. The calls would keep her from spinning off into outer space. Yet part of her was still running a loop, laying out all the facts, examining the clues, sifting through them like a rag picker.

"It's as if everything is happening in slow motion," she said.

"That feeling is understandable," Marilyn said. "I remember when your father died, there was this vacuum you told me that had to be filled. Filling it was called 'taking care of Rokhl.' Now there is only the vacuum."

↩ It was true. After Barak's death six months to the day of his diagnosis, Hannah had quickly fallen into a routine, making certain Rokhl's fridge was stocked, that she was taking her medication, and that she heard a human voice at least once a day, sometimes twice. When she could manage, she would get her mother outside the house for more than the purchase of a loaf of fresh bread.

"I remember how composed you were when your father died," Marilyn said. "Everyone commented on it at the funeral."

"What else could I do with my mother more silent than ever? People asked me how she was doing, and I would have to make things up because I had no idea. It was like Barak had gone on an extended trip and was eventually coming back. Sometimes, it was like he had never left. We didn't talk or reminisce about him. The silence was eerier than ever."

Marilyn put her arms around Hannah and squeezed hard, her eyes brimming, but when she looked at her childhood friend, she found Hannah dry-eyed.

After her father's funeral, there had been moments when Hannah was overcome by a strange ache. There were bouts of longing that usually came on after she'd seen a man with Barak's shape or his cocky walk. But where Rokhl was concerned, in the ocean-like expanse of the days since her mother went missing, there was nothing to grab on to.

Suddenly rising, Hannah said, "I'm heading to the office."

Marilyn nodded her understanding that Hannah needed to keep moving to stay calm.

"Thank you," Hannah said reaching for her friend's hand. "You cannot imagine what you mean to me. You remind me I'm not alone. I need to remember that. You know, it's only in the first moments of the morning, before I remember Rokhl is missing, that I feel any calm."

Without Rokhl, the magnetic pole by which Hannah had oriented herself all her life, something to pull against or hug fiercely close, had evaporated into thin air. But in the office, the only thing keeping Hannah tethered was a length of telephone cord and the photo on her desk, taken the year before Barak died when her mother occasionally remembered how to smile. The photo had been snapped at Passover, and the three of them were at the Seder table, the remains of the meal not yet cleared away. A moment after she had set up the camera's timer, Barak had pronounced a compliment on the roast chicken. When there had been no reaction from Rokhl, he said, "I know what you're thinking ..." A Mona Lisa smile had crept across Rokhl's face just as the shutter snapped. And a moment later, it was gone; and all that remained was the enigmatic and unfathomable face that her mother wore day in and day out. Hannah never even thought to ask what her father meant. She had long ago learned the futility of asking. It was wiser not to question, not to stir the pot where memories always simmered on a back burner. But she cherished the photo, a testament to the possibility of happiness, no matter how fleeting.

"Couldn't we ask the papers to run your mother's photo?" Danielle suggested and not for the first time. "You know like they do sometimes, under the word: MISSING/DISPARU?" She religiously read the French tabloid, *Journal de Montréal*. "Our agency certainly spends enough advertising dollars with the *Gazette* and *La Presse* to warrant a favour."

Hannah shook her head. How could she do that? Rokhl would be mortified. The thought came despite her inner censor, a relentlessly rational voice, discrediting this line of thinking as nonsense. Even with Rokhl missing, Hannah continued to follow her rules of conduct. Just as her mother followed Barak's rules in the years after he was gone. She stared at the photo, scanned it with the intensity of a lighthouse beam searching through fog. *What's wrong with me?* She admonished herself; she was the one everyone relied on to take charge in an emergency. Where was that Hannah now? The best she could do was to identify what was not going to happen: no radio bulletins, no sad newspaper photo with a plaintive call for help. Not for her mother, not for this Holocaust survivor living in a bubble, not for this silent woman whose life was a mote, a single ash wafting up above the chimneys of Auschwitz-Birkenau. All she could do was stay true to Rokhl, and patiently wait.

↝ "Mme Baranowski?" A stone dropped on Hannah's chest as she recognized the gravelly voice of Det.-Sgt. Desjardins. Over the past three days, she had imagined this call a hundred times. She gently replaced the spoon in her cereal bowl. Breakfast was over.

"Ms Baran, please," she said, correcting him. Her hand grew clammy as she clutched the phone. She reached up and tucked her hair behind her ear.

"Yes, excuse me. Mme Baran. This is Det.-Sgt. Patrice Desjardins. I took over your file? We spoke …"

"Yes."

She knew who he was, had known from the first intake of his breath.

"Yes, I remember."

"We think we have some information about your mother. I am sorry. It may not be good news. When can you come down to see us?"

"Where?"

Desjardins provided an address.

"I'll be there in 15 minutes," she said and hung up without a thank you or a goodbye.

Hannah pulled into the parking lot of the shopping mall where the police station was located. Despite all her haste to get there, for a moment, she couldn't for the life of her recall how she had managed to drive to the station from her condo on the canal. A crazy notion took hold, the idea that she might be asleep and having one of her 'ordinary' nightmares, those dreams that had haunted her since childhood. In them, sad things happen but nothing so frightening as to warrant screaming or even waking up. The nightmares were most often filled with an escalating series of appalling events, not physical but always dreadful. Like the dreams where she has a baby. She is so busy with work or travel that she forgets to feed or bathe the infant for days. Or the dream where she misplaces the child and must keep reminding herself to look for it. In a way, that's what the last three days felt like to Hannah, a nightmare in which, through her neglect, she had misplaced her mother. What about her pledge to Barak? Hannah had only that one responsibility and she had failed to carry it out.

Nearby, a car door slammed shut snapping Hannah out of her reverie. She took a deep breath slowly letting the air slip out. How long had she been staring out the window? It didn't matter. The dread of not knowing could now only be made more awful by the news that

Rokhl was gone forever. The day had been hot and sticky—Hannah remained barely aware of the weather until a thunderclap rattled the car window. Beneath the sound, she thought she heard Barak's angry challenge: *What's the matter with you? If not you, who? If not now, when?*

Det.-Sgt. Desjardins shook Hannah's hand then led her down a hall into a windowless cubicle where he asked her to take a seat. Even with her eyes aimed at the floor, she knew this office looked nothing like those she had seen on TV, yet the man in front of her, medium height, in his fifties, with a receding hairline and a slight stoop, could have been any number of performers playing the role of the gruff but kindly police detective. Hannah tried to imagine how she might perform in the role of the distraught daughter. So far, her ability to remain outwardly calm had been disturbing to those closest to her.

"Mme Baranovsky?" Desjardins said.

"Baran," Hannah said. "That's my legal name."

"Mme Baran, my apologies. I know you must be distraught, but can you answer my question?"

"I'm sorry," Hannah said, "would you be good enough to repeat it?"

She had momentarily detached from her body and taken up residence in a corner of the ceiling, like a spirit after death. From there, she was keenly observing both herself and the detective.

"Was your mother depressed?" the detective asked slowly, as if to allow her to read his lips. "Do you think she was capable of killing herself?"

Hannah looked at the man whose job it was to tell her that her mother was dead.

"Monsieur, my mother was a Holocaust survivor," she said in a voice so laden with sympathy that the detective grew uncomfortable.

Undaunted, Hannah recounted her mother's history as if reciting a childhood poem: "My mother survived Auschwitz. She lost her entire family, every single member. My father died two years ago and I'm an only child. So yes, she may have been depressed but I never believed her to be suicidal." Hannah moved to the edge of the chair and leaned forward. "And as I said, my mother is a survivor. I think survival for her is an instinct; it's as if her whole system is somehow programmed to keep her alive, despite the losses and the horrors of life."

"Does she take any medication for depression?" the Det.-Sgt asked.

"Yes, she does," Hannah said, "but she is closely monitored, and the dosage is often reviewed to make certain she is not over- or under-medicated."

"But you do not seem surprised by my question, Mme Baran. Do you think it is possible your mother might have decided to end her life?"

Hannah had not told the detective about the purse still hanging in Rokhl's hall closet. Nor about the note. It was not a suicide note; she was sure of that. It was merely one more cryptic message for Hannah to decipher. She looked down at her hands where her fingers had been busy at work, picking away at a cuticle. Hannah was tired of holding back, she was tired of the dread. But she had no choice.

"What have you found, sir?" she finally asked keeping her eyes on her hands.

"Three days ago, there was an accident on Côte-des-Neiges some blocks from your mother's home. Witnesses said that, without looking, a woman stepped out in front of a bus. She was killed instantly but caught under the front wheels, her body was dragged for several metres. The woman was wearing a blue dress and ... and this is the part that we are not certain about, you said that your mother had a scar on her right forearm ... You had noted this identifying scar in the same location when you reported your mother missing ..."

The stone that had lodged itself in Hannah's gut on entering the police station was suddenly a boulder rolling downhill. For a moment, Hannah went careening with it but, in the face of the inevitable, she proved to be her mother's daughter. Her look remained impassive. Only her lips moved, imperceptibly, as if testing her memory for a recital, gathering together the rehearsed words to make an acceptable and coherent sentence.

"When my mother was liberated from Auschwitz," Hannah quietly said to the French-Canadian detective who likely had heard worse, "my mother scraped and cut the skin off her arm where she had been tattooed with a number."

Hannah called Marilyn from the police station. Her hands were trembling as she jabbed at the keys. She could not go to the morgue only in the company of the detective. She wasn't sure she could go at all but there was no choice. No choice. All the big moments in her life always seemed to end like this. For years, she had imagined this day when she would be all alone, when she would have to deal with the loss of her parents. Along with an odd sense of disconnect, there was a vague sensation of disappointment.

She felt let down by all the systems she had so carefully constructed to help make order out of the chaos of her life. In her thirties, she had embraced Taoist philosophy in preparation for this very moment. Yet she was now unable to invoke anything that could keep her steady. She needed to regain her balance. Taoism had helped her form a mantra: Accept everything that happens because who is to know what's good or bad? This was the rule she had determined she would live by. It should have prepared her, but she didn't feel equipped, only detached.

A story appeared to be unfolding while somewhere high above the changing scene, she hung suspended as if clinging to the riggings above a large stage. Looking down, she could see the players enter and exit, but she was growing exhausted waiting for a cue. Was Rokhl's disappearance, possibly her death, Hannah's fault? It all started with this Heilemann business. She should never have agreed to go to Germany for Sonenshein. That was the cause of her mother's despair. Rokhl had killed herself because of their quarrel right after she had shouted, "I do not want you to go to Germany. If you go, it will be over my dead body, do you hear me? Over my dead body ..."

ROKHL WACHSBERG BARANOWSKI

1928–2000

If you are reading this, Hannaleh, I have gone to the other world, to where my beloved Papa has been waiting so long to greet me. Perhaps I can finally rest now. I have failed you in so many ways, I know. Yet, I cannot abandon you forever and take my story with me. It is your story, too.

CHAPTER FOUR

I **was an** *only child, like you, Hannah, but not spoiled as you were by Barak. My papa doted on me but he set strict rules that I lived by. And though he did not often say so, I knew he loved me very much. It was a secret we shared. Sometimes, he would whisper in my ear, 'Du bist der* oig in meine kop,' *the apple of my eye. How that thrilled me. And when we talked, he would crouch down and make himself small so we could be closer as equals, conspirators. His breath smelled of tobacco and something else, something sweet. When we were eye-to-eye, he would run his hand over the tangle of my curls as if he could smooth my hair down by some magic and, at the same time, tame the wild thoughts racing around inside my head. Somehow, he understood I would tame my thoughts to please him if I could.*

Papa was very different when he was with Mameh. Near her he somehow swelled and became taller, straighter. He treated her as if she was a fair damsel, gallantly taking her hand whenever she rose from her seat. He would slip his arm around her small waist, helping her to navigate past obstacles with authority, like a captain steering his ship through the difficult straits of our sitting room. When she spoke, he wrapped her in his gaze as if no one else existed, as if protecting her fragile nature from a harsh world. And when she played her violin, he would sit in utter rapture as she became one with her instrument. When she was finished, he would take her hands and kiss them, whispering, "Such beauty from such fragile fingers."

Fragile was not how I would ever describe my mother. To me, Mameh had a core of steel. Papa looked at me when we spoke, but Mameh hardly acknowledged my existence, especially when Papa was not in the room. And when we were all together, all I ever received from her were little drops of poison coated in sugar and wrapped like pretty sweets.

"Oh, look at that hair, Shimon … what can we do with our little vilde chayeh. *How did such a wild animal come to live among civilized people like us?" Here, she would wink at me and then look at my father with a little smile that slipped into me like a knife.*

"Gotteinu, wherever does that hair come from?" she would ask. "Not my side, that is for certain. If only it was smooth and shimmery like our copper pots instead of this mass of curls. You could be so pretty, my child, if only …" My father, the only possible source of my red hair, would toss me a little smile of apology. In contrast to my wiry curls, my mother's hair was a lustrous, honey blond, beautifully coiffed in soft Marcelle waves. These were carefully arranged around her delicate features and tawny skin in thick folds of melted nectar. In her kinder moments, she would smile at me as if I was an orphan. With a degree of cruelty, I only came to understand later, she would bring her face close to mine to compare our features in the mirror. This she did as if playing a little game that might entertain my father. He always nodded indulgently at her efforts. She'd run her hand around the perimeter of my face, stopping at my cheekbones to press her fingers against the roundness there as if she was a potter able to alter the shape of my contours with her artistry and force of will. Her hands, small and delicate, felt cool upon my skin and always left me wanting. When it came to music, again I took after Papa. Piano lessons were a painful weekly reminder that I could never aspire to reach any degree of my mother's artistry. Or so she said.

My parents had married against the wishes of my mother's family. She came from hoicheh fenster, *Papa said, a well-to-do Warsaw family; both her father and brother were medical doctors. They thought that Papa, an accountant who tracked the progress of other people's money, was not as important as those who had money and the position it brought. We lived* in Krakow which my mother's family deemed a provincial town compared to the cultural richness of Warsaw with its Jewish population second only to New York. She never said so, but there were times I think my mother agreed with her family about my father, but there was no doubt that she adored him. "You have two completely different women in love with you, Shimon," she said one night. Papa smiled at her but there was sadness in his eyes, and when he turned them on me, his smile softened. Early on, I understood that I could never best my mother when it came to comparing beauty but, in my heart, I was certain that my father loved me best.

We lived on ulica Florianska in the heart of Krakow's Old Town shopping district. On Shabbos when I was young, I would put on my finest dress, one my father had brought home for me from Au bonheur des dames that imported its dresses from Vienna. I would pull on my white stockings and the shiny black shoes that Papa had also bought for me. Determined to tame my hair, I would rip the brush through the tangle with a furious determination. When I could finally make something of the unruly mess, something that might have pleased my mother—if my mother could ever be pleased—I topped it with a white satin bow that my father taught me how to tie. I was frustrated that I never managed to get it quite right because, as the day wore on, the bow always began to list to the left. When my hair resumed its natural buoyancy, the bow would slowly sink into the spongy marsh of curls like a ship taking on water. Every once in a while, as we walked to the Isaac shul, the most wonderful synagogue in all of Krakow, my father would stop to straighten the bow. I loved our shul and my father often told me the story about how it came to be built. As we walked, my mother's arm would be firmly looped through my father's left elbow and my child's hand, securely planted in his large right palm. The walk from our apartment was pleasant and, after the service, on our way home, my parents would nod at acquaintances or stop to chat with friends. We would sometimes visit their homes and, while my parents spoke about the world at large and the troubles at home, I would sit quietly. I liked listening to the adults, aching to grow up faster so I could become one of them. I did not want to be a child. I did not want to be helpless. And I did not want to be excluded from my Papa's world. Once in a while, during a discussion on this or that amongst the grown-ups, my

Papa would turn and say, "Rokhleh knows the answer to that." I would sit up and deliver the answer my father expected. Even before Papa nodded his head in approval, I knew I had done well by the tight smile on my mother's face. She wanted the other adults to think she was proud of my cleverness but what she would have preferred was to take pride in my beauty.

In hindsight, I was not so much clever as determined. To please Papa, I applied myself at school as he expected. I was first in my class of girls but could have beaten any of the boys as well. I had a good head for languages. They came easily to me, and Papa would help. By the time I was twelve, I spoke Yiddish, Polish, German and I could read Hebrew. Why am I recounting all this now that it is too late? Now that I occupy another world? I should have shared these stories long ago. Perhaps I would have if you had asked? Probably not. Perhaps I was afraid that you might learn too much about who I was. Maybe it is true that beginnings can help you to understand endings. In a life torn between having love and wanting love, what are the rules? What is fair in love? In war? Maybe I am recalling all these stories so you will know that the world I came from was a place of culture, of refinement even, not a pillar of smoke blotting out the sun. I came from Krakow, a city that had once been the seat of kings who ruled an empire that sprawled over half of Europe. In school, we learned about Poland's hardships under the rule of successive conquerors while, in my home, I learned about betrayal and the politics of love.

MAXIMILIAN MOHR
JULY 2000

CHAPTER FIVE

O**utside the offices** of M.F. Flaubert Realtors in downtown Montreal, Max Mohr took a moment to shake off the weariness of the transatlantic flight. It was late afternoon, and he could have waited. There was no pressing need for this appointment to take place on the very day he arrived, but it was a good time to get a first impression. At the end of the day, people were less guarded, more likely to reveal themselves. He was restless to get going. The call he had received from Heilemann before leaving Köln was nagging at him. It was most uncharacteristic for Heilemann to repeat himself or to press for action. This sudden emphasis on expediency had taken Max by surprise. To hurry things went against his nature and he had always thought, against Heilemann's nature as well. It was what had informed their success. Heilemann was renowned for his languorous approach to business. It made for interesting tactics when negotiating, a challenge that Max looked forward to with relish.

"What's the hurry?" Heilemann would say. "The building will not uproot itself and walk away. The land is not going to disappear down a hole. Time is always on the side of the buyer."

What had suddenly changed? Max wondered. He firmly believed that regret is the usual end result of a hurried process. This sudden push to action niggled at him but he knew better than to ask. One didn't question Heilemann's strategy without having more information, in the event advice might be requested or required. Heilemann, his most lucrative client, was not a man who suffered being second guessed. Max stepped into the coolness of the Flaubert offices and slowly surveyed the room, taking in the rich sheen of the leather Barcelona chairs and the naïve paintings on the walls depicting young children with rosy cheeks playing hockey on a city street. They made him smile as he approached the receptionist. She looked up and, for a moment, appeared to have forgotten her lines.

"Bonjour," Max said, letting the *r* roll off his tongue. He enjoyed the sound of French and the opportunity to practice the little he had left. He gazed down at the middle-aged blonde seated behind the reception desk, and patiently awaited her response. He saw a slight flush rise in her cheeks but made an effort not to let on that he had.

"Bonjour, est-que je peux vous aider? May I help you?"

Max smiled and the receptionist flushed again. He was accustomed to this odd effect he had on women although he was careful not to take it for granted. He would be the first to admit that there was a world of handsomer men, most of them much younger. But he did take some pleasure that the attention he elicited from the opposite sex had not diminished much, and he thought that maybe it had even grown when he hit his forties.

"I certainly hope so … Estelle …" he said, reading the name plate on the counter. "My name is Mohr. Maximilian Mohr. I have an appointment with Mme Baran."

"Uh … yes, thank you. *Un moment, je vous en prie.* Please, won't you have a seat?"

"Thank you, but after seven hours on a plane I much prefer to stand. I should have taken the Concorde but alas, I didn't. I'll just wait here, if I may. Besides," he said with a dazzling smile, "the view is so much nicer from up here."

The woman looked up in surprise but Mohr was not looking down but past her, through the floor-to-ceiling windows behind the reception area. From where he stood, Max could see the curve of what passed for a mountain in Montreal, and the large iron cross facing eastward. Perched on the edge of Mount Royal, Max thought, it looked like a talisman thrust out as if to protect the city from evil.

"Ah, so you've just arrived in town?" Estelle said. Max smiled and looked down at the intercom. Nonplussed the receptionist remembered her duties. "I'll let Hannah ... I mean Mme Baran ... know that you are here."

Estelle adjusted her headset, giving her hair a quick pat in the process, and buzzed Hannah's extension. Although the receptionist sat facing her computer screen, Max felt himself being scrutinized. He turned to smile at her once more, but she now appeared totally engaged with her work.

⤳ Taking a moment to collect herself, Hannah strode out of her office and down the hall at a clipped pace. She heard Marilyn's voice buzzing in her head, asking what's the rush? Marilyn was always chiding her about not taking the time to be in the moment. Her latest passion was a book called *The Power of Now* by Eckhart Tolle. Heeding the voice in her head, Hannah slowed her progress for a second to smooth the sweater she had taken so much care in selecting that morning. It was not her habit to fuss over clothes but this meeting seemed to call for it. Her closet was stuffed full of business wear, mostly suits, but that morning, she had chosen a less formal look. Thinking back, it struck her that she had stood in front of the bedroom mirror way too long wondering if the V in the baby blue sweater was revealing too much (or not enough) cleavage. With a wry smile at her foolishness, she had to acknowledge that the need for fussing was moot since she didn't have that much to reveal. Still, her trim figure gave her a reason to smile. As she moved through the hall, Hannah inhaled slowly to allow the breath to calm her. She dropped her shoulders before entering the reception area, pleased that the morning had deliberately been kept light to ensure she would be at her sharpest for the meeting with the German agent. She was always better in the afternoon, she knew, and that sometimes gave her a small edge. It was still irritating, however, that there had been so little time to prepare. The call, one of those windfalls that catch you completely by surprise, had come three days earlier. Despite Mohr's careful description of why he was coming to Montreal, Hannah still wasn't thoroughly clear how—or why—he had chosen her from the crowd of agents in the city. He had called Flaubert Realties and asked for her by name, Estelle had reported.

Hannah viewed windfalls with suspicion. And as if nature had not made her cautious enough, whenever she was 'handed' a golden opportunity, a note her mother had written years earlier came to mind. She discovered it shortly after she placed first in her Grade Eight class when Evie, the brightest student, had fallen ill with mononucleosis. The note from Rokhl read: *What good comes too easy often goes very fast.* Sure enough, she lost the top position when the school allowed Evie to take her exams at home under the teacher's supervision.

Despite her cautious nature, the little flutter in her belly and the nervousness of having to deal with a German, Hannah was not about to look a gift horse in the mouth. Furthermore, the man that Maximilian Mohr was representing was no ordinary gift horse. Hans-Georg Heilemann was a rare Arabian stallion type of gift horse, a man with a fortune estimated in the billions. Hannah recalled his name being mentioned years earlier in a *Forbes* article so, when Mohr called, she had set about doing some research on Heilemann at the library. What she found was relatively meagre, most of it gleaned from a story in an old issue of *Travel and Leisure* magazine that Danielle had found in the office. Born in 1944, Hans-Georg (Ha-Gay) Heilemann had built his fortune—and reputation—buying up and renovating relics. Most were dank, decaying *schlösser* and derelict religious buildings—monasteries, convents, churches—located throughout central and western Europe. He had started with one dilapidated manor, an estate he had inherited that was worth less than the crippling taxes. It seemed Heilemann always had a vision of what he wanted from a luxury hotel. To ensure his vision was realized, he worked side-by-side with stonemasons, carpenters, and designers. Upon the opening of his first property, he immediately began work on another. It was grudgingly granted that he had a talent for unlocking the hidden value in neglected buildings and developing them into eclectic, high-end properties. As he expanded his chain, it seemed he had acquired the knack of turning stone to gold. He created the wildly popular—and obscenely expensive—Luxury Historic Hotels, LHH, a chain of trendsetting resorts, by utilizing his other talent—the design and implementation of marketing strategies.

Not much else was known except that he was Catholic, a widower, and the scion of a long line of Bavarian *Junker,* barons who along with the rest of Germany's aristocracy had been disenfranchised by the Weimar Republic in 1919. Sometime in the early sixties, however, he suddenly surfaced as a player. From what Hannah knew of the hotels, it was clear that Heilemann's vision was brilliant. He had chosen to buy properties that were strategically located in hamlets, villages, and towns near—but not too near—major centres in Germany, Austria, Italy, France, the UK and Ireland. The quaintness of the locales, contrasted by the extravagant hotel properties, worked as an irresistible draw for a mix of celebrities and the truly wealthy who enjoyed spending time in fairy tale surroundings equipped with state-of-the-art amenities. And as Heilemann offered private hotel management and culinary training programs for any talented young locals, small town politicians were always eager to adapt whatever laws necessary to clear the way for Luxury Historic Hotels' job-creating ventures. One last stroke of genius ensured Heilemann's phenomenal success. Once a hotel was breaking even, the real estate mogul would buy up much of the land in the village to ensure that the 'authenticity' of the locale remained unaltered by those seeking to capitalize on the wealthy clientele. No fancy franchises could lease retail space, no developers were able to buy up large tracts for condos or competing hotels and restaurants. The LHH remained the focal point of the area's cottage industries. Still what Hannah could not find an answer to was what Heilemann's sudden interest in Quebec was all about. After several days of research, Hannah was no closer to an answer about the purpose of Mohr's trip to Montreal. There had never been any indication that Heilemann considered making a foray into North America. Since there were no castles anywhere near Montreal, Hannah decided it must have something to do with non-operational church properties that had caught his attention. In Quebec, there was no shortage of religious properties, convents, monasteries and particularly churches. Mark Twain had once famously observed of Montreal: "This is the first time I was ever in a city where you couldn't throw a brick without breaking a church window." Since the Quiet Revolution of the sixties, however, Quebec's churches had been suffering from a steady loss of congregants. A number of the greystone, tin-roofed giants had already been converted into condos, but what was going on in Quebec did not fit with the profile she had cobbled together on Heilemann. And then, there was that other question: Why had she been singled out? It couldn't be her connections. There were loads of agents better connected to the Catholic church then Hannah Baran.

This Maximilian Mohr had indicated he wanted to explore the terrain in the outlying areas around the metropolis. Another mystery. Heilemann was notoriously passionate about his privacy. Hannah suspected that he was not so much a recluse as a man who chose to remain unknown. He shunned the celebrity his money attracted. She could find only one photo of him; it accompanied the magazine article she had found in *Travel and Leisure* and was somewhat dated. The out-of-focus paparazzi shot revealed a man of medium height but well-built with a Freud-like beard streaked with grey. He looked nothing like any real estate developer Hannah had ever met, most of whom barely reached her shoulder. Apparently, Heilemann's wife had died in 1985 while giving birth to their fifth child. He had remained unmarried and was raising his children on his own. Without any rhyme or reason, Hannah had been entertaining peculiar fantasies tied to some possible future meeting with Heilemann. It had been so very long since she had been intrigued by anyone, and even longer since she had entertained romantic fantasies. But the whole thing was absurd. A German! And a baron to boot! This morning, she had laughed aloud when she caught herself taking extra care in applying her eye make-up and then using the diffuser on her hair for more than her usual perfunctory five-minute fluff-and-run. Instead, she had tried to emulate her assistant Danielle's technique for creating curls fat as babies' fists, the kind that bounced when you tossed your head. She wanted to make a good impression, one that Mohr might convey to Heilemann. She convinced herself that all the fuss was just business, about attaining the upper hand. As she neared the reception area, she shook her head to toss off silly fantasies about German real estate moguls. It didn't take a major in psychology, like the one she had acquired, to recognize that she had chosen the most unlikely of scenarios about which to fantasize. If Barak was alive, this meeting would not be taking place. Even if he would never learn of it, any dealings with a German would have been a serious crossing of the line, a betrayal of all her father stood for. As for her mother, who knew what Rokhl stood for? She never said, making it much easier not to weigh the consequences.

↝ Max Mohr was lost in thought when a glint of copper caught the corner of his eye. The late afternoon sun flashed off a head of lush curls, a suitable frame for the attractive, triangular face belonging to Hannah Baran.

"Herr Mohr, I presume," Hannah said, thrusting her hand out and giving him a warm, welcoming smile.

Max reached down to take the proffered hand and was surprised at the firm grip from such a small palm but the wince on her face reminded him how strong his own grasp was. With an apologetic smile, he immediately loosened the pressure on her hand and said, "Please, it's just Max. I prefer the informalities of North America. And may I call you Hannah?"

She nodded, warmth flooding her cheeks. For a moment, Hannah was thrown by her body's visceral reaction. Max Mohr stood, smiling down at her.

"Of course, Max, please do call me Hannah. Uh …"

She dropped her eyes until Max, slightly abashed, realized he was still holding her hand, so small, it was lost in his own. With some reluctance, he let go. Hannah experienced relief followed by a surprising sense of loss as if she had found something valuable and then, had to return it. Handshakes were important, Barak had always insisted.

"When you are presenting yourself in life, in business, when you touch someone, make sure it is with authority so that they know you cannot be

taken advantage of too easy. A strong handshake is a mark of confidence. It says, I know who I am and now you know I know."

"How was your trip? Uneventful, I hope," she said turning with a small gesture to indicate Mohr should follow her down the hall. Walking beside her, Max slowed to take in the paintings that were artfully hung between the office doors. He stopped a moment to admire a canvas of brilliant hues depicting a village scene in winter. Hannah stopped as well, and they stood for a moment gazing silently at the painting.

"The colours are so vibrant, the strokes so bold, so exhilarating," Max finally said in genuine admiration. "This is not at all how I know winter. In Köln—what you call Cologne—we have mostly frost, not mounds of snow."

"The artist is Canadian, the late Sam Borenstein. As you can imagine we Canadians have a special relationship with snow and winter. Borenstein did numerous paintings of Montreal and villages in the Laurentian mountains. He is one of my personal favourites. That particular painting is of Ste. Agathe des Monts which hardly looks like that anymore. Are you interested in art, Mr ... uh, Max?"

"I am interested in everything that reminds me to stop and pay attention to life ... art, music, dance, food ..." He gave her a look that seemed to say: You ... you are most interesting.

"... and philosophy ...?" Hannah said with a quick smile. Keeping it light was turning out to be relatively easy with Max Mohr. Of their own accord, Hannah's shoulders dropped slightly.

There was something puzzling about this man, although it was nothing she could put her finger on immediately. Maybe it was the way he walked, loose-limbed and unhurried, back and shoulders ramrod straight. Like a man strolling on the beach. Or maybe he was just a man worn out from a long flight.

"Your offices are lovely, Hannah. I think it's important to have a workspace that is congenial."

"I never quite thought of this office in those terms, but you are right. It was decorated with care by M. Flaubert's daughter. She is one of Montreal's best-known decorators and, as you may have guessed, an art aficionado. She is partial to Quebec artists and so all these works you see here originated in this province. And if I may, I must compliment you on your English, Max. It is so..." Hannah suddenly blushed realizing that she was about to say something stupid.

"Do you mean my imperceptible *Zherman* accent?"

"No ... uh ... I didn't mean ..."

Max laughed at Hannah's attempt to protest but she was chagrined at her faux pas. What was she thinking?

"My facility with English began in my youth. I had an English friend; his father, an engineer with the British army, was stationed in Köln when I was young. When he left, we corresponded for years. I've also spent many years living abroad in the UK and Ireland. I have had Mr. Heilemann as my principal client for almost two decades. His interest in attractive properties, no matter where they may be, has afforded me tremendous opportunities to work on my English."

"I am envious of your facility with language ..." Hannah said and stopped when she suddenly realized they had been standing in front of the boardroom door for too long. Oddly, it seemed the most natural thing in the world to be exchanging personal information. But Hannah knew it wasn't.

"Please," she said opening the door, "come in and have a seat, Max."

A moment of confusion ensued until Hannah realized Max was waiting for her to enter first.

Taking a seat, she asked, "Did Estelle offer you a beverage?"

"No, but that's okay ..."

"Some coffee, perhaps, or sparkling water?"

"No, really nothing for the moment. Perhaps we should be getting down to business."

Max lifted his briefcase onto the boardroom table, opened it and withdrew a business card and slid it towards Hannah. Hannah took the card and produced her own from a cluster of stands in the centre of the table. She folded her hands in her lap and leaned back into the tall boardroom chair that she knew made her look small and childlike.

At the moment, she hoped she looked composed although it was not how she was feeling. What was unsettling her was how Max Mohr's eyes, a startling deep green with gold flecks, were so like her father's.

"Montreal is a lovely city," he said, glancing out the boardroom window. "This is only my third visit to Montreal but from the little I've seen, the city seems to have blossomed since I was last here some 15 years ago, sometime in the mid-eighties. I detect a moderate air of prosperity."

"Well, ten years ago we were in an economic slump," Hannah said. "We had come off the 1980 referendum to decide whether or not Quebec would separate from Canada. It was close enough—60 to 40 against separation to send a new wave of corporate head offices heading down the Trans-Canada Highway to Toronto and points west. It was obvious that investment in Quebec would stay on hold until the ground stopped shaking beneath developers' feet. However, I like your characterization as 'Montreal's moderate air of prosperity.' Things have started to pick-up. We're beginning to get the hang of building and buying condos. And young people find Montreal exciting. It used to be that our youth left to get their education someplace else like Toronto or the States. Now we have students from all over the world choosing Montreal, not only for the quality of education but for the three F's ..."

"Three effs?" Max looked at her quizzically.

"Food, fashion and festivals. You can't beat Montreal for its *joie de vivre* ..."

Hannah stopped short, a little chagrined for letting herself take off like a runaway horse.

"Please forgive me, Max, I am quite enthused about my hometown."

"No apologies necessary," Max said, a smile playing at the corners of his mouth. "I love passion in people ... especially women."

Hannah looked at Mohr, straightening her back against the chair. Is he flirting with me? she wondered. But when she looked again, Hannah could find no trace of lewdness or condescension on Max Mohr's face.

Pull yourself together, Maidelleh, Barak's voice thundered in her head.

Don't ever let your guard down, with no one, certainly not a German. Any sign of weakness and they will eat you whole.

"I am sorry if my comment was crude. It was not meant to be," Max said, running his palm along the top of the briefcase now in his lap.

"Perhaps we should get to the business at hand," Hannah said, "although you must be tired from your journey. We can hold off until you've had a refreshing night's sleep. But if I may have some idea ... the reason for your visit ... I can be better prepared for our next meeting."

Hannah quickly glanced at Mohr. His face revealed nothing but a calm demeanour.

"*Ach, quatsch!* You're right," Max said. "We should get down to business. I am only mildly tired. Jet lag has no effect on me. Although I am ... how do you say ... rambling a bit. My business, representing Mr. Heilemann, has to do with a property belonging to one of your clients, ah, Mr. Chaim Sonenshein. It is a large tract of land in the Laurentian mountains."

So that was it? The anticipation of a big windfall, building steadily since she first spoke to Max, was suddenly as flat as a collapsed balloon. Still, Hannah kept her voice neutral as she asked, "Which large tract are you referring to? Mr. Sonenshein has several in the area we call *Les Laurentides*."

"Yes, I believe I am familiar with Sonenshein's many holdings in the Laurentians, but this particular tract is northeast of the town of Lachute, around Lac de Trois-Îles."

"Ah," she said, "that prime piece of land."

Hannah's eyes shifted to her hands resting on top of the board room table. She gave it a moment and then said, "You have done your research well but it's in the middle of nowhere and long ago, Mr. Sonenshein made it known to me that that particular piece of land is not for sale. I wish you had let me know before you had come all this way. I could have saved you the trip. I'm afraid you've come a long way only to be disappointed."

Mohr smiled a small smile that, despite its lack of smugness, reminded Hannah of the Cheshire cat in *Alice in Wonderland,* so enigmatic yet honest. There but not. As a child the Cheshire cat was one of her favourite Disney characters. As if he hadn't heard her bleak pronouncement, Max Mohr gently pushed back from the boardroom table and crossed his long legs. He looked down as he ran his hand along the crease on his light grey trousers and then shifted his weight. Unsettled, Hannah focused on the cut of the double-breasted linen jacket. A persistent clicking sound suddenly alerted her that she had been absent-mindedly snapping the cap of her fountain pen. Off. On. Off. On.

Max noted her fidgeting fingers and the way her facial expression, although seemingly immobile, could change as fleetingly as open fields under a passing cloud.

"Well then," he said with an easy smile, "the least you can do is offer me a cup of coffee."

"But of course. How about an espresso?" she said, pleased when Max's face lit up.

"Ah yes, please, a double."

Hannah buzzed Danielle and put in Max's request, and a rooibos tea for herself. She clicked the intercom off and turned to Max who had been watching her closely. His gaze was disconcertingly intense. She touched her hair as if to pat it down but quickly caught herself and brought her hands onto the tabletop. Max Mohr smiled that smile she was finding both attractive and irritating.

"I understand the situation," he said, "but I must confess I am not easily disappointed, Hannah. Furthermore, I would never categorize meeting you as a waste."

A brief glance assured her there was no 'funny business' as Barak called it; all she saw was a kind of open admiration that was unassailable.

"In any case, you should not be concerning yourself about disappointing me. This is business and I have come to Canada to conclude a number of contracts with Canadian companies for Mr. Heilemann's ventures in the UK. This is just one aspect of my reason for being here. And Montreal is such a lovely city, especially in the summer," he said, gazing out of the window onto the billows of green treetops scaling the southern slope of Mount Royal.

"Nonetheless, I am truly sorry, Mr. Mohr ..."

She caught herself as he gave her a playful scowl.

"... I mean Max. Mr. Sonenshein was clear that he may never sell Trois-Îles."

A knock on the door was followed by Danielle carrying a tray which she placed on the table between them.

"Thank you, Dani," Hannah said as her assistant quietly retreated, but not before catching Hannah's eye, however, and miming the word: WOW.

As Hannah handed the espresso to Max, the cup tilted against the saucer, but he saved the day with a firm grip on the plate. He lifted the cup and took a sip.

"Excellent espresso. Montreal is one of the few places in North America I can count on for that. Tell me, Hannah, in all seriousness, do you believe Mr. Sonenshein would say 'no' to an offer that has not yet been made?"

Hannah didn't answer right away; not so much for dramatic effect but to choose her words carefully. "Do you mean by that you think he could change his mind for the right price?"

"Of course, he would," Max said, affably. "He's a real estate developer, a highly successful one at that. I can't imagine that Mr. Sonenshein is emotionally attached to the land he is holding. It is property, meant to be bought, developed and/or sold for a profit. So, if my client were to ensure that your client makes a handsome yield on this property, why would he not sell?" His head cocked slightly, and his gaze remained steady. Hannah's face betrayed no disagreement.

Ah yes, she could hear Barak roar. *Don't they believe that the Jew is always driven by money. Offer him enough and he will sell his soul to the devil.*

Hannah smiled sweetly, "For the most part that's true, Max, for most people. It doesn't always work that way for Chaim Sonenshein. He can be surprisingly sentimental despite his success in business ... but I am curious. My understanding of Mr. Heilemann's business model is that his interests run to old properties he can renovate. There is nothing of the kind in or around Trois-Îles."

Neither Mohr's smile nor gaze waivered. "You will understand that, at this juncture, Hannah, I am not at liberty to discuss Mr. Heilemann's intentions for the property. Ours is but a preliminary meeting to establish contact."

"You've come a long way just to say hello."

"—And I have no regrets yet. But since I'm already *here*, could I tour this property that is not for sale?"

"I cannot answer that without discussing it first with my client. I will contact Mr. Sonenshein and try to have an answer for you by tomorrow. How long are you planning to remain in Montreal? I don't want to waste your time unnecessarily."

"No concerns. I plan to remain for two more days, and I have no regrets about this meeting. That would be especially true if you agree to have dinner with me tonight. I could tell you a little more about Mr. Heilemann's 'vision' and you will have time to think about bringing a serious offer to Mr. Sonenshein. What do you say?"

Without thinking, Hannah answered, "Yes, that would be lovely ..."

"I am staying at the Ritz-Carlton ... shall we dine there, let's say at 7 p.m.?"

"Certainly. That's perfect."

"Nothing is perfect," Max Mohr, replied with a Cheshire grin, "but some things come close."

Hannah slowly put the receiver back in its cradle and looked down at the pad on her desk where she had been drawing spirals during her conversation with Chaim Sonenshein. She had been expecting a Barak-style tirade—at times Chaim could be so like his old friend, but instead of him taking Hannah's head off, he had merely asked a few calm questions. "Tell me what you know about this Heilemann, and what kind of interest does he have in Canada?"

Hannah answered the first question based on her research but couldn't answer the second.

"I'm having dinner with Max Mohr tonight and hope to have more information for you by tomorrow. But are you even open to a bid on that property? I don't want to mislead him if that's not a possibility."

"Did I say that it was NOT a possibility?" Sonenshein said. Ah, that's the man I know, thought Hannah.

"You didn't say yes, and you didn't say no," Hannah said with a sigh. It was a game Sonenshein liked to play.

"You're such a clever girl ..."

"Don't patronize me, Chaim. I'm 45 years old, hardly a girl. We know each other too long for that. So, what do you want to know from Max Mohr to get this negotiation off the ground?"

"Simple," Sonenshein said. "How much money does Heilemann have to spend and what's his intention for the land? You know that particular property has special meaning for me ..."

"I know that's why I ..." Hannah started to say, but fell silent when Chaim, as usual, interrupted.

"... it was the first piece of land I ever purchased. And from the greedy, bastard son of that *paskudniak* ... y'know, the one who vowed no Jew would ever step foot on his land or poison his water. Such a long time ago ... I've owned that land for ..."

"... fifty years, I know."

"No, you don't know, *Maidel*. How could you know what it was like? I worked three jobs to *zammel* enough money. My wife didn't see me for more than an hour a day for years, but she understood, we had survived worst. I worked hard and then, a little *mazel* came my way, the reparations money from the Germans. I took it because I was alive. Your father was a real *shtick aktion*, stubborn as a mule, refusing to take what belonged to us. He called it blood money. I told him, 'Yes, blood money ... it is giving me a new life.' I had been robbed, we had all been robbed of our families, our homes, our youth ..." He stopped, and Hannah could hear his breathing slow. "*Nu*, never mind that. When I got that money, I bought my first piece of land. You should have seen, all around, how those Jew-haters panicked. *Un maudit juif* in the neighbourhood. Imagine! I bought them out, too. *Nu?* You don't know from such things, *Maidel*."

The spirals had filled Hannah's blotter as she waited patiently for Sonenshein to finish the familiar rant. She had had to run the gauntlet of these tirades but thankfully, they were different from what

Barak would spew out like poison. Her father could not say the word, 'German' without spitting.

"OK, Chaim, I will see what I can learn. He has asked if he could tour the property and I will tell him you have agreed but I can tell that this man, this Mohr, he's a good card player."

"You're not so bad yourself," Sonenshein said and hung up. Hannah had long ago grown accustomed to Chaim Sonenshein's practice of never saying good-bye.

CHAPTER SIX

Hannah pulled the Subaru up to the front door of the Ritz-Carlton and turned off the ignition with a flourish. She was feeling a little giddy having decided on valet parking. And why not? It was part of the adventure, this dinner with Max Mohr, a walk on the wild side. When the liveried doorman opened the car door, Hannah handed him the keys and entered the lobby of the city's Grand Dame of hotels. The Ritz-Carlton, opened in 1912, was the first hotel in North America to bear the iconic name, and was Hannah's favourite by far despite some evidence that the gild may have worn off the nameplate. It was the hotel's depth of history that appealed to Hannah, evidenced by the long list of famous guests from Winston Churchill to Marlene Dietrich and Maurice Chevalier. It fed into Hannah's love of Old-World glamour although she was less impressed that it was the hotel where the first of the Taylor-Burton marriages took place. Marilyn had argued in her no-nonsense way that the famous wedding had given Montreal a certain cachet in 1964 that it had not enjoyed before and not again until Expo 67.

"Those were the days when Montreal was excited about the future," Marilyn said with a touch of bitterness over her daughter's upcoming move to Toronto, "and not the battleground for separatists and petty politicians plotting how to divide up a fiefdom."

Passing the gold-veined lobby mirror, Hannah caught a glimpse of herself and experienced a moment of satisfaction at how the little black cocktail dress hugged her body. She smiled and glanced down at her watch. Too early, she thought. Usually punctual, tonight Hannah preferred to be a few minutes late. She stopped at the entrance to the Palm Court and stood for a moment looking down its length to where it opened onto the blue-walled Oval Room. The doors were closed but she easily recalled the layout of the superb salon where she had once accompanied Barak to the wedding of Lilah Sonenshein, Chaim's daughter. Chaim had made sure to let everyone know that the kitchen was 100% kosher, the joke being, Barak told Hannah, that Chaim was himself not so kosher. Despite doctor's orders, he loved his bacon and eggs.

Suddenly, the hair at the nape of Hannah's neck stood on end as a deep voice rumbled in her ear and a warm exhalation of breath flushed her cheek.

"It is peaceful this artful arrangement, is it not?" Max Mohr asked.

Hannah spun around, disconcerted by Max standing so close behind her.

"Pardon?" Her voice was barely a whisper.

"The way the palms, so out of place, complement without overpowering the décor of the room. You can almost see the ladies in their ball gowns, men in their smokings ... standing about socializing, *ne?*"

"Smokings?" Hannah felt a little like Alice tumbling down the rabbit hole.

"Yes ... uh, I think you call them tuxedoes," Max said.

"Oh, I understand. A scene from days gone by," Hannah said, stepping back. "I think I detect a hint of the romantic in you, Herr Mohr." Joke, tease, taunt, deflect, that had always been the weapon Hannah used against business situations that threatened to become too personal. Hannah raised her eyes to see the wry smile on Max's face. She hadn't noticed before that he had a dimple, only one, in his left cheek and a slight cleft in his chin, as if the renegade right dimple had found another, more interesting location.

"I'm afraid it is much more than a hint, Frau Baran. I think you can call me, as you say in English, a hopeless romantic … it's probably why I have been single for so long."

"Strange," she said returning the smile, "I would have thought it would have worked the other way around."

"Well, probably once burnt, twice shy," Max said.

"Perhaps we can explore that after we have discussed our business," she said. "After all, that is why we're here, is it not?"

"Is it?" Max Mohr asked and placed his hand on Hannah's back, turning her in the direction of the Café de Paris dining room. Once seated, Max had proposed that their meal not be marred by business talk.

"Fine food must be given its due, savoured and enjoyed without any distractions other than that of a pleasant conversation. In short, business can wait, don't you think?"

Hannah tilted her head in a gesture that could be mistaken for agreement. Instead of answering, she ran her fingers over the starched white linen cloth and eyed the elegance of the place settings, acutely aware that she was being examined by the man seated across from her. Had it been someone else who made the suggestion that their business discussion be sidelined, Hannah might have bridled. She didn't take well to pre-set rules but something about Max, a certain openness, belied any likelihood he was jockeying for the upper hand. Acknowledging that, Hannah relaxed and smiled at her dinner companion. It made for a pleasant meal with Max talking about some of his favourite trips: Tibet, Ireland, and Hong Kong, but Hannah was relieved when the remains of her arctic char and Max's sirloin steak were finally whisked away. The dessert menu was presented, and a perfunctory perusal of the mouthwatering descriptions ensured that Hannah would fall back on her old standard, crème brûlée. When tempted, Hannah always clung to the tried and true.

"This is a charming setting for a restaurant," Max said, expansively, looking out at the garden and the several ducks paddling in the pond. "I must say, these are the last things one expects to find outside of a city park, and in an inner-city hotel. It would seem Montreal has many hidden treasures." He caught Hannah's eye and smiled broadly.

"I think you're not only a romantic, Max, but a bit of a flirt," Hannah said. "But if it's urban nature that you want, you might, if you have spare time, visit the Hotel Bonaventure with its two-and-a-half-acre rooftop garden filled with mature trees, waterways, and even more ducks than the Ritz."

"Clearly you love your city. I like that. You were born here?"

Hannah looked down at her hands. There it was. The moment she had hoped would not arise. She imagined Barak leaning back in his chair, folding his arms across his chest, the corners of his mouth set in a grim line. She knew she should sidestep the question. It would be so much easier than telling the truth. Hannah recalled a note that Rokhl had written her when she had made friends in Grade 6 with Marianne, a blond, blue-eyed Christian. *Trust only your own* was all it said but even then, Hannah understood its intent; that you did not share what went on in your home with anyone, especially a non-Jew.

"Actually, I have lived here all my life, except for the first three years ..."

"Really, so where were you born then?"

Hannah took a breath. "I was born in Landsberg am Lech," she said.

"You're German?" Max looked surprised, even pleased, Hannah thought.

"No, I am not. My parents were refugees ... refugees in the DP camp there ..."

Hannah watched Max's expression closely but saw nothing to betray a look of surprise.

"So they were not German. Where are they from, your parents?"

It was becoming what Hannah had feared, a conversation about origins. The irony was that he could ask her where her parents were during the war, but she had no such license. She could not very well enquire, *"And what did your father do in the war? Where was he stationed? Did he murder any Jews?"*

She had been boxed in like this once before. When she was married, Hannah and Albie were touring southern Europe and were on a Danish cruise liner from Malaga to Genoa. They had been travelling on the cheap so were assigned to different berths. The Danes had

paired the passengers according to their country of birth and so Albert
had ended up sharing a cabin with three French-Canadian males and
she, with three young German women. She was 23, and for some reason,
terrified that the German girls would discover she was Jewish. As if
they might lock her into that tiny cabin and turn on the gas. When
she conversed with them, she hoped it sounded like German but was
certain they knew she was speaking Yiddish with a German accent.
The girls expressed polite curiosity about where she was from because,
they said, they found her dialect a little confusing yet intriguing. Like
Max, they had asked where she was born and when she answered
truthfully, their faces betrayed no guardedness at learning she came
from Landsberg. They had no idea that there had been an American-
run DP camp there after the war. When she finally admitted that she
was speaking Yiddish, they looked at first surprised and then delighted, asking her countless questions about Judaism. She was willing to
answer but it eventually galled her. There could be no questions about
what they thought of being German. They had no issues.

"Ah, so you are Jewish," Max said breaking into her reverie.

"Yes, I am Jewish."

"Do you remember anything about Germany?"

"No, I was just turning three when we left."

"But you've been back since then, no?" He looked so earnest Hannah
was a little taken aback. Was he playing at being naïve? She looked
around the genteel dining room. There were couples in animated but
muted conversation, others too long married to have anything left to
say, and groups of men, well-dressed, exchanging polite conversations
about what Hannah imagined were business matters. At that moment,
she would gladly have switched places with any one of them.

"No, Max," she said, "I haven't been back. My parents are Holocaust
survivors. There was never any possibility of me going back to Germany.
When I travelled to France, Spain, and Italy with my ex-husband some
20 years ago, Germany was never even considered an option." She did
not add that neither had she ever been allowed to own a product
manufactured in Germany.

"But why not?" Max said. Hannah was bewildered but certain

that Max was not being disingenuous. What could she say? She settled for part of the truth.

"It would have caused my parents great pain."

"So then," he said, looking chagrined, "they would not be very happy that you're sitting here with me, having dinner, would they?" There was no smile on Max's face as he waited for Hannah's reply.

"I believe in taking each person individually," Hannah said, carefully rolling her linen napkin along the tablecloth. "My father passed away several years ago and my mother doesn't have much to say on any subject."

"I'm sorry about your father," Max said. "I grew up without one. He left when I was two." He said this watching Hannah's restless hands. When she noticed, she quickly unrolled the napkin and laid it back in her lap. "Hannah, I was born in 1948. What happened in the war is not part of my life. It has nothing to do with me."

Hannah shook her head at his response.

"We need to talk about something else, Max. This is not a subject for a beautiful evening at the Ritz and it's not the topic of our business. We should get to that."

Reluctantly, Max agreed.

CHAPTER SEVEN

The next morning, Max was unable to shake the feeling that he had inadvertently stepped into quicksand. How did that happen? The business he had come to conduct was not being conducted in the manner he had anticipated. Something about Hannah Baran had managed to distract him. There was no doubt she was an attractive woman, but he had known and been intimate with many such women. Nadya had been stunning but that did not a marriage make. Alexander would be fifteen now, probably still unaware that he had a biological father who had been eliminated from his life soon after he was born, cut like the excess fat Nadya would trim from her steak. And Nicole, well, she came close to perfection but sadly, he did not rise to her standards. She found him too … too … what was the word she used? Oh yes, repressed. The French are so emotional, especially about love and how it must be expressed. It would never have worked. And since her, none had succeeded in accomplishing what Hannah Baran had in less than a day, without any artifice he could detect. He had let his guard down, but it would not happen again. It was merely a question of maintaining a proper distance because, without it, any project becomes an uphill struggle.

What disturbed him most was how he had inadvertently opened the door to territory he should have known was *verboten.* He had meant the evening to be pleasant, light, filled with social chitchat. All it took to complicate matters was a simple assumption on his part. *So, you were born here?* was all he had said and, suddenly, he fell into that black hole in history called the Holocaust. A small, nagging voice raised the old familiar question: Why can't we live in the present? Why not was truly a mystery to him although he considered himself an astute fellow and a keen observer of human nature. But he should have been prepared for this off-limits territory. It was for most people but most especially for a German.

Would he never learn? He had done his research on Sonenshein and knew the man's history: a child survivor who had not only endured the Lodz Ghetto but lived through several concentration camps. Given that history, Max could not help but wonder why Heilemann had been so specific about going after this man's property, especially since there was so much land currently for sale in that region of Quebec. Not to be overlooked was his client's puzzling shift. Why this property? One which Max Mohr was convinced had nothing in common with Ha-Gay's typical acquisitions. But these were questions Max could not raise, thorny problems which he understood innately that he was expected to resolve without any specific directives. It was his client's modus operandi to develop the big picture, the visionary aspects that had made his empire such a success, and Max's job to take care of the fine details.

Lately, however, Max had begun to feel there was something imperious in the way Ha-Gay did not trouble himself with intricacies of the deals he initiated although he was always there for the final negotiations. And as per usual, every deal was concluded in Köln as Heilemann, the owner of so many famous hotels, disliked travel.

This time things were even more complicated as Max felt surrounded by so many unknown quantities—Heilemann, Sonenshein and Hannah Baran. He was treading water for the moment. To succeed, he had to concentrate on what he knew. There was a piece of land he needed to inspect and determine what it would cost to purchase. His client had not asked for more than that. Perhaps, Max thought, and not for the first time, it was best that he didn't know the 'big' picture. It could get in the way of any successful negotiations. He needed to concentrate but Hannah was not making that easy. Suddenly, he had a vision of her standing at the edge of a silvery lake, the wind combing through her hair and bright sunlight making it shine like fine threads of copper. Last evening, standing behind her in the lobby, he had felt an irrepressible urge to slip his hand beneath the fall of those copper curls and grab a handful. The memory was so visceral he was startled by the tug in his groin.

Ach, quatsch! This was dangerous territory. What he needed was a good walk to clear his head. Having made up his mind to move, he quickly changed into light cotton slacks and a polo shirt, ran his fingers through his thick hair to give it a semblance of orderliness and headed for the lobby. He approached the concierge who quickly gave Max his full attention and an obsequious smile which normally would have annoyed him but today Max was more preoccupied with getting out and clearing his head. He asked directions on how to reach Mount Royal. He had studied the work of Frederick Law Olmstead as part of his MA at The Bartlett School in London. He was a great admirer of the parks Olmstead had designed—Central Park, Golden Gate Park and Montreal's Mount Royal. The concierge assured him it was an easy climb.

As Max exited the Ritz, he spied his destination. Walking towards it, he eyed the architecture and examined the houses in the area the map labelled The Golden Mile. In sharp relief against a bright blue sky, the elegant grey and red stone mansions of long dead industry barons stood shoulder to shoulder, now serving as university faculty and fraternity houses. The climb towards the mountain was not too steep and most welcome. Physical exercise, Max believed, always helped make for clear thinking. That's what Omi Edda would say when she took him for long walks while his mother was sleeping through the morning, and Leni and Eva were at the *Schule*. It sometimes surprised Max how much more he remembered of his grandmother and his twin sisters than his mother. He had adored them all, but Omi Edda had been more than grandmother.

In a way, her fierce nature and willingness to battle for what she thought was right filled the vacuum left by the father who had disappeared from his life when he was a toddler. According to Omi Edda and the *Zwillinge* that was to Max's good fortune. Eight years older, the twins refused to talk about what they remembered of their father. *Mutti* wouldn't either, waving him away with a hand that was rarely without a cigarette between stained fingers. Anyway, there was precious little opportunity as she was so rarely awake during the day or at home in the evening.

Max climbed steadily up Peel Street until, as the concierge had instructed, he reached the castle-like structure of the Royal Victoria Hospital. It loomed over the downtown area like the queen it was named for, she who had loomed over an empire on which the sun had never set. This city, Max thought, suffered from a split personality. The French factor was always butting up against some relic of the British Empire. He continued to climb, up past the hospital and behind it, eventually finding the steps that led up the southern slope. It felt good to be stretching his legs as the Americans were wont to say. Lately, too much of his time was being spent in front of computers or on planes.

The sun warmed his back, and a light breeze riffled his shirt as he reached a wide path that led him to something called Lac aux Castors where he saw a few fat ducks swimming in the man-made lake but no beavers. He turned to the higher ground and headed up a steep road that led him at last to a belvedere overlooking the southern end of the city. At the concrete balustrade, he stopped to take in the panoramic view. Next to him some Japanese tourists were taking group photos and a young couple, decked out in Lycra, were astride their trail bikes, enjoying the view.

Max stood looking out at the downtown area and beyond to the river and the low mountain ranges on the horizon. The scene spread beneath a clear blue sky reinforced his affection for the city. He liked that it seemed to stand with a foot in two camps—the European and the American. It didn't feel much like any other city in Canada. There was an air of calm that lay like a silken scarf on the treetops below the balustrade, disturbed only by the faint clink of hammering. Not far below, workmen were laying a new copper roof on a church, the glint off the red metal immediately conjured up Hannah's hair. He turned away and headed down the stairs, back to the hotel.

CHAPTER EIGHT

"**M**aximilian Mohr."

"Hello, Herr Mohr ... this is Hannah Baran, Flaubert Realties."

"Well, Hannah Baran ... hello, hello. Please, it's Max, remember? It is so very good to hear from you. I was beginning to think you may have forgotten me."

Hannah felt the morning sun as it poured through her office window, baking her back and colouring her cheeks. The voice on the other end of the line, nearly 6,000 km away, was resonant and carried with it a genuine smile. She visualized the face, how Max Mohr had looked as he stood in the reception area weeks earlier, his hand outstretched in greeting, the handshake crushing. Barak would have said that by his handshake Max Mohr knew who he was.

Images of Max flashed. She remembered his easy smile and the way it cracked his cheeks as it widened, his eyes that crinkled at the corners when he looked at her with a gaze that was congenial yet somehow self-effacing. During the weeks since, thinking about him, she finally pinpointed how that look had made her feel: gathered in, accepted. It was nothing like the wolfish looks she often got or the condescension which she encountered more often. Whatever the look that Max gave her translated to, it had made her feel at ease. The memory of Max Mohr had become a guilty pleasure. Hearing his voice on the line, Hannah felt the corners of her mouth lift.

"I'm pleased I caught you in the office, Max," she said. "I know it's late."

"Not so late and I have no reason to rush home. How are you, Hannah? I was beginning to doubt we would ever be in contact again."

She wondered why there was no reason he needed to be home.

"I apologize it's taken so long to get back to you, Max. My client was away and had not yet made a decision. But it has worked in your favour. I am happy to report that, much to my surprise, Chaim Sonenshein has decided he will consider your client's offer. That is if the inspection met with your approval. If it did, as proposed, I am prepared to come and meet with you and Herr Heilemann by late September. I'm afraid though, that I cannot be there for the realtor's seminar as you suggested."

"*Ach, quatsch.* I meant to write you that, in the end, the seminar was cancelled but if you're still willing to meet with my client and me, that is wonderful news. Only yesterday, Heilemann was asking after our progress. I look forward to your visit and to a fruitful negotiation, mutually beneficial."

The unchecked enthusiasm in Max's voice sent another wave of heat across Hannah's cheeks. Disconcerted, she whispered a hoarse 'thank you,' then sat silent for a moment, embarrassed by such a foolish response. What on earth was she thanking him for?

"Well, then," she said, fighting to recover her composure. "I will wait until you confirm your client's availability before booking my ticket. As this is my first trip to Germany, Max, I would appreciate any suggestions as to a preferred airport. I'm not sure if there is a direct flight to Cologne from Montreal. If there isn't, what would you suggest as the next nearest airport?"

"Düsseldorf or Frankfurt."

"But isn't Frankfurt quite far from Cologne?"

"With hardly any speed limits most of the way, nothing is too far."

As Max described the travel time between cities, Hannah was surprised to find that she was deliberately prolonging the conversation. She imagined Max standing on the other side of her desk, his stance loose and relaxed, his head bent slightly forward, attentive, and his smile rearranging the contours of his face.

"—But it does not matter where you arrive, Hannah Baran. Whether Köln, Düsseldorf or Frankfurt, you can be certain I will be there to collect you at the airport."

She smiled. He would 'collect' her. She would be collected. It was something she had not been for some time, certainly not since Barak's death, and wondered if she ever could be again. She realized she had stopped listening to his words but was simply enjoying the music Max was making in her head.

"Hannah?"

"Yes?"

"So, we are talking about sometime in the second half of September?"

She sat up in her chair and breathed deeply to get back to reality. She needed to get a grip on herself if she was to adequately represent her client.

"Yes," she said with more certainty than she felt, wondering how she would break the news to Rokhl that she might be gone for a week. And about where she was going.

CHAPTER NINE

I **would hear** *Papa talking about Hitler. Not just Papa, of course, Hannaleh. Everyone was talking about Hitler and his Brown Shirts. Their voices dropping to hushed whispers when we children were near so as not to frighten us, but we heard them. After a while, when I was around, they no longer resorted to whispers although they were careful to keep their voices well-modulated, matter-of-fact. It didn't matter. I was not paying attention as they argued about whether things would continue to grow progressively worse for German and Austrian Jews or if those practical, intelligent Germans would rise up against the National Socialists once and for all. I took no notice because I was almost 11 and there was this young boy, a neighbour who lived in the apartment above us. Oskar Liebner and I were friends. Or so Oskar thought. He couldn't know the part he played in my nighttime fantasies where I imagined us meeting in smoky cafés or secretly holding hands at the movies, maybe one starring my favourite actor, the handsome Clark Gable. Oskar was very handsome, too, with a full head of curly black hair and large green eyes. He was to be bar mitzvahed in a year and had confided in me that he was terrified his voice would break as he sang his* parshah. *We giggled when his voice cracked as he told me this. Oskar liked me. I know he did although he never said so. He was very polite around me but would become loud when he was with a group of his friends, pushing each other and laughing at their silly* *jokes, mostly about girls. I know, I watched him through the lace curtains that covered the window of our living room.*

↝ *"What is so interesting outside there that you forsake your precious studies?" Mameh asked one day, startling me. I pulled back from the window, but she swept the curtain aside and smiled her knowing smile. Just then Oskar looked up and Mameh moved aside so that he could see me looking down at him.*

"You have set your sights too low, my darling daughter," Mameh said, releasing the curtains and straightening the lace with care. "You will do better, I promise you."

She left me standing there wondering what was wrong with Oskar and who she thought might be better. As Fate would have it, better would one day prove to be an unwashed, fierce partisaner who rescued me from a nightmare, a prison which I have to admit to you, meine kindt, I helped build myself. But that came later, much later, in another lifetime far away from those days of innocence and even farther from the world you grew up in. After that day, however, things between me and Oskar slowly changed. He had less time for me, running down the stairs two at a time to meet up with his friends, flying past me without a sideways glance. He was also spending extra time at the shul in preparation for the day he would become a man. I thought carefully about that. He would become a man, but I would still remain a girl. Soon that didn't matter so much as I began to see that he would never be much of a gentleman, not like my Papa was. Once, when he thought I wasn't watching, he wiped his nose on this sleeve and often he laughed with his mouth wide open so you could see all his teeth, like a horse. Gentlemen did not laugh like that. And I began to notice that he was growing gangly, not as good looking as he had once been.

↝ *All of that—fantasies, childish crushes, inattentive boys never to become men—all of that changed on the day—September 6, 1939—when I turned 11. Papa and Mameh had planned a party for me; my school friends were already invited in late August and Mameh didn't see why* we had to cancel. But Papa suggested that we could hold just a small celebration, with something bigger later on. Just as well. That was the day that the Germans, with their shiny boots and flower pot helmets, goose-stepped into Krakow and down ulica Florianska, our street. Their appearance should have come as no surprise. We had known for five days that we were at war, well, invaded really by the Third Reich, but for some reason which I have now long forgotten, we never imagined that war would touch us in Krakow, Poland's cultural centre, the seat of a famous university, of the Jewish intelligentsia. For one thing, not a single cannon was ever fired because our brave mayor surrendered the city without a shot, to save us he said.

Well, to save some of us anyway.

CHAPTER TEN

Looking back on that night, it was clear the whole thing had begun badly. Hannah suspected as much but had deliberately blinded herself to the danger. There was no way out, as Marilyn liked to say, except through. Rokhl had to know about Hannah's travel plans.

"Ma, I have something to tell you," Hannah had said, watching her mother bend to straighten the hall runner at the entrance to the living room. After a week of agonizing over how to introduce the news that she was planning a trip to Germany, I-have-to-tell-you-something was the lamest approach in her arsenal. Yet, there it was. Something in Hannah's tone made Rokhl turn to take a closer look at her daughter. What she read there in that concerned face with the large violet-blue eyes must have somehow suggested that she should sit down. All Hannah wanted to do was prepare Rokhl for her physical unavailability for a week, something that had not happened since Barak had died. Moving into the living room, Rokhl had placed her palms on the sides of her favourite armchair and slowly eased herself onto the worn seat. Hannah waited for her mother to settle down, noting again how fragile she was looking these days. It pained Hannah to think that she knew women older than Rokhl who were energetically playing tennis, taking yoga, remaining vital. But not her mother who seemed to be growing weaker with each passing month.

After so many years, the burgundy chair Rokhl sat in had faded to pink in patches where the velvet had worn away, but Hannah had long ago stopped trying to convince Rokhl to replace it. And the chair was not the only thing needing to be refreshed in the sparsely furnished living room. As a teen, Hannah had measured what they had against the homes of her peers. There was never any comparison. What chagrined Hannah the most was her parents' casual disinterest in spending money on appearances, especially where furniture was concerned. When Hannah hinted that the living room needed some additional pieces, Barak wearily maintained that the money he earned had better uses than to be spent on décor to impress the neighbours.

Stacked up against what some of her friends had, her silently submissive mother, the unadorned living room, even the lack of an annoying sibling, failed miserably. Marilyn's mother, Mrs. Lehrer was Hannah's ideal, always happily chattering away even when no one was listening. She took fitness classes at the Y and volunteered at the Jewish Public Library and the Hospital of Hope. And though other mothers weren't as cheerful as Marilyn's, back then they had furnished their living rooms in a style worthy of Versailles. They had curvaceous sofas arranged in spacious rectangular, suburban living rooms beneath tinted portraits of bar mitzvah boys. These treasured French provincial couches were tightly fitted in gold and white brocade as if competing with courtiers attending Louis XIV. Or they had avocado cut velvet, the latest fashion, all carefully encased in thick, fitted plastic covers that clung to the back of your bare legs in summer. The Baranowski couch upholstered in a nondescript, scratchy beige material had always been covered by a *shmateh*, intended to keep the fabric fresh for company. But company rarely if ever came especially after Hannah stopped bringing her friends home. The matching beige armchair where Barak had sat for over 30 years now sagged sadly in the seat as if lonely for the bulk it had supported. The cream and beige Persian rug, bought at Eaton's and centred perfectly in the small room, lay beneath a long maple coffee table also perfectly centred. Early on, her mother had silently trained Hannah and Barak to circumvent the carpet in order to save it from being worn out. Over the years, it was the parquet floor around it that had eventually lost its varnish creating a cartoonish effect as if a path had been worried away.

"—Worrying about the carpet," was Barak's wry joke.

Rokhl's chair was near the window, under a bronze and milk glass floor lamp that Hannah had once offered to sell as a genuine antique after seeing something similar on the Antique Road Show. But Rokhl refused. It was one of the few things Rokhl seemed to cherish, the lamp bought in a second-hand store and the burgundy velvet armchair which she had seen in an Eaton's flyer and had uncharacteristically insisted she must have. The night before she disappeared, Rokhl had sat down in her favourite chair, raised her chin, and lowered her eyes to indicate that she was paying attention while Hannah scraped away at the raw cuticle on her thumb using the nail of her crooked middle finger. Her mother waited but Hannah was finding it difficult to start the usual string of patter that passed in lieu of conversation between them. Rokhl coughed softly but did not look up.

"I'm going on a business trip ... to Germany," Hanna finally blurted out.

A strange silence ensued, markedly different than Rokhl's usually wall of dead air. This felt somehow charged.

"Ma," Hannah said, "I plan to leave in three to four weeks. And I'll be gone for at most a week, well, maybe a little longer. It will be sort of a vacation too because you know, I haven't had a vacation since Papa died and this is a golden opportunity for me to combine business with a bit of a holiday. I'm meeting with a German real estate developer who is interested in buying a piece of land from Chaim Sonenshein to build a luxury resort in the Laurentians. They're paying all my expenses. Do you remember the German client I told you about? Maximilian Mohr? From Cologne?"

Hannah was lying. She had never mentioned Max before, but she barrelled on hoping the speed of her delivery would pave over any upcoming bumps in the road.

"Ma?" Hannah was unable to look at her mother. "Anyway, I'm going to Germany and even though it's a business trip, I decided it's crazy not to take advantage of being in the country where I was born so I thought I would ... I mean, well I thought that I should ... go ... uh ... back to Landsberg, y'know, to see the town, the area."

There. Done. It was all out and over. Hannah wrapped her arms around her chest, a chill running through her despite the humidity in the room. The worst was over, Hannah chose to believe despite the eerie calm. Telling her mother what she was planning had always been the hardest thing for her to do, even harder than telling Barak, or actually *doing* it, whatever "it" was. Sharing news with Barak had been easier because you always knew where he stood. He attacked right away. His face would flush and framed by his thick white hair it would take on a purplish hue as he discharged whatever fury he had gotten himself into over whatever major or minor action Hannah had proposed. That had been easier to deal with than her mother's silence. *You cannot argue with a stone,* Rokhl had written in a note when, as a teenager, Hannah had grown too vocal about their inability to have a conversation. Hannah believed that the worst-case scenario was she might be punished by an extended period of Rokhl saying not a word. But what transpired on that night was a heat-guided missile from the other end of the spectrum.

"You are not going to Germany," Rokhl said sharply, biting off the words as if each was a piece of her daily ration of RyVita toast.

Suddenly, Hannah was eight years old again, holding the cheek that had just been soundly slapped by her mother's hand. A slap from Barak was never a surprise. But that slap? The pain had been unbearable, due as much to the revelation that Rokhl was capable of such forceful contact as by the sting of the smack itself for such an innocent question. All Hannah had asked was: How could *all* Germans be bad? Not since that day so long ago, had she seen Rokhl so fierce, or so deeply sensed the gathering of the magma that usually flowed deep below the surface of their lives.

With the news that she was planning a trip to Germany, Hannah had somehow affected a rupture in her mother's world. Tectonic plates grinding against one another could not have been more earth shattering then the sound of Rokhl's voice that night.

"Over my dead body will you go back to that land of demons and monsters that took us so many years to leave behind."

There was no warning, no internal signal and, if there had been, she would still have been unarmed. Hannah had never learned how to swim in turbulent seas, had never had to, not even with her father. Up until then she had only needed to be skilled in treading water. But her mother's raised voice, issuing a direct command and most shocking of all, the emotion in it, were beyond Hannah's imagination.

"But, Ma ..."

"*Nein!*" And the words came spilling out of her mother's mouth in such a steady flow, Hannah was staggered.

"*Du bist eine narish kindt*, how can you be so foolish? After all these years? Do you think I would permit such a thing, to go back to a place that wanted only to starve and kill us? Their people came to beat us, gas us and turn our parents, our children, to ash? Do you think I would let my only child go back to the land where they tried to exterminate us? What kind of a daughter have I raised?"

"But Ma ... that was in the camps over half a century ago. Things have changed; things DO change," Hannah said, afraid to raise her voice above a whisper.

At the mention of the camps, Rokhl's eyes grew unfocused; her face flushed. It was as if Hannah had broken some spell. During her tirade, Rokhl had thrust herself from the chair, stood with her fists clenched by her side, quivering in the grip of some fever raising her colour to a dangerous level.

"Did we teach you nothing? Did you learn nothing from the past? *Gottinu*, why am I still being punished?"

Rokhl's face contorted. She threw her head back, raised her eyes heavenward and wailed, "Barak, come take me to Gan Eden. Take me, I beg you. Take me away from this world of pain."

Hannah stood stupefied as her mother called for Barak to relieve her of life. Did she really wish she were dead? How could she, after half a century, react so violently to a mere business trip?

"It's just a week ... and it's been 50 years," Hannah said feebly.

"Nothing has changed, do you understand?" Rokhl turned and said in a strangled voice.

"You have lived too long in bright sunlight, so you are blind. Oh, if only my enemies could lick my heart, they would die on the spot from the poison stored there."

Rokhl fell backwards into her chair, the colour draining from her cheeks.

"*Mein Gott*, what do you know? To have lived so long and still remain a child. You say fifty years ago? Fifty years? Fifty years or five minutes, what is the difference? Believe me, they are the same. Nothing grows old but the body. My life is dust and ash if not for you. You are all I have to show that I did not die in a black pit. And you ... you ... YOU cannot go to *Deutschland*. You will not go, not to the land of murderers. There is nothing there for you. No one and nothing. *Nein. Nicht mueglicht.* Over my dead body, do you hear me? Over my dead body!"

Black hole? What black hole had Rokhl escaped? But Hannah asked no questions, taking a leaf from her mother's book she chose silence. There had been so many words ... and none of them on paper so that Hannah could read and re-read them, searching for the meaning. These words had been flung at her; their import wreathed in layer upon layer of code she could not understand. The very sound of the words as if they had been stones shot from a slingshot had caused her physical pain. Where had they come from? Hannah had always believed that Rokhl's voice was unable to project above a certain soft range like that kitten Hannah had found while walking in the woods outside Magog. She had rescued Putzi from a leg-hold trap. The kitten had been there about a week, the vet had speculated, and had cried so long and hard, his voice had cracked and broken, never to return.

The night before Rokhl disappeared, Hannah was forced to acknowledge the depth of her self-deception. She thought she knew her mother's story, but there was Rokhl keening, a sound Hannah had expected after Barak's death, but had never come. After her father died, Rokhl had only grown more silent and her notes, the only connection Hannah could count on, less frequent. For some reason, what wounded Hannah most was that Rokhl had never before scolded her, never given her a direct order. Why? What did Rokhl think could happen if Hannah went back to Germany, back to the town where she was born? Shaken by the force of Rokhl's dictum, Hannah had made her mother a promise that she knew she would not keep. She lied saying she would respect her mother's wishes.

Within 24 hours, the lie no longer mattered.

CHAPTER ELEVEN

The sun was high in the sky and fierce as they stood outside the Montreal morgue on Parthenais St. Marilyn placed an arm around Hannah's waist and pulled her close.

"I will see to it that we have ten men for Kaddish at the cemetery," Marilyn said. Despite the heat, a shiver rippled across Hannah's rigid back. The memory of her mother's stone-cold arm remained on her fingertips like a touch of frostbite. Marilyn rubbed her upper arm, trying to generate some comfort and Hannah leaned into her friend's solid body, wondering if she could ever shake the chill creeping through her. Maybe that's why she had not yet shed a tear, she thought, maybe they're frozen in place. By contrast, Marilyn's cheeks were glistening as a stream rolled unimpeded to her chin. Hannah looked at her friend and was grateful. In the end, it had been easier to ask for her help than she had imagined. And ever dependable Marilyn, taking the request to heart had considered it a green light to indicate that she could take charge. She had already insisted on making the funeral arrangements. Numb, Hannah acquiesced without protest.

➢ Standing on the sidewalk outside police headquarters Hannah was attempting to reconstruct the chain of events that led them to this spot. She remembered talking to the detective, Desjardins, and then thinking that, after the morgue, she would have to go to the funeral home. She remembered what it was like when Barak had died two years earlier—the trip to Paperman's Funeral Home, the agonizing march past the selection of coffins and the silent (perhaps imagined) reproof from the undertaker when she had chosen the plain pine coffin.

"It's what my father would have preferred," she said, having felt compelled to explain.

The undertaker had nodded with a knowing look as if to imply that's what they all say. The funeral home was going to be difficult but in no way could she go to the morgue alone. What if they didn't speak English at the morgue? What if they asked her to look at several bodies? What if Rokhl wasn't there? What if she was? 'What ifs' zoomed through her head until Hannah had to swallow her pride and reluctantly, greedily, reached out to Marilyn who was in the car before Hannah had finished the phone call.

They had entered the Montreal headquarters to the Sûreté du Québec at Parthenais and Ontario, not an area of Montreal either was familiar with, and gave their names to the officer at the front desk. Soon enough, someone came to escort them to a cubicle where for about half an hour Hannah answered a barrage of questions about Rokhl. When all the answers had been recorded, they were handed passes which they had to present to an armed officer at the elevator. As the doors closed, Marilyn could not resist tossing off an acerbic, "Do they think people are dying to get in?"

Hannah managed a wan smile. The doors opened followed by a sudden blast of cold air filled with the weight of chemical agents. It made their eyes instantly water.

"If you're not dead already," Marilyn said, mumbling, "this smell could kill you for sure."

For a moment, Hannah was disoriented by the colour combination of the floor—white walls, blue doors, and blood red floors but Marilyn soon steered her to a door on the right. After pressing a buzzer and showing their passes, they were ushered in. Without thinking, Marilyn stretched out her arm so Hannah could steady herself. Inside the morgue, Hannah surveyed the walls of stainless-steel lockers. Once again, she felt as if she'd stepped into an episode on a crime series. It was all so familiar and yet so foreign. Her eyes darted around the room and only came to rest when she spied a large, zippered bag on a gurney. After a brief exchange, it was rolled into the centre of the room by a young man in a blue smock and a shock of black hair. Marilyn took the reins and answered the pathologist's questions.

"Are you ready?" Marilyn asked.

"Please ask them if I can see only the right arm. I don't need to see everything." She kept her head turned until she heard the zipper sliding down releasing a whisper of finality. As the arm was carefully slipped out, Hannah turned slowly to catch a glimpse of the pale flesh, translucent as ice but for the ridge of scarred skin. Again, she remembered the arm in motion as it had arced gracefully over her head, the gentle brushstroke to her hair. The memory evaporated in a moment and all that was left was the lifeless arm.

From that moment on, Hannah used all the silence she had absorbed in a lifetime of living with Rokhl. She felt her organs liquefying at a remarkably rapid pace; only a skin made of silence prevented them from leaking out. She heard someone ask her to look at the face, but Hannah shook her head and turned away. Marilyn did it for her and calmly confirmed that yes, this was Rokhl Baranowski. Her teeth chattering, Hannah made it into the hall and to the elevator only by hanging onto Marilyn. Outside, the heat enhanced the odour of death that had remained clinging to their clothes. For days, Hannah would be convinced it continued to rise from her skin.

The morning of the funeral, it was Hannah's turn to be calm and collected while Marilyn was coming apart.

"I'm so sorry I've let you down, Hannah, I tried and tried but could only come up with eight men. I even called Albert but it's the last week of August and everybody is out-of-town for the Labour Day weekend."

"You called my ex-husband?" Hannah was incredulous at the lengths to which Marilyn had gone to find ten men for a *minyan*.

"Well, he and Rokhl did used to be thick as thieves ... I thought he'd want to know. You're not upset, are you?"

Hannah shook her head remembering how Albert would sit in the kitchen for hours as Rokhl prepared the Friday night supper. It had been the ideal set-up. Albert talked and talked, and Rokhl, unlike her daughter, never interrupted or lost interest. Theirs was a match made in heaven.

"No, of course, I'm not upset ... how could I be after all you've done to get me through this? I can only imagine how hard this has been for you, juggling your volunteer work and the house, and now me. You have done so much."

"Stop it," Marilyn said gently. "Don't you dare start comforting me when you're the one who needs to be consoled. Don't you go doing that, do you hear me? Let someone take care of you for a change. And if I want to feel bad, please let me, Hannaleh. Okay?"

Hannah nodded wearily and felt the fist inside her chest open a little. Only Barak and Marilyn had ever called her Hannaleh.

The funeral service, like the thin crowd scattered through Paperman & Sons' smallest chapel, was meagre. Again, the box was plain. As the rabbi had never met Rokhl, a total stranger to syna-gogues, he gave a brief eulogy using a description that Hannah had provided. All this despite Rokhl's insistence after they buried Barak that her funeral should be totally private. She had only agreed to a public funeral for Barak because he had friends and acquaintances—his union comrades, his Sunday night card players, his co-workers—as well as all of Hannah's friends and business associates who attended out of respect. But Rokhl's secluded life was evidenced by the sparse assembly of elderly Jewish men and women—a few neighbours, the kosher butcher with whom they had travelled to Canada on the U.S.S. General Black troop ship; Maria, the Portuguese cleaning lady that Hannah and Rokhl shared, and surprisingly, Betty, Dr. Rubin's recep-tionist. There was just one or two unfamiliar faces that Hannah could not have placed. Dani, Sam, Jean-Marc and Irv, fellow agents, and work buddies, had come out of support for a lady who was one of the best, they told Marilyn. Some even came in from the country in the hopes that they could help make up a *minyan*. They sat in the front pew and when they could, caught her eye and smiled self-consciously at Hannah who sat by herself in the area reserved for family. This was it, the way it was going to be for the rest of her life, she thought. *I am now nobody's daughter.* It was a phrase she had read in a book, maybe it was the title. She would occasionally remember it, wondering what it would feel like to be an orphan.

Nobody will ever again look at me and remember what I was like the day I was born or remember the first words I spoke. Those who loved her were gone—first Barak, now Rokhl. They were the two extremities of her life to which she had been tied—and had pulled against.

After Barak's death, she had experienced the same numbness but had focused all her energy on Rokhl. Now with her mother gone, Hannah was adrift.

~ As kids, she and Marilyn used to stand in a doorway, pressing the backs of their hands against the frame. The trick was to press as hard as you could and then step away to allow your arms to rise, floating up of their own volition, as if any minute, you could fly away. Sitting alone, facing the foot of Rokhl's plain wooden coffin, Hannah was unattached from everything that mattered. Led by the Paperman hearse, the small cavalcade of cars turned off of Sources Blvd. and onto the grounds of the Kehal Israel Cemetery. The motorcade proceeded cautiously down the narrow road barely wide enough for two vehicles to pass each other. When the procession reached the centre lot, the cars broke formation to park. The lead limousine with Hannah and Marilyn, and the hearse with Rokhl's coffin, circled the copse of mature birches that stood guard over the centre lot. Doors opened, legs and arms sprouted, followed quickly by bodies assembling themselves into a small crowd gathered in the dusty lot. Together, the group set out down the road. Nearby, a freshly prepared plot was waiting. A rectangular hole, a mound covered by a bright green carpet of Astroturf, a wooden marker and ten men to say the prayer for the dead were all the preparation needed to bury Rokhl.

Hannah was twelve years old the first time she stepped foot in a cemetery, in that very cemetery, the one where Barak now lay and where Rokhl would soon be settled in beside him. One of her father's co-workers, a Holocaust survivor without family who had sometimes

76

taken walks with them on Sunday afternoons, had died. Barak had insisted on bringing Hannah to the funeral despite Rokhl's silent agitation and a flurry of notes. Hannah told her mother she wanted to go; wanted to see how people were buried in the ground. By then, Hannah had already read all about cremation, about the extermination procedures at Auschwitz, Dachau, Treblinka, and Chelmno; as a teenager, she had wondered if Death wasn't the fourth member of their small family, the other silent one. That first time, she had watched with insatiable curiosity as the coffin was lowered into the ground and heard the first clump of earth hit the wooden box with a dull thump. She remembered the chill, the finality that sound had conjured and how she had cried. Her reaction was the same for every burial she had witnessed since.

"We will all lie together," Barak had told Hannah that day. He said that all three of them—he and Rokhl and Hannah—had plots reserved at Kehal Israel. They were members of the Hebrew Protective Society; the first organization Barak had joined upon arriving in Montreal. Every month, her father had doled out a fee, albeit modest, to secure their burial plots. Only years later did the action strike Hannah as bizarre, ironic even, that her immigrant parents should arrive in Canada, the land of hope, and make their final resting place their number one priority. Before saving a penny or investing in a house, they had made sure they had someplace to rest when they died.

☞ The sky was a clear, bright blue on the day they put Rokhl in the ground next to Barak. A refreshing wind riffled the birch leaves that fluttered like angel wings. Rokhl was buried in her pre-paid plot despite the rabbi's concern, addressed and dispelled by Hannah, that the death may have been a suicide. If it had been, Jewish law stated that Rokhl could only be buried on the edge of the cemetery. Inside the boundaries of the cemetery, no trees grew to overshadow the rows of low gravestones lined up as if for roll call. Rokhl had had enough of ominous shadows, Hannah had said to the rabbi. She had earned her right to be buried with dignity.

Eight men carried Rokhl's plain pine coffin to the freshly dug hole but even with the rabbi there was not enough for a *minyan* at the grave. That meant there could be no Kaddish, no prayer for the dead. Suddenly, Marilyn broke rank and abandoned Hannah to stand alone staring into the hole in the ground. When she pulled her eyes away, she saw Marilyn ushering two old Chassidim over to the grave. Her friend had found a way to keep her promise for a *minyan*.

"At least Rokhl will have Kaddish said for her," she whispered into Hannah's ear. The 'at least' was a gentle admonition. Despite Marilyn's chidings, Hannah had decided that there would be no *shiva*. How could she sit *shiva*, sit in mourning for seven days all by herself, sit on that short-legged chair with nothing but a few friends dropping in after work? What good would that do her? *Shiva* was meant to honour the dead and comfort the mourners. No comfort would be derived from the constant reminder that she was all alone and that there was practically no one left to honour Rokhl.

⮐ On the way home, sitting in the cool interior of Paperman's limousine, Marilyn announced that she had made plans to sleepover at Hannah's for the next few days. Startled, Hannah shook her head.

"No," she said in a whisper.

"No?"

"No, Marilyn, I understand your motives," she said, gently, "and I love you, but you'll want to help me. You'll want to talk things out."

"It's important ..."

"I know ... that's what makes you such a good communicator and such an invaluable friend but ..." Hannah laid a cool hand on Marilyn's tanned arm. "But what I need now is *not* to think but to feel. I need to feel something other than this numbness. I don't know why but I don't feel sad. What's wrong with me? I don't even feel anger. I haven't shed one tear over Rokhl. What's wrong with me?"

"There's nothing wrong with you," Marilyn said, leaning into Hannah, hugging her hard. "Your father, may he rest in peace, was sick for months. That gave you time to prepare, to absorb the fact that he was going to die. Nobody beats pancreatic cancer, so you had time to ... to ... to get acquainted with your grief. It may have been only six months, but you saw him physically fade away. There was a transition. That's different than what happened with your mother, *halova shalom*."

Despite not wanting to, not wanting to show her emotion, tears trickled down Marilyn's cheeks. She pulled a tissue from her pocket.

"I know you," she said. "It'll take maybe three days, three weeks or three months, but suddenly, it'll hit you and you'll be emotionally overwrought. It took you months to get angry about Albert and his betrayal. Remember? So, I promise you, you'll be crying long and hard when the time comes." Marilyn reached out to hug her friend again, but Hannah put an arresting hand against Marilyn's chest and slid herself into a corner of the limousine's backseat. In the cool dark, Hannah shivered.

"It's as if I've waited my whole life for this moment, and now that it's arrived, I'm unable to understand what is happening. Maybe it's so big I can't see it ... I'm too close. I don't know. It's like there's a vacuum inside me and if I open any window even a crack, the outside world will get sucked into this black hole."

She heaved a sigh and stilled herself, examining her hands and the self-inflicted damage of tattered cuticles, the only visible testament to the stress of the last few days.

"Maybe when I'm alone, things will sort themselves out. The police have closed the investigation but there is something that I need to figure out. I can't talk about it now because ... well, because I don't understand it myself. It's ... it's ... it's like a riddle ..."

"What are you talking about? A riddle? Do you mean why your mother left the house without her purse and was wandering on Côte-des-Neiges?"

"Yes, yes ... that's what I mean ..."

"Oh, Hannah ... how many times have you yourself told me that we can never know what goes on in a person's head, that we are the only ones who can see the world through our eyes? That has to be doubly true of our parents after all they lived through."

Hannah sucked in the scented air of the limousine. It gave her a moment of comfort. She wondered how many conversations this vehicle absorbed ... how many words of grief, bitterness, anger, guilt.

"I told my mother I was going to Germany on business and ..."

Marilyn waited for the end of the sentence. When she saw Hannah unable to finish, she suddenly sat up.

"You don't think that's what set her off, do you?" Marilyn, her back rigid, towered a little over her friend. "Tell me that you haven't convinced yourself of that."

"She yelled at me." Hannah's voice was barely above a whisper.

Marilyn stopped in mid-protest. "Rokhl?"

"She yelled in a fury and told me that I was a child and that I could not go to Germany ... except ..."

"So, she was upset, Hannah. You know how they get. They get adamant about ..."

"She said if I went to Germany, it would be over her dead body."

Marilyn slowly leaned back against the soft grey velvet interior and closed her eyes. The set of her mouth said that was that. There would be no arguing with Hannah now that those were the last words she would ever remember from a mother forever silent.

CHAPTER TWELVE

The day after Rokhl's funeral, Hannah drove down the ramp into the gloom of the office garage and pulled into the stall with her name, painted in large, white letters. Seeing Hannah Baran writ so large, she experienced another moment of surprise at no remembrance of how she got there. Staring at the wall, images of her mother's pale face, the scarred arm, and the words *"I am not her"* flickered in her mind. She squeezed her eyes shut as she used to when she was small. Behind scrunched lids, starbursts and whirling galaxies appeared. She breathed in and they slowly faded to black. There was comfort in the darkness. But she had to go to work, couldn't just sit there in the gloom for the rest of the day.

Following the funeral, Hannah had slept for eighteen hours straight and although she recalled no dreams when she finally awoke, she was exhausted. Since standing over Rokhl's grave, there was a dull, intermittent ache in her chest. Her condo, that treasured refuge, the one place where she could just be, where the mask she wore in business was laid by the door, was suddenly a foreign landscape. A kind of hollowness had been growing. Hannah's passion for minimalism in décor, the absence of colour and clutter, was now disturbing. Her refuge suddenly felt like one more empty space in her life. The thought depressed her but not to the point of tears. Dry eyes stared back at her accusingly from the bedroom mirror. *No tears for Rokhl?* No tears for Rokhl? Leaving for the office was the only thing she could think to do. Maybe it was too early to return but she didn't care. People talk no matter what you do. The only thing she was sure of was that she needed order in her life.

Hannah shook the thought off and picked up the phone. She called the office. "Get my things in order," she told Dani, "I'm on my way."

Danielle jumped up from behind her desk as Hannah entered the office.

"Hannah, oh, are you OK? Are you sure you should be here?" Danielle started to move towards her boss, but something prevented her from reaching out. Hannah offered up a small smile.

"I'm fine. And yes, this is the only place I'm sure I need to be."

Hannah reached for the door to her office and rested her hand on the handle. She inhaled deeply before opening the door. She thought about Rokhl's one and only visit to her offices, how she had been both awed and intimidated by where her daughter worked.

"Your office is so big, bigger than our living room," is all Rokhl had said before asking to be taken home.

"Your messages are on your desk. And you have one from Albert," Danielle said, closely watching Hannah standing frozen on the spot. Danielle reached out to touch her boss. "Did you hear me? You have a message from Albert."

"What?" Hannah turned her head as if to hear better.

"Albert? Your ex-husband? He called twice."

➷ A sigh escaped Hannah's lips when she saw the large pile of contracts stacked on the centre of her desk, threatening to topple. Has it only been a week since she left her office in a rush to pick up Rokhl? She despaired for a moment but was comforted that there would be no time for wallowing. Sitting down, Hannah eyed the neat piles of phone messages laid out as Danielle was instructed to do—in alphabetical order, one slip per message. Hannah riffled through the pile noting how many calls per person. She had always hated voice mail and the effort it required to take the information while trying to catch every nuance of a hurried voice. A written message sidestepped all the unnecessary guesswork.

She turned away from the notes to scan through a pile of offers and counteroffers that colleagues had handled for her while she was away. When she felt settled, she turned back to the phone messages and worked her way through the pile, prioritizing the calls. At the top of the list was Max Mohr in Cologne, at the bottom, Albert. How long had it been since she and Albie had exchanged pleasantries? Years maybe, certainly not since that scene that erupted in the restaurant with Joani getting hysterical. Hannah flushed at the memory of people staring mouths agape when her ex-husband's new wife called her a selfish bitch. Marilyn had told her that Joani was a big-time drinker, but Hannah never expected to see it firsthand. Such unseemly behaviour, and all over the sale of a piece of property that didn't even belong to the Mrs. Zelig Number Two, as Marilyn called her. It had been the semi-detached cottage in Snowdon that she and Albert had lived in but had always been in her name. Throughout the scene, Albert had pretended that he was in another room, and that this shrieking woman had nothing to do with him.

"Your ex is on line three." Danielle was standing in the doorway. Startled, Hannah looked up. "Why didn't you just buzz me?"

"I did. Why didn't you answer?"

Hannah shook her head to clear the images running through her mind like a horde of unruly children.

"Sorry, I guess not all of me is back here yet." She gave Danielle a small smile by way of an apology and waved her off. Hannah regretted not making the call to Mohr while she had had the chance. Punching line three with more force than necessary, she decided to make the call brief, like her marriage to Albert.

"Hannah Baran," she said.

"Hannah, it's Albert. I'm calling to say how sorry I am for your loss. I heard about Rokhl and wanted to let you know how sad I was to learn about her death."

"Thank you, Albert. That's very thoughtful."

"We always got along so well, Rokhl and me." He paused. "It kind of made up for Barak."

"Albert, please don't. Barak, may he rest in peace, just had my best interests at heart."

"Yeah, I guess. But I'm really sorry I wasn't at the funeral. Rokhl was very special to me, y'know but ... well, we were in the country."

Hannah had to fight the urge to tell Albert it was all right, to let him off the hook. Instead, she remained silent, letting him dangle on the other end of the line. She was not feeling charitable about him missing the funeral. Although it meant nothing to her, and she knew Rokhl had not even wanted a funeral, Hannah thought maybe it would have meant something to her mother if he had made the effort. She still wondered what Rokhl had seen in Albert. They had connected almost immediately. Puzzled at seeing Rokhl so animated whenever Albert came to pick her up for a date, Hannah first suspected that it was one of those ways her mother devised to defy and irritate Barak who had had a very negative reaction to Hannah's new boyfriend. That didn't explain, however, Rokhl putting on her best dress or taking out dishes Hannah rarely saw to serve coffee and cake to Albert. She even exchanged pleasantries with an ease Hannah had rarely witnessed.

These were things that Barak would berate Rokhl for *never* doing. This could have merely been another deliberate irritant on Rokhl's part yet, somehow, it never felt like that. It was almost as if Rokhl had taken a fancy to Albert. It had been abundantly clear that, on first sight, Barak was opposed to the man Hannah would marry. Somehow, he had known that they would not be a good match—that was a time Hannah would do anything to contradict Barak. Maybe, in that respect, she was a little like Rokhl.

➷ Albert first walked into her life some 25 years earlier accompanying an elderly aunt who needed social services. Five years later, he walked out of her life with the daughter of his senior partner hanging off his arm.

"There's something intriguing and yet familiar about Albert," she told Marilyn a few days after their first meeting. These were not words she ever expected to use in describing an accountant.

"Intriguing, eh? Curiosity about a man ... how thrilling. Tell me more," Marilyn said.

Hannah just laughed. She'd had only two lovers at that point and although she cared for them, neither inspired her to let loose as she had with Albert. Their lovemaking may have lacked tenderness, but there was wildness in it that excited her.

"He howls like a wolf when he comes," she told Marilyn shyly when pressed how the affair was going. "It scared the hell out of me the first few times, but I like it. It kind of sets me free to make all the noise I want without feeling foolish."

After three months, Albert proposed, and Hannah accepted despite Barak's express wishes to the contrary. He despised Albert, a case of familiarity breeding greater contempt. Somehow, though, that only increased Albert's hold on Hannah, that, and his remoteness. At times, he seemed as unreachable as Rokhl. And then one day, after about a year of marriage, Hannah realized she did not care if she ever reached him. She never knew whether it was his lack of interest in the marriage or her lack of interest in him that had come first. When after five years she learned about Joani and knew it was over, the hardest part was telling Barak. He hit the roof.

"You see," he said, "from the beginning I told you that he was a *paskudniak,* a man without honour. I was right all along. You deserve better."

"This is not about you being right or wrong. This is about my life and my marriage. Why can't you just be supportive and give me some comfort instead of more proof that you're smarter than me?" It was one of those rare moments when Hannah had won a grudging silence from her father. That night, after leaving her parent's house, Hannah was looking for a handkerchief and instead found a note in her coat pocket.

It read: *You cannot lose what you never had.*

At the divorce hearing, Hannah remembered the note, remembered the frustration reading it back then, and began to wonder to what else did those words apply to in her life?

CHAPTER THIRTEEN

Hannah **woke slowly** to the warm caress of the sun on her cheek. She lay with eyes shut, reluctant to relinquish the shred of a pleasant dream. Her sleep had always been filled with cinematic scenes and often so realistic that she half believed she inhabited two worlds. At times, she was uncertain as to which one was real. This morning, she hung on for a moment before crossing the bridge into her other reality, the one which Rokhl no longer inhabited. The sunshine streaming in through the bedroom's four floor-to-ceiling windows drew a smile from Hannah, and the resolve that she would make the most of the day. Lacking curtains or shutters or the inclination to cover the view, Hannah rose with the sun. Beyond the door of her bedroom, sunlight spilled onto the ornate Turkish rug in the living room, setting the rich orange and red weave ablaze, and burnishing the blonde oak floor into a sea of iridescent honey.

Hannah stretched and smiled. For days, the rains had dampened leaves exhausted by a brutal summer. The stormy weather had signalled the early onset of fall but in typical contrarian style, Montreal's forecast for the next few September days called for full sun and warm temperatures. It was possible that summer had time for one last fling.

Standing by the window, Hannah tried to recapture the dream that had left behind a vague sense of happiness. What was it about?

Had she dreamt about Max Mohr and, as soon as the thought arose, she wondered why it had popped into her head. The thought of him made the corners of her mouth curl up. Not for the first time she questioned why that kept happening. Earlier that week, she had called Max to reschedule her trip to Cologne. He had not asked for details when she said the delay was a family matter. He had offered her comforting words instead, saying that whatever the situation, he hoped the outcome would be a good one.

Again, a smile came unbidden until the memory of Rokhl's arm in the morgue rose up like a spectre as if separating itself from a foggy corner of her brain. The smile had slipped from her lips. A memory of Rokhl sitting in her favourite living room chair formed. Her face was immobile, and her eyes fixed in that way she had of being and not being in the room. Rokhl had always been something of a ghost, an ever-present riddle that haunted Hannah even before her inexplicable death. Hannah shook her head and her unbrushed curls bounced against her cheeks. It was a reminder of what she needed to do to regain her calm. Stop. Breathe deeply. Focus. Recapture the moment of well-being. Climb into that moment. Erase the events of the past month. Respire. Respite.

I am not her.

Since the visit to the morgue, it seemed the air was forever tinged with the smell of death. It somehow clung to her. For as long as she could remember death had been a constant companion in the home where she had grown up, where every story narrated by Barak seemed to be about someone or something that had died: a sister, a brother, parents, a way of life once so sweet with innocence. She wondered how much time it would take to dull the ache of Rokhl's death although this morning felt different.

She padded barefoot up the spiral staircase into the spacious living room and planted herself at the panoramic window. Looking out on the gentle contours of the Montreal skyline, she was reminded of all the reasons why she loved her condo. The light dancing on the murky waters of the Lachine Canal in summer. The leaves ablaze along the opposite bank in the fall. The twin steeples of St. Patrick's on the other side poking holes into a clear blue sky. The elongated shadows of cyclists doing their morning tour along the bike path that stretched from one end of the island of Montreal to the other.

Before she had seen this property, she had never imagined herself living on the southern edge of downtown, home to antique shops, the Salvation Army, rowhouses one step from the sidewalk, and clumps of crumbling, derelict factories. When she received the referral for the listing, she had every intention of representing the seller. But the more she prepared to show the newly renovated, two-story condo, the more she fell under the spell of its industrial austerity: the exposed brick walls, the iron and wood spiral staircase, the expansive view of the canal from the bedroom on one side, and from the kitchen, the secret garden of the property's enclosed courtyard.

A half century before, the Steel Company of Canada had forged the rails that ran parallel to the building along the banks of the canal. In Montreal's heyday, the area was crowded with factories and goods delivered via the port and the man-made waterway. When Hannah purchased the condo two years earlier, the area around the Atwater Market and the canal was just beginning to go 'pink'. Gays were moving in, renovating inexpensive spaces with high ceilings, lots of light, that artists had been happy to use as low-rent studios. But as it evolved, the area took on the patina of industrial chic and values began to creep up. Now there was even talk that Parks Canada might be opening the Lachine Canal to pleasure boating.

The idea of living in an emerging neighbourhood appealed to Hannah. It intrigued her how something so worn down and seedy could be given a new lease on life. As a child, she liked tracking the progress of green shoots as they emerged through cracks in the sidewalk. Once she even built a tiny fence using Popsicle sticks and Elmer's Glue to protect a cornflower pushing its way into the world in the laneway where she played. Blue was still her favourite colour.

Around her 38th birthday, she had begun feeling the pressure to make a change in her life. The ticking clock had gone quiet and there was no man on the horizon to raise the possibility of a relationship. The condo appeared at just the right moment, the way some things do, in the same way she chose to go into real estate after giving up her job as an administrator at the Marvin Silver Seniors' Centre. Sometimes, the stars align, she had told herself and, in a moment of excitement, had shared her plans with Marilyn who listened silently, then cocked her head and looked at Hannah hard as if she was trying to find a way to understand where such an idea had come from. Marilyn worked hard at trying to see the world through other people's eyes but by her own admission, did not often succeed.

"Are you really going to live in a neighbourhood where you don't know anybody and nobody you know also doesn't know anybody? Why do you want to live among strangers?" Marilyn asked, her eyes wide with surprise.

Why indeed? She had not thought about not knowing anyone. But there was something about being anonymous that was not unfamiliar territory for Hannah. Aside from Marilyn, who even had a clue what her life was like? Marilyn's questions created a brief bout of self-doubt but then the business side of Hannah's brain took charge. She did the math and speculated that the property was a sound investment with the possibility of yielding an excellent return in years to come. But Marilyn's negative reaction to her news was the determining factor for Hannah although she decided it was best not to tell Barak about her intentions until after the deed had been notarized. When she finally did share the news, his reaction was no less than what Hannah had expected. Pure disgust. *Arois gevorfeneh gelt,* money down the drain, is what Barak bellowed.

"Did you hear what your daughter did, Rokhl?"

He spoke as if his wife had not been sitting there in the living room the whole time. Her response was one of pure economy, a mere shifting of her gaze from Barak to Hannah.

"Your daughter, she paid good money to live in a factory. *Nisht zu gloiben.* Can you believe? More than 30 years I work like a *ferd* to get OUT of a factory and that's where our Hannah has decided she is going to live. There, in a neighbourhood with the *shvartzeh* train porters and a bunch of *feigelach*. I saw at least three of them prancing around with their little dogs. *Feh!*"

It got worse when he saw the proximity of the railway tracks and derelict buildings a few blocks away.

"With just a little more cash, my big shot daughter could have a whole new house in Côte Saint-Luc or New Hampstead. But no ... that's too close to her own kind."

Through every meal they shared for the next two months, he never failed to ask the same question: "How are you enjoying life next to what is little better than an open sewer?"

Taking a leaf from Rokhl's notebook, silence became Hannah's best defense but, just when she was ready to scream if she heard the question one more time, Hannah found a note. It was after a family supper. She had stopped at the dépanneur for some sugar and found it tucked in her wallet. It read: *It does not matter where you live only how that is important.*

The calm Hanna struggled to reclaim was fast dissipating as she munched on her toast. In an attempt to recapture the good humour she had awoken with, she slathered the rye slice with fresh yogurt and Marilyn's homemade blueberry jam. It failed to change her outlook. There was more on her mind than the events of the past. Looking ahead, Hannah struggled to see a hopeful future. Despite being certain there had to be a light at the end of it all, she knew she was not on solid ground if anyone was to ask what she foresaw. Juxtaposed to her cautious optimism was the belief that there were dark and hazardous twists in the road ahead. The only way to still her jumpy brain, she decided, was to take advantage of the weather and walk to the office. Maybe it would help clear her mind or even dull the shard of anxiety jabbing at her whenever she thought about the pending trip to Germany. Or the question never too far from her thoughts, about the claim: '*I am not her*'.

Hannah set out down Rue Vinet to Notre Dame, the sun once again warming her face. She stopped a moment to look into some the windows of the antique shops that were slowly disappearing, making way for funky cafés like Quoi de N'Oeuf and high-end restaurants like Le Boeuf Qui Rit. Meandering through the neighbourhood, so bright and cheerful, her step lightened. As she turned the corner onto Atwater, Hannah eyed the overgrown plantings in the wide median running the length of the avenue, the spill of flowers in their autumn colours and the lush vines escaping over the concrete sides of the beds. At the beginning of the summer, they had been so tame and orderly but now seemed to envy the weeds their freedom as they grew alongside the graffitied overpass.

Climbing steadily, she entered the coolness of the tunnel perennially littered with chip bags and flattened cigarette packs. Out at the other end, Hannah quickly sidestepped a brown pile of something and when the odour reached her nostrils, she immediately knew that someone had relieved themselves in the shelter of the tunnel. The odour jarred her out of the lull she had fallen into with the rhythm of her gait. Unbidden, her thoughts suddenly rushed ahead to what lay waiting at the office for her. Today had been blocked off Hannah's calendar to allow her to work on travel plans. As she climbed up the hill past René-Lévesque towards Ste.-Catherine Street, she ran through the list she had been formulating since her call to Max Mohr. Once again, a smile crept across her face although it worried her a little how easily her moods fluctuated these days. By the time she arrived at the office in Westmount Square, Hannah was winded but looking forward to getting down to work. "Good morning, Dani. How are you on this beautiful morning?"

Her assistant smiled broadly. Hannah thought she detected a look of relief flicker across her assistant's face.

"I'm especially fine to see you in such a good mood," Danielle said.

"Yes, I am in a good mood and, to keep it that way, let's hold my calls to a minimum. I have a trip to plan."

"Aye, aye, *ma capitaine*." Danielle threw her a playful salute. "Your decks are clear. You only have one message. Sheryl, your mother's cousin called."

"Who?"

"Your mother's cousin?"

"My mother's cousin?" Hannah repeated, her eyebrows drawing together.

"Yes, Sheryl. She's calling from someplace in New Jersey. She said she was anxious to speak with you. The message is on your desk."

"My mother's cousin?" Hannah said once again as if deciphering a foreign language. "But my mother has no cousin. My mother has no living relatives."

CHAPTER FOURTEEN

When Barak died, Marilyn had sent Hannah an Eckhart Tolle quote: "The past has no power over the present moment." Marilyn intended the thought to be inspirational but what on earth was she supposed to make of such an assertion? Did Marilyn really believe that the present stood on its own two feet and that the past held no sway over the moment? Not with their background, it didn't, couldn't. To Hannah's way of thinking, time was akin to threads drawn taut on some giant loom. She had seen a documentary once about the making of tapestries and now imagined time plaited from a myriad of delicate strands, so tightly interlaced that it was impossible to separate them. Hannah believed herself a captive of the past as sure as if she was surrounded by a barbed wire fence: the past, the war, the dead. Barak spoke of it too much and Rokhl not at all, but it was always there, in the present. What holds us in its grip more tightly, what you know of the past or what remains unknown? Why had she not asked more questions?

Every January 27th, the day the Soviet Army accidentally liberated Auschwitz, Barak would recount for Hannah—whether she wanted to hear it or not—the story of how he found Rokhl. Barak would settle his square bulk into the armchair and begin, as if reading from a script about a scene from his life. The wording never changed.

He would explain how at 16, he had become attached to the First Army of the Ukrainian Front.

"Y'know, I was fierce in a fight and so the *Roussins* took me on willingly. I had, of course, not shared with the *tovarishchi* that I was a Jew. Why give them cause for concern? After all everyone knew that the Jews prefer running to fighting. Jews were not to be trusted, they said, and then would spit to get the bad taste that the word *Zhid* left in their mouths. Me, I didn't care. I wanted nothing more than to fight, to rip open the throats of every Nazi and collaborator I could find. I wanted to tear apart the bodies of those who had murdered my family and stolen my life. You think me bitter, Hannaleh, and that I exaggerate, but let me tell you how I came to be this way. It was 1941. We had been in the ghetto in Vilna, maybe six months. The winter was bitter cold. I was returning from the construction site where I laboured for a little bread. I remember I was carrying broken furniture for firewood when I saw them—the Ukrainian *Hilfspolizei*—with a group of people they had rounded up and trapped between a fence and a wall. The pigs were laughing as they pushed around a little boy. As I came close, I saw it was my brother, Srulek. They shot him as he was running to my father. They shot my father, too. My mother was screaming and then one of them slapped her. She fell down and I stood frozen as I saw those filthy pigs rape and murder my mother. When they left, laughing, I ran to Srulek who was barely alive. He bled to death in my arms and, for months, I refused to remove the jacket, the sleeve stiff with the life that had drained out of his little body. On that day, the day my family was killed, I knew I would do whatever I was able to avenge them."

Silent tears filled Hannah's eyes at this point in the story, the part where her grandparents and uncle, her family had been murdered. Each time, she thought about how she would never know them or what they looked like. And they would never know her.

"I joined the FPO, the Vilna resistance. Everyone talks about the uprising in Warsaw, but we had one too in Vilna except we were sold out by those cowards, the *Judenrat* who thought they could save lives by cooperating. I knew better. Me and two friends escaped through the fence and ran into the woods as if the *tavel* himself was chasing us, which in fact he was. In the dark, we found the Bielski brothers watching over a flock of cowering women, children and old men that they were keeping alive in the Naliboki Forest. At first, they thought I was just one more mouth to feed but Zus Bielski, he saw I was burning for revenge. We shared that fire—a desire for retribution that burned like coal. We wanted to kill Germans, for sure … but also those *paskudniaks,* the *Ukhrainer* who saw an opportunity to better their lot in life by ridding the land of every *Zhid* they could find. These people, they were our neighbours, sometimes our friends even, people we had helped out in bad times …"

Hannah who knew the stories by heart, had learned never to interrupt. As Barak described who he had been, Hannah would imagine her father as a teenager, living like an animal in the woods, stealing chickens and tearing vegetables out of the ground, running from farmers who would have turned him in for no reward, merely for the pleasure of cleansing the world of Jews.

"After a while, Zus and a few of us left the woods to join other partisans but he never let on to them that I was a Jew. He said that was my decision. He eventually returned to the forest and his brother Tuvia, but I stayed on."

There was but one photo of Barak from that time. In it, he stood with his arm around some older men all wearing the same weary faces. He was bundled in layers of clothes that gave his square frame the look of an immoveable object. Tucked into his belt, with the handle angled for easy access, was the butt of a pistol. As a child, Hannah was mesmerized by the fierceness she saw in her father's eyes. When she grew older, she noted that her father's eyes had lost their ferocity, but the grim line of his mouth had remained unaltered.

"I knew I had proved myself when they attached me to the 322nd Rifles. I was fighting side-by-side with Ukies who I knew would kill me if they ever saw my circumcised *schvantz* and yet, I survived. We were fighting our way through Poland when one bitter winter's day, a strange smell settled on us like a damp rag. We didn't know where it was coming from. We were in our winter white camouflage and approached carefully when we saw the guard towers. But they were empty. Behind the barbed wire, were rows of scarecrows dressed in stripes standing by the fence. We had no idea. There was nothing like this on our maps. Yes, we knew there were death camps because Majdenak had been liberated by the Russians the previous summer. But who could imagine such a nightmare in front of our very eyes? All around me, with each breath, men were gagging. You could taste death on your tongue. The skeletons—standing, sitting, lying—their eyes frozen in their skulls, were watching us as if we were the ghosts. That's what we were, Hannah, standing on either side of the fence—a collection of ghosts and skeletons. We stumbled over the railway tracks that led through an entrance like the gaping mouth of a sleeping *golem*. From the gate, and as far as the eye could see, stood row upon row of barracks. Perfectly straight. Neat lines—everything neat—except for the bodies leaning or lying here and there, some dead and some welcoming death. That was when I knew that we had entered through the gates of hell.

"As we walked down the tracks, those skeletons still standing reached out as we passed by, maybe to make sure we were real. On the other side of the tracks, we saw what looked to be women, their faces gaunt, their heads shaved and some wearing outsized boots. We knew they were women because they weren't wearing pants, and some had rags wrapped around their heads. From the corner of my eye I saw a young girl standing in the doorway of a barracks with only her head visible. Although she was half-hidden, I saw a pair of bright eyes enlarged by terror. I started towards her but she did not move. The men were stopping now, sharing water and some rations. I slowed as I came nearer to the doorway, like I would if I was approaching a strange dog. She did not shrink back. She stood staring at me with her great, big blue eyes. Even from a distance I could see the gold flecks, like sparks. And that, *meine teireh tochter,* is how I decided to choose life over revenge. Later, when we learned that your mother also had no family left, she too made a choice."

CHAPTER FIFTEEN

What cousin? The question was like a tire in mud, spinning like crazy but making no progress. Outside her office window, Mount Royal was a palette daubed with red, orange, and gold running together at the whim of the fall wind. Hannah stared out the window to bring her attention to some point where she might stop feeling as if the world was conspiring against her moving forward. Rokhl had no living relatives was what she had been told. No family at all. Just like Hannah, her mother had been an only child, and both parents were dead. After the war, Barak had explained that none of her relatives had survived. But what if her mother did have a cousin, and if she did, why had she kept it a secret like all the other secrets she had harboured from Hannah? All these questions spiralling made her think of a Slinky toy. As a child she had loved to watch the little perpetual motion machine make its way down the steps of their front porch. It was only a coil of thin steel wire that, once set on a path, kept moving without any real purpose except to demonstrate the law in physics about a thing in motion ...

What was that law? she wondered. Hannah snatched at bits of memory. She was drifting. These days she was forever on the verge of but never grasping her reality.

Reality. The word stopped her cold. That's what's wrong. *My sense of reality has gone astray.* Nothing has felt real since she walked into her childhood home and found it empty. It seemed to have begun with Max Mohr and that dinner.

⮑ A mere few hours earlier, the morning had started off so fine, the closest thing to calm she had felt in ages. Rokhl's death was beginning to sink in. She was learning to acclimatize her emotions. This morning Hannah had hopes of being able to stop and reassess how things might unfold. Just as she was making some sense of her feelings for Max Mohr and that whole business between Sonenshein and Heilemann, another tsunami landed on her shore. And Hannah suddenly recalled Newton's first law: An object at rest stays at rest and an object in motion stays in motion with the same speed and in the same direction unless acted upon by an unbalanced force. Rokhl was at rest but since her disappearance Hannah had been an object in motion. A part of Hannah wanted to give up and let go; she so wanted to stop struggling. But she was the daughter of Barak Baranowski, the partisan, the freedom fighter. In his name, she could not surrender. She punched the intercom on her desk.

"Dani, I'm sorry to ask but please bring me one of those good strong coffees, the kind only you can make. I think I really need it."

Ten minutes later, her nerves soothed by an espresso, Hannah picked up the message slip and began to key in the number for some woman named Sheryl somewhere in New Jersey. As it began to ring, it occurred to Hannah that this supposed cousin might help her decipher the words that had been on the edge of her consciousness, day in, day out, since Rokhl disappeared. Maybe she would hold the key to the meaning of the words: *I am not her.*

CHAPTER SIXTEEN

"**H**ello." **The voice** was soft, hesitant, with a pronounced New Jersey accent, decidedly youthful.

"Hi, Sheryl, my name is Hannah Baran, originally Baranowski. You left a message for me earlier today, making some reference to a cousin …"

For a moment it was so still on the line Hannah thought the connection may have been lost.

"Yes, hello. I'm Sheryl Shapiro and it seems that we are second cousins, according to my late mother, *Olav ha-shalom*, may she rest in peace, who was first cousin to your mother, Rokhl Wachsberg."

"I'm afraid there must be some mistake. According to my late father, we had no living relatives. I am sorry. There must be another Rokhl Wachsberg."

Although she had spoken the words, Hannah was more than ready not to believe that there was no other Rokhl Wachsberg. Her hand on the receiver trembled and she thought she heard a catch in the breath on the other end of the line as if this Sheryl person was preparing herself for something arduous.

"My grandfather and your grandmother were siblings," she said, quietly. "My mother only told me about *your* mother, this long-lost relation, as she was struggling with the final stages of cancer. You can imagine I was stunned. We have always had a fairly small family so the news that there was someone my mother had not shared with us came as a shock."

A long silence followed while Sheryl waited for Hannah to say something. When she didn't, Sheryl moved on.

"According to my mother, who was born Fenia Wachsberg, she had only just learned that her cousin Rokhl had survived. The news, it seems, came as quite a shock."

Hannah finally found her voice. "This all sounds so fantastic. How did your mother learn of her cousin's survival, if in fact, my mother was your mother's cousin?"

Hannah had not meant to sound so disbelieving but this story was not making any sense. It was some fifty-five years since the end of the war. Relatives don't suddenly pop up overnight like mushrooms on a damp lawn.

"At a wedding in Lakewood, here in New Jersey where I grew up and my mother still lived. It was about two years ago that my mother met a woman from Toronto who had a cousin living in Montreal." There was something cautious in Sheryl's voice as if she was making a report of no consequence but of some possible interest to Hannah who made not a single sound to encourage the continuation of the story. Sheryl soldiered on.

"They got to talking about the war. They seem to do that a lot once they grew older ... the survivors, I mean. It seems to me the older they get, the more time they spend lost in the past. But maybe that's true for all of us; I suppose we'll find out."

"You were saying ..." Hannah said.

"Sorry, yes ... I'm a bit nervous. Anyway, they were talking about how some people never seemed to have recovered from what happened. And this woman my mother was talking to mentioned her sister's next door neighbour, a Rokhl Baranowski, who never talked about the war or, in fact, about anything at all. According to the sister, this woman felt her neighbour was an example of one of those people permanently damaged by what they had experienced. For some reason, my mother asked if she knew anything more about this woman Rokhl because, although certainly the name wasn't uncommon, she had had a cousin by that first name whom she believed she had once caught sight of at Birkenau but could not find after the war. I guess hope never dies. Like so many others looking for family, many of my mother's relatives were never confirmed to be alive or dead. Of course, this woman could offer nothing more than her sister's address and one thing she remembered. Her sister had remarked how her neighbour had a daughter with the most beautiful copper-coloured hair. My mother recalled how envious she had been of her cousin Rokhl's thick and curly red hair."

Hannah almost dropped the receiver as her free hand flew to her head and gave her hair a pat as if to ensure herself that she wasn't dreaming.

"That time, in Auschwitz-Birkenau, my mother thought she spotted her but wasn't sure. For one thing, her beautiful red hair was shorn. And she wasn't wearing a yellow star but a red triangle. My mother said the woman she thought was Rokhl was standing by the side of the commandant Mandl, the one they called The Beast. After liberation, my mother searched for relatives and especially your mother because they were about the same age. She never found her and so thought she was dead like all the others. You can imagine then how this idea that her cousin was alive and that she had found her took hold of my mother until she couldn't stop talking about it. Finally, she had me call Montreal's Jewish Community Centre to get an address. They found one under the name of Barak Baranowski. That was about a year ago."

Oh my God, thought Hannah, the sister of that Toronto woman must be Rokhl's nemesis, the nosy Mrs. Orenstein. But what did that prove? Nothing. Two women called Rokhl Wachsberg? Wasn't it Jung who said that there are no coincidences but often, synchronicity? Given that, how many Rokhl Wachsbergs were there in the whole wide world —and with red hair? Hannah struggled to keep her voice level.

"Sheryl, may I call you Sheryl? All that could be coincidence. There are many women named Rokhl that came out of the war." She decided to keep the advent of red hair to herself for the moment. "So why did your mother think she had found her cousin, that my mother was her relation?"

Hannah was growing hot, ambushed by the possibility that this story was leading to something good. All her instincts were geared to anticipate disappointment if not disaster. Surely, the other shoe would drop when she least expected it.

"My mother wrote Rokhl Baranowski a letter."

"She did?" Rokhl had never mentioned a letter but she felt no compunction to reveal anything to this woman, certainly not that her mother never shared anything of consequence with her only child.

"In fact, my mother wrote her several letters. She read them to me because they were written in Yiddish and I can't read Yiddish. She recounted moments from their childhood, reminisced about Rokhl and her *fetter* Shimon, Rokhl's father, how she always felt a little intimidated by him and her cousin when they were together. She said they seemed to have a secret language between them, a private world. She envied Rokhl that. But when *fetter* Shimon was not around, that she and Rokhl were good friends and shared secrets."

"Oh my God," Hannah whispered. Shimon was her grandfather's name.

"What?" Sheryl asked.

Ignoring the question, Hannah asked, "What happened after your mother sent the letters? Did she receive any response?" Hannah was now sitting on the edge of her seat, her elbows planted on the desk, one hand holding the phone, the other resting on her hair.

"My mother's cancer had been in remission when all this started. The prospect of reuniting with her cousin gave her a kind of energy I hadn't seen in her in years. She told me that she was not surprised that Rokhl wasn't responding right away, that she had always taken some time to warm to Fenia. It seemed that in this, she took after her mother, Tante Liba, who apparently was not as loveable as her name implied.

Hannah's hand shook as she held the phone. There could be no doubt now that Sheryl's mother and Rokhl had been first cousins. She knew little about Rokhl's life before Canada except for how Barak had met her, but she did know that Shimon and Liba Wachsberg had been her parents.

"Your mother never responded to any of the letters, so my mother finally wrote her to announce that she was coming to Montreal in August for a reunion with one of the few blood relations she had left in the world before it was too late. And nothing was going to stop her. And then, something did."

There followed several beats. Hannah tried to imagine this woman, her relation, sitting somewhere in New Jersey, trying to collect herself to finish this story. But Hannah already knew how it ended. What had started out as cancer in her breasts ended up in her pancreas.

"She was gone in a matter of weeks before we knew what had happened. That was two months ago. I forgot all about the letters and Rokhl until now."

"I am so sorry for your loss, Sheryl. Truly sorry. This is a tremendous shock to me, as you can imagine."

Not a soul in the world related to her by blood … and now this. She felt something tickle her chin. When she brought her hand to her cheek, it was wet. She breathed deeply, exhaled slowly.

"So why did you decide to call now?" Hannah asked, her voice thick with emotion.

"A few days ago, I was going through my mother's mail from the last month and found a letter from that woman in Toronto. I guess they must have kept up a correspondence. Anyway, inside the envelope was a clipping from the newspaper about your mother's death. I too am sorry for your loss. Something told me there was no right time to reach out. We are two motherless cousins. Perhaps we can meet, get to know each other?"

A giant sob escaped Hannah's lips, her face slippery with tears.

"I'm sorry if I have called at a bad time," Sheryl said, her voice suddenly scratchy. "Maybe we can try to talk again later."

"Yes, please." Unable to say anything else, Hanna pressed the button and ended the call.

CHAPTER SEVENTEEN

Inside **Chaim Sonenshein's** private office, Hannah grew restive. She had been summoned by Chaim whether to discuss the strategy for the upcoming trip to Germany or to be briefed on the negotiations —she didn't know. Perhaps Chaim thought she already had a strategy worked out. The thought of disappointing him added to her agitation.

Situated atop the 36-story Tour Soleil, Chaim's inner sanctum invariably put Hannah ill at ease. At two-stories high, the walls looming over her were hung with portraits by some of the world's most famous painters of the late 19th and early 20th century—Renoir, Matisse, Modigliani, Picasso, Soutine. There was something about the innumerable pairs of eyes bearing down on her, their fixed stares held fast for eternity in gilt frames. The whole effect made her antsy. What's more, the sum of the immeasurable value of these works was unnerving. Amongst these art treasures, she was an interloper, a cat burglar trapped inside a vault with no way out.

"That room makes me really uncomfortable," she had told Marilyn after her first visit to Sonenshein's private office. "I get claustrophobia, hemmed in by all those long-dead eyes looking down on me from four walls."

Marilyn was clearly mortified at Hannah's attitude. Oh, what she would give to spend a couple of hours locked in with so much prodigious art. Confessing as much to Hannah, she took the opportunity to gently chastise her foolish friend who clearly had no appreciation of the privilege she was being afforded. What really amazed her, Marilyn had said, was that someone in little ol' Montreal—Chaim Sonenshein no less—had the panache (she acknowledged he had the money) to acquire such a prestigious collection.

Waiting for her client, Hannah paced around the elegant Jacobean coffee table in the centre of the room that held a massive vase filled with an impressive bouquet of exotic flowers. A whiff of the powerful scent caused Hannah to step back. So much beauty was proving more than Hannah could handle. She went back to pacing and thinking about why she had been summoned. Chaim Sonenshein, one of her father's oldest if not closest friends, was something of a mentor, her first and her most important client. Still, it was unusual for him to call Hannah to his office. Their business was normally conducted by phone and email although they had a standing date the first Monday of the month to meet for breakfast at Modigliani, the upscale restaurant located on the ground floor of the Tour Soleil. On those days, Hannah looked forward to their meeting with anticipation because it was an occasion for her to have her favourite breakfast: *pain perdu* with goat brie melting in its centre. Nobody made French toast or an espresso allongé like Modi's.

The request had come through Chaim's private secretary, Rose, who had been guarding the door to her boss's office since Hannah was a little girl clutching tightly to Barak's hand. In those days, Chaim's office was a converted construction trailer and the door Rose guarded, a thin partition. Only one thing had remained unchanged from those days, Rose's hairdo combed off her face with a flipped wave on either side of her forehead like two clamps. The 'do always reminded Hannah of Queen Elizabeth. And Rose was just as unflappable as the long-reigning queen. Mum was the word. No unnecessary information, like why you had been invited to the inner sanctum, would ever slip through Rose's pursed lips.

As much as she didn't want to be there, Hannah would not deny Chaim Sonenshein anything. When she had realized that social work and Albie were not going to take care of her in her dotage, she asked

Chaim's advice about going into real estate. Long hours in a Sisyphean line of work had convinced her that she did not want to be an old lady living on a government pension, but rather doing the kind of work where her income would reflect her output. Chaim had encouraged her saying she had what it took to be a success in the real estate business: She was presentable, personable, and clever at reading people. Added to that was her desire to please, so he said, she had chosen wisely. From that moment on, he had taken her under his wing and became a catalyst for her success.

"Hannah!" came the shout from the doorway. Sonenshein entered the room with arms opened wide and one hand reaching out for her shoulder. In his early seventies, Sonenshein radiated the energy of a man twenty years younger, with a physique to match. The telltale signs that he was not as young as he looked resided mostly in his dark brown hair too evenly toned to be natural. Fit and slim, he seemed taller than five-foot nine, Hannah's height, something that always surprised her as they stood side-by-side waiting to be seated for their breakfast at Modi's. He was also a man of fashion. This morning he was wearing a dark blue-grey Versace and his signature pale blue shirt with his initials stitched in red on the cuff. He walked towards her, a look of concern etched into his tanned face. "*Maidel*, I am so sorry that I was away when Rokhl passed, *olava sholem*. Did you get my note, the platter from Pierre Olivier, and the flowers? I could not believe that something so terrible should befall you, especially so soon after you just buried Barak, may he rest in peace. Do you know what happened? How did she end up under a bus? What was she doing wandering into the street anyway? She was always so hard to read. Tell me, is there is anything I can do?"

Hannah's shoulders sagged. The barrage of questions fell like hammer blows around her ears. He had called her by the name her father would have if he still lived. Her throat constricted. Chaim put one arm around her shoulder and with the other took hold of her hand. Hannah tried to step back, to find a place from which to gather her composure and respond but his hand on her shoulder did her in. A sealed door was flung open, and a terrible sound escaped. She leaned into the nearby shoulder and began to sob like a child.

"What a fool I am. I am sorry, so sorry. Too many questions," he said pulling a linen handkerchief from his pocket. He dabbed at the tears on her cheek and handed her the hankie without letting go of her shoulder. After a few moments, Hannah calmed herself, hiccupped twice, and wiped her eyes carefully to avoid leaving mascara on the linen. She pulled away slowly and Chaim led her to one of two leather armchairs on either side of a small table with a carved elephant head as its base. Chaim Sonenshein opened the button on his jacket, pulled on the crease in his suit pants, and sat down beside her. He patted her hand as if to say, take your time, and waited for her to speak.

"I have no answers to your questions, Chaim," she finally said, feeling the eyes of all the portraits staring down accusatorily. "I wish I had even the slightest idea of what happened, but I have nothing, not from the police and not from anything I've found in the house so far." The thought of the house, an accumulation of some 35 years, was like a deep cave once inhabited by bears. It stood waiting to be scoured to rid it of the smell left by its former inhabitants.

It crossed her mind that she could share with Chaim everything that had taken place since that day in August when Rokhl and the life Hannah had known went down the rabbit hole. The note her mother left. The cousin who appeared out of an obscure past. The trepidation she felt about the trip to Germany. Max Mohr. Her heart ached to unburden itself of the chain of events that some would deem too bizarre to be real. Instead, she chose to turn that organ into an implement with which to bury her fears and confusion. Barak and Rokhl had taught her how to play her cards close, to keep things to herself. Now was no time to break the mould if that was what was holding her together. It was so much easier to reveal the mundane aspects of death's chores.

"I've tried twice to make a dent at emptying out the duplex but each time I had to leave. I can't explain why but I just can't bear being in there alone. Chaim, you know me to be a practical woman, right?"

Sonenshein nodded his assent and patted her hand again to encourage her to go on. She hesitated knowing that, out of respect for her privacy, Chaim would not question her too closely.

"But it's been one thing after another and none of what has happened, none of the pieces of this puzzle fit together. I keep thinking that if I don't look too closely, perhaps if I let some time pass and allow some distance, I'll begin to see a pattern, that something will reveal itself. But so far, the mystery just keeps getting deeper. Maybe that's why I'm looking forward to this trip to Germany, although that is a little daunting. Anyway, at least it will give me some physical distance."

She gave him a little smile. Her shoulders slumped a little. Looking down at her hands, she realized that she had been twisting Chaim's hankie until it now looked like a corkscrew. She dropped it on the table and glanced up at Chaim and wondered how he had managed to open the door to the frustrations and grief she had successfully kept under wraps. Not even Marilyn, with all her hovering, had managed to pry it open. But she had no answers. Being uninformed was anathema for Hannah because she always made it her business to have answers for her clients before they even asked the questions. However, this was not business. It was her life.

Sonenshein looked at her closely and suddenly changed the subject.

"Have you made your arrangements with the Germans for your trip? Are there still plans for you to address the realtor seminar on Quebec opportunities?"

Hannah sat up and quickly regained her composure.

"Yes, Mohr and I discussed the best time to come. Originally, we had planned for September but now ..." She stopped a moment. "So now we're talking about late October. That's too late for the seminar but he's confirming with Heilemann which day or days would be best. But Chaim,"—she hesitated a moment—"I still don't understand why I'm going in your stead. I am flattered by your trust in me but ..."

Chaim waved his hand as if to bat away any false modesty on Hannah's part.

"So, you will fly to Cologne or Frankfurt?" he said with a twist to his lips.

"I think Frankfurt because Mohr has kindly offered to pick me up."

"Oh, you think he's being kind? It couldn't be that he's interested in an attractive, clever woman?"

Hannah sat up, turned to face Sonenshein, her demeanour changing as she gave him a hard look. "Please, Chaim, if you trust me to negotiate this deal for a piece of land you swore you would never sell, you should trust me to know how to handle a man who is a little too cavalier for my taste. Have you forgotten whose daughter I am?"

Sonenshein eyed her closely and shook his head, unable to suppress a wry smile. "No, I have not forgotten your father and his stubborn ways. I've told you how often I had tried to bring him into my business so he could make a better life for all of you. He always said he lacked the killer instinct I had. Him! A *partisaner* who had killed so many Germans."

"So how do you think he would view my business dealings with this *yecke*?"

Hannah shifted in her seat and grimaced in a way that made Chaim laugh out loud.

"Exactly! I suppose, though, I owe you some explanation as to what I have planned as you will be my alter ego and believe me, there's a reason for that as well. Let me tell you a story, a very sad story about how a young boy survived the war. A story about me and a Nazi, *Oberstleutnant* Heilemann."

HANS-GEORG HEILEMANN

NOVEMBER 2000

CHAPTER EIGHTEEN

Max Mohr eased off the A555 from Köln, heading towards the scenic *Bundesstrasse* 9, direction Koblenz. He was on his way to Bad Breisig, making the hour-long drive in response to Heilemann's invitation to dine at his home, Heilemann's home being an impressive Schloss. No reason for the invitation had been provided but it was certain his client wanted an update on the Sonenshein dossier. There was something else, Max suspected, an underlying agenda attached to the summons. Relaxing into the soft leather upholstery, Max shrugged. There was no point to this speculation because trying to second-guess Heilemann was a fool's game.

Putting the whole business out of his mind for the moment, Max gave his full concentration to the marvellous machine he was driving. Without a girlfriend or wife to bake him a cake, the car had been his *rundes yahr* gift to himself. After all, fifty was a momentous age, one worth of celebrating particularly as he was in good shape both physically and financially. For almost a year he had lusted after this beauty rumbling beneath him, touted as the super sedan of all time—the new BMW M5 with a 4.9-litre, V8 engine and 400 horsepower. From the moment he had seen it showcased in the weekly issue of *Auto Motor und Sport* he knew some day it would be his, and what better timing than a special birthday. He smiled with satisfaction at the sound of the engine throbbing with power. Open it up and it thrummed like the music of the heavens. He knew its power, its ability for speed but today, had no need to exercise it.

In this new decade of his life, the first year of the twenty-first century, a certain awareness had suffused his consciousness entering as if by osmosis. It quelled any need to prove himself. He had arrived at a place where he was secure in his skill as a negotiator, knowing that he had the foresight to anticipate all possible routes of a negotiation and an innate ability to design a strategy for each eventuality. Difficulties and obstacles would most certainly lie ahead but these challenges were what he relished, the battle of wits and the patience. Yes, the serenity with which to persevere.

Unbidden, a memory of sunlight glinting off of copper strands flashed through his mind, distracting him. He brushed the image away, raising his right index finger from the steering wheel as if to say, *oh no you don't*. He sat back, signalled right and moved into the middle lane. He had decided on the scenic route and was leaving himself plenty of time to get to his destination.

Driving was one of life's greatest pleasures according to Max. The simplicity of allowing rubber to fly along asphalt, steering a potent machine so it moves in tandem with the contours of the road, making it respond immediately by the mere flick of his wrist on the steering wheel. It was something visceral and soothing at the same time. If only life was as simple. Why are we not able to plot a course, follow the signs, and with the exception of the weather and the stupidity of some individuals encountered along the way, arrive at our destination? He resolved to enjoy every minute of the ride despite not looking forward to the meeting. He liked Ha-Gay and enjoyed their collaboration, but he bridled at being summoned without an explanation.

Max gazed out at the countryside so familiar to him yet always stimulating. To his right, the Rhine flowed stolidly on its way to the North Sea, a steady travelling companion whose shores sprouted towns and villages along the way, their peaked church steeples and half-timber *fachwerk* buildings gleaming in the afternoon sun. On the opposite side of the road he sailed past vineyards, their slopes lush and velvety as corduroy, gorged with Riesling grapes ready for harvest. Around Königswinter, the rolling green hills rose gently to form an undulating outline of low mountains reminiscent of the area around Lachute he had seen in the Lower Laurentians during the site inspection. Max briefly wondered if Heilemann had ever noted the resemblance between those ancient mountains in Quebec and the wooded *Siebengebirge*. And what did it matter if he had? Max thought. What difference would that make?

As he had been instructed to do, he had inspected the Trois-Îles property. Nothing he saw there recommended itself to the LHH brand. It was a heavily wooded, somewhat marshy land perforated by three very picturesque lakes and inhabited by hordes of hungry biting insects, among them black flies that viciously left welts wherever they took a piece of him. The surveyor accompanying him, however, seemed inured. But Max had never in his life experienced such vicious insect attacks, recalling too late Hannah's suggestion that he arm himself with Deep Woods insect repellent. He could not understand Heilemann's sudden interest in a property visibly devoid of any connection to his current business.

Ach Quatsch. Why was he even trying to puzzle this out with so little information? Max shook his head. Recently he had grown impatient with the paths down which his mind wandered, areas of thought that he had never rummaged in before. Was it age? he wondered. Truth be told, he felt no different than when he was 25. Well, maybe a little different. Perhaps he had been more hopeful in those years, like believing that two fully formed people could come together and meld into one happy couple. He had been quickly divested of that idea. Although he had been unsuccessful at making personal relationships flourish for long stretches, each decade had brought other opportunities. At twenty he had been a hungry, young student with a degree in medieval history that prepared him for absolutely nothing but teaching, not a route he was inclined to take. Time and again, no matter how hard he tried, he could not recall why he had chosen that discipline to pursue, or why his sisters who should have known better, had not stopped him. Certainly, the history of that era had always fascinated him but even before graduation, he saw no opportunity to apply what he had learnt. Instead, thank God, his brother-in-law Hans, Leni's first husband, a successful architectural landscaper, gave him a job.

"*Ach,* what are older sisters for?" she had said a little embarrassed when he thanked her with a single red rose.

Hans owned a firm that had both private estates as well as public lands as clients. It suited Max who enjoyed being outside and didn't mind hauling bags of soil or carting two-metre-high trees around. The hard labour somehow was a help when it came to him choosing a new path. He was earning a good salary and living with Omi so managed to save enough to change course. Almost thirty, he landed in London and the Bartlett School of Architecture where two things happened: He got his MA and he met Nadya. She left him three years later taking their infant son with her, accusing him of being an inaccessible cold fish.

After that, he threw himself into his work, moving from small jobs to progressively bigger, more complex contracts, designing gardens on large estates, and experimenting with creating controlled natural settings. His specialty was fashioning landscapes for large properties that were being put on the market. And that turned his interest towards real estate sales. Without much effort, he silently slipped into that field where he met Ha-Gay Heilemann just as he was turning another *rundes yahr.* That had been his 40th birthday present from the gods.

Max let the M5 edge up to 120 kph without the slightest effort. The car could easily do twice that on the Autobahn but the trade-off for taking the *Bundesstrasse* to enjoy the scenery was a reduced speed limit. Still, the heartbeat of the M5 engine was as hypnotic as a siren's song. A deep sigh escaped his lips. His eyes swept across the sleek dashboard with satisfaction, a place for everything and everything handily in its place. He pressed the radio on and a smile crept across his face as Foreigner's "I Want to Know What Love Is" sprang from the speakers:

In my life there's been heartache and pain
I don't know if I can face it again
Can't stop now, I've traveled so far, to change this lonely life
I want to know what love is,
I want you to show me.

The breath he had been holding whistled through his lips. He reached out and snapped the radio off. Was there no escaping Hannah Baran even here on the road in his brand-new toy taking a leisurely *Kaffeefahrt*? It had been three months since their meeting. How was she still lurking in the shadows, ready to leap out at him from some corner he had pushed her into with such determination? Maybe, he thought, he should stop trying and just follow the road to wherever it leads.

In the distance, Max recognized Bad Breisig—a picture-perfect German town with an abundance of pristine *Fachwerk* buildings proudly showing off their best craftsmanship along the banks of the Rhine, some *deutsche* eye candy to the river cruises heading to and from Mainz. He knew Bad Breisig to be the kind of place that sixty-something Germans came to for a getaway weekend at the Roman baths or the destination of a leisurely Sunday drive. Swerving smoothly off the main thoroughfare, the M5 began to climb the serpentine road towards Heilemann's hilltop chateau. Reflected in the rear-view mirror, the late September sun was a lover rushing to meet his mate. Max tilted the mirror to get a better view of the blaze as it slipped below the horizon.

At the entrance gate, Max rang, announced himself, and was buzzed in. The massive wrought iron gates split and spread wide as angel wings, gaining him entry to the cobblestone courtyard. Max took a minute before turning off the engine, reluctant to leave the comfort of the car. Peering through the windshield, he suddenly caught a glimpse of Heilemann standing at an upstairs window. With a sharp tilt of the head, Ha-Gay acknowledged Max, then disappeared.

As he headed in the direction of the massive front doors, Max stood a moment in the courtyard to survey the three-story main building, its crenelated roof and the two building wings that extended to left and right, enfolding the courtyard in an embrace. Its open square likely held as many as fifty horsemen when the Schloss was built in the early 1800s and every Christmas since Ha-Gay purchased the Schloss, the courtyard played host to a *Weihnachtsmarkt*. Heilemann, in the fashion of bygone nobility, would invite local artisans to put up booths and sell their wares to the nearby townsfolk and occasional tourists.

"Why are you lingering out there, Max?" Heilemann was standing legs astride in the doorway, calling out. "It's getting chilly. Come in, come in."

Dressed in grey slacks, a navy fisherman's sweater over a crisp white shirt, Hans-Georg Heilemann looked every inch the lord of the manor. He reached out with his trademark firm, warm handshake, reaching up to pat Max, a half head taller, on the shoulder.

"*Herzlich willkommen.* Have you grown taller, Max, or am I shrinking?" This was Ha-Gay's standard greeting of late along with complaints about growing older.

Max smiled.

"Well, it must be you, Ha-Gay. You must be shrinking because I stopped growing about 25 years ago. It can only be your advanced age. What are you now, 66?"

Heilemann frowned and wagged a finger at Max. "You're lucky you are such a good broker, or I would be forced to make you seek a new source of income." And with that, Heilemann pulled Max into the ornate entrance hall and closed the door.

❧ The simple supper that Heilemann had promised consisted of the biggest slab of filet mignon that Max had ever seen; it must have been eight cms thick. They were seated on well-padded, high-backed leather chairs in the cavernous kitchen of the Schloss where Ha-Gay had setup a chef's table near the gas grill. With a theatrical flourish, he had flung the steaks onto the flame. The sound of the meat sizzling elicited a deeply satisfied chuckle from Heilemann and Max thought once again about how short men had these deep voices. The seared rare meat was accompanied by a baked potato and a huge dollop of *Rotkohl,* made just the way Max liked his red cabbage. Ha-Gay had paired the steak with an excellent Musigny Pinot Noir which they drank slowly, giving the wine its full due.

Throughout the leisurely dinner, the conversation catapulted from topic to topic: the joy of the M5 on the Autobahn and the shame that the chip, factory-installed by BMW, prevented the engine from going beyond 250 kph; how Gerhard Schroeder was no Helmut Kohl and whose protégée, Angela Merkel, was beginning to show promise; the state of the euro against the soaring dollar; and oddly, Ha-Gay's ruminations on Pope John Paul II's apology to the Jews on his visit to Yad Vashem earlier that year.

"As a devout Catholic, I hold the office of the Holy See in the highest regard. He is our shepherd. And of course, I have nothing against the Jews. They make wonderful lawyers and doctors. If I have the option, I will always choose a Jew." Heilemann leaned back and offered Max the remainder of the wine.

Max demurred, conscious that he still had to drive home when Heilemann finally got around to the reason for the dinner. Ha-Gay filled his glass with the last dregs then turned the bottle to silently examine the label.

"This was a very special bottle, Max. I've been saving it, but I didn't know why. I just knew we had to share it tonight. I feel the same way about that piece of land in Quebec, the one I want you to get for me, no matter the price. But I do not want Sonenshein to know you are willing to pay his price. You know how they are." He looked at Max whose eyes betrayed his confusion. "Why, they are crafty as foxes." Heilemann said with a snicker. "Like foxes."

CHAPTER NINETEEN

It **was the** end of 1939. Things continued to grow worse yet somehow, Hannaleh, my papa remained calm even as he lost one Christian client after another. Then one night, the pharmacist, Tadeusz Pankiewicz, Papa's Polish friend, came for dinner and warned us that times would soon grow very bad for the Jews. Krakow had been named the capital of the Generalgouvernement, a part of our country that suddenly was no longer Poland. I could see that Tadeusz was very upset but Papa, who revered the work of Schiller, Heine, and Goethe which he would read to me in German, refused to believe anything really bad would happen. He said that the Germans were a people one could reason with. A small noise made me turn my head towards Mameh who had been silent through most of the dinner. It was then that I had my first hint that my mother was in a panic, although she sat quietly at the end of the table, as genial and beautiful as ever. Her eyes were hooded but her mouth was slightly twist-ed as if she had tasted something sour, and her hands were buried in her lap. When I looked more closely, I saw she was slowly wringing them as if trying to rid herself of something. Deep in conversation with Uncle Tadeusz, as I called him, Papa didn't notice anything wrong with Mameh, not until two days later when he came home from the office looking hag-gard to find Mameh packing her suitcases. It was the alarm in his voice that brought me out of my room to stand in their doorway.

"Meine hertz," *he said, his eyes sweeping the wardrobe and bed.* "What is all this?"

"I'm going home to Warsaw," *she said calmly.* "I cannot stay here. You cannot protect me."

"Protect you? From what? The Germans?" *Papa said, looking from Mameh to her dresses laid out on the bed.*

Although I was standing in the doorway, I could have been invisible because neither seemed concerned that I was listening.

"I'm going home to my father and my family there. I am not safe here with you."

"But *meine Teireh* Liba, *how can you just leave us like this? One does not run at the first sign of trouble. How can you abandon me? And what about our daughter? What about Rokhleh? To prevail through this time of trouble we need to remain together as a family. We can only stay strong if we stay together."*

Standing behind her, I saw how my mother was holding herself rigid. In a fury, she rose and whirled around to face Papa. It was then, at last, he saw in her eyes what had long been familiar to me.

"You and your precious daughter have no need of me," *she spat out with disdain.* "You are your own cabal. And you want to keep me here like a Dresden doll until they break the door down. I am leaving while I still can. My father will protect me, perhaps get me to Paris where I can be safe."

And with that, my father was struck dumb by this strange woman who had replaced his fragile wife as my mother began to methodically fold her finest dresses in preparation for departure. Papa sat down and watched until he found his voice. He stood up slowly to face Mameh. Softly, he said, "Liba, this is madness. Stop this immediately. You are having a little bit of a nervous breakdown. I will get you some laudanum from Tadeusz. After you have rested, we will discuss your concerns."

Mameh laughed, a hard vicious sound that I felt slice like a cold blade between my budding breasts. "I think not. Stop deluding yourself that I have any affection for you. Nothing could be further from the truth, and nothing could induce me to stay."

Papa stood rooted to the spot, colour draining from his face, his eyes sweeping the room as if looking for the woman who had once been his wife. Not finding her, he turned and saw me standing in the doorway. Tears sprang to his eyes and for a moment, I understood why Mameh could do this to him. He was weak. But I loved Papa and I would never abandon someone I loved; I would never do what my mother did. She left the following morning without a word. I would not see her again for another four years when circumstances had twisted that blade in my heart until there was nothing left inside. And the shoe was on the other foot.

From then on, it was just Papa and me. Those first weeks without her as the whole of Papa's world—our world—crashed around his ears, were painful but I was not unhappy. I ached for Papa, but my mother had been right; we were fine without her. Until the day, a few weeks later when Papa was rounded up and ordered to report for work in a labour camp. Luckily, he was able to convince the Nazis he would be of much more use as a bookkeeper and accountant, and so avoided being sent into the fields or the quarries.

Soon after they took over our city, the Germans closed and emptied all the synagogues but in Krakow they didn't burn the books. Instead, they confiscated and stored them in warehouses along with all the Torahs and menorahs and other beautiful things that had been in our shul. Papa was one of the people who kept the inventory of everything they stole from us. I don't remember if Papa told me this or I learned it after, Hannaleh, but the intent was that when Krakow was judenrein—*cleaned of Jews—it would become a German city with museums of artefacts of the dead race. Us. The dead Jews.*

During those early days, I was still able to attend school but, by December, there were all kinds of laws that we had to follow, or we would get in trouble. Worse than anything, we had to wear the yellow armband with the Star of David. For my 11th birthday Papa had given me a Mogen Dovid that I wore around my neck, close to my heart. I had loved it so. Until I had to wear the armband. That's what the Germans did to us. They took everything away, sometimes little by little and sometimes all at once. And eventually, they made us hate who we were. With Mameh gone, and the world upside down, Oskar and I began to spend more time together. He still ran off to be with his friends in the Akiva Youth group but what he did there, this we did not talk about. He said it was better if I knew nothing about what went on. When it came time for his bar mitzvah it was a very small affair. Ten men, mostly family, gathering in the Liebner's apartment upstairs on a Shabbat morning. As I stood by their front door, I could hear Oskar singing the portion of the Torah he had studied. I waited but his voice didn't crack once. I believed it was because he had become a man. It was Papa's voice that cracked as he tried to assure me that everything would be okay soon. We just had to be patient. And smart.

CHAPTER TWENTY

"**W**hat about this?" Marilyn asked pointing to a cupboard where three shelves overflowed with plastic cottage cheese containers, glass jars and neatly folded bags once filled with sliced bread or apples.

"It looks like I hit Rokhl's treasure trove," she said with a sigh.

"Green garbage bag for whatever can be recycled," Hannah said over her shoulder, "and orange for trash."

Marilyn had showed up without an invitation after Hannah mentioned she was finally going to tackle clearing out Rokhl's home. Hannah had not a word of protest for her impetuous friend, only a smile of gratitude. Now after five straight hours, both betrayed the deep exhaustion that came of going through someone else's cupboards and drawers. To start, they had just put their heads down and burrowed into the work. Yet after a full morning they had managed to only make a minor dent in Rokhl's kitchen.

Hannah stood in a circle of boxes, her fortress against the chaos. All the cupboard doors were wide open, and several drawers pulled out. There were boxes marked for the Jewish charity depot Mercas, filled with mismatched dishes, glasses, and cooking utensils still in reasonable shape. One large plastic container, filled not only with Rokhl's pills but medicine that had belonged to Barak, was marked for the pharmacy. Hannah could have sworn she had got rid of all her father's medication and, shaking her head, wondered if Rokhl had hidden some and if so, why.

The two friends worked in tandem, striving to be methodical in their approach but every cupboard, drawer, and pantry, the fridge and freezer, held some element of surprise. Hannah had never realized how much of a hoarder Rokhl had been. Like everything else, she had done it quietly. In the freezer were plastic containers of chicken soup, each neatly labelled with a date in Rokhl's European slant; some had been there for more than four years. Rokhl also found a Ziplock bag with $1,255 in bills and another with loose coins.

Among Rokhl's stockpile were at least twelve giant packs of paper towels and roll upon roll of toilet paper distributed in a variety of places as if it was necessary to secrete away this commodity. They found a dozen packages of Manischewitz lima bean and barley soup, tins of Camel halvah, Chicken of the Sea tuna and Heinz vegetarian baked beans all neatly stacked at the bottom of the broom closet. There were aluminum frying pans blackened with use and cast-iron pots that Hannah knew had been brought from Germany when the family had immigrated some 45 years earlier, Rubbermaid bowls and colanders in olive green from Hannah and Albie's first kitchen, and a cast iron meat grinder that she remembered her mother anchoring to the edge of the kitchen counter fastened by a giant screw.

Hannah was unable to stop although every once in a while, something—often nothing special—roused a memory and left her motionless, lost in thought. A scene would unfurl in her mind's eye like a time lapse photo of a bud becoming a bloom, and she would get sucked into the black hole of memory. Hannah was reliving such a moment when Marilyn called out. She turned around to see her friend on the stepladder, one hand on the top shelf of a cupboard and in the other a pair of baby shoes partially wrapped in a piece of worn fabric.

"Well. Would you look at these?" Marilyn said, steadying herself as she descended. She held the shoes out to Hannah. "Why on earth would Rokhl put these on the top shelf and at the back of a cupboard … in the kitchen?"

Hannah turned the shoes over in her hands. They were so soft, kid leather probably, pale blue and very small. She had never seen them before.

"Ask me, Marilyn, like I know anything about what went on in my mother's head," she said exasperated.

"I bet they were yours."

"Who knows. I don't recall ever seeing them and, if they were mine, it must have been when I was a newborn."

Hannah cradled the shoes in her palm lost in thought when she felt Marilyn's arm around her.

"It's okay, go ahead," she said. "You've needed a good cry for a while."

"I'm not crying," Hannah said weakly.

"Well then, it must be raining indoors because your face is wet."

Hannah's hand flew to her cheek damp with tears. She raised a forearm and quickly wiped it over her face but didn't shrug off Marilyn's half embrace. It was all Hannah allowed as she stood gazing at the little leather booties. She felt Marilyn's gaze on her but kept her focus on the object in her palm. No memory surfaced. Now what? she wondered. Should she add these booties to the heap of mysteries her life had become. Why was Rokhl hiding these? How do you have a relationship with someone your whole life and still know so little about who they are and why you don't know?

Questions whirled around in Hannah's brain, along with Barak's admonitions about never sharing what went on in the home with outsiders. That effectively raised the drawbridge and kept Marilyn, her oldest friend, on the outside and so she went back to sorting and packing. Marilyn did the same. In all the decades they had known each other, Marilyn had never succeeded in convincing her friend that she was 100% trustworthy. Some part of Hannah, some chamber of her heart, was forever kept under lock and key. It wasn't a question of love but rather trust. She knew that Hannah loved her, in her own way, but could never completely reveal what lay in that secret chamber. Marilyn believed it was her vulnerability. For Hannah, raised on the paranoia of two people who believed the world to be a treacherous place, it was anathema to be unprotected.

Marilyn bent down to toss some old containers into the recycling when she saw something red on the floor.

"And what's this?" she asked picking up a triangular piece of red cloth. The fabric was old and frayed at the edges where some remnants of black thread remained.

Hannah turned to look.

"Where did you find it?" she asked.

"It was on the floor ... I think it was wrapped in the cloth with the booties."

Marilyn examined the fabric that had protected the baby shoes and found some of the same black thread that hung from the triangle.

"Something about this looks familiar, doesn't it?" Marilyn asked. Hannah just shook her head in disbelief. The list of unknowables never seemed to end.

"Let's get back to finishing this kitchen," Hannah said taking the red triangle and slipping it into her jeans pocket. "At this rate, I'll never get the apartment ready for the new tenants before I leave for Germany."

"You're going to Germany?" Marilyn said, her eyebrows rising up to her hairline. "When were you planning to tell me that?"

CHAPTER TWENTY-ONE

Light slipped through the Venetian blinds like a thief through the forest. It was late afternoon and the autumn wind had picked up, hustling the last leaves off the sugar maple in the backyard. She had planted that maple sapling with Barak over 30 years earlier when it was no more than a foot high. Spent from a day of packing, Hannah lay stretched across her childhood bed feeling every muscle in her arms, legs and back strained beyond endurance but it was worth the pain knowing that she and Marilyn had not only finished the kitchen but the bathroom and living room as well. Thank God Rokhl wasn't one for *tchotchkes* or wall décor; after the kitchen there was a lot less to pack. In two days Mercas was sending a truck to pick-up the furniture, carpets, beds, linens, and the fridge. That allowed her a week to clear out the bedrooms and closets. She had thanked Marilyn with a strong hug and convinced her she could do the rest on her own.

"I know you can do it alone, but why should you if I can spare the time to help?"

Hannah just shook her head, gave a kiss to her on both cheeks and shoo-shooed her out the door. Marilyn left reluctantly but not before offering to have Hannah join her, Bram, and the girls for supper. When Hannah turned her down, Marilyn exacted a promise.

"Call me if you decide you need help. I mean it."

Hannah smiled and nodded. Marilyn had barely changed in all

the years they had been friends and recalled the epithet Marilyn's daughter, Ella, had for her mom: Mrs. I'm-In-Charge. Her daughters and Bram had long ago stopped resisting her efforts to 'do' for them. Not one of her girls knew how to cook. But then neither did Hannah, as much her fault as her mother's. The few dishes that Rokhl had made were nothing anyone would ever ask for the recipe. The best home-cooked meals Hannah had ever eaten came out of the kitchen of Marilyn's mother. Eventually, Barak took over the Baranowski kitchen, but he was a master of *schitt arein*—a little of this, a little of that, no discernible recipe. He went by feel and taste, never making a dish the same way twice.

Food was a necessity but not something Hannah had ever found interesting enough to learn how to manipulate. When she and Albie had married, Marilyn had proudly gifted her with a copy of "Second Helpings, Please," a compendium of recipes put out by a local chapter of B'nai B'rith Women. Albie criticized everything she tried to prepare, especially if the recipe required that you open a can of something. Where he got his snobbery about food was anyone's guess, Hannah never knew. But he made it clear he would rather eat out or order in than suffer through a meal she had cooked, and that was just fine with her. She sometimes envied Marilyn's natural skills for homemaking the way she used to envy the large family she was a part of, but not enough to do anything about either.

At the thought of family, the telephone conversation she had had several weeks earlier with her newfound cousin came to mind. It had been running on low wattage in her subconscious for weeks although she theorized that Sheryl Shapiro probably knew no more about Rokhl than she herself did. Hannah wondered if maybe her mother Fenia had shared some information about Hannah's grandparents, Shimon and Liba, something that could provide some insight about what had gone into forming Rokhl.

Since her mother's funeral, Hannah had limited the time she allotted to think about what had happened, about why and how. She did this by focusing on just one aspect of the events at a time. That's when Hannah had decided Rokhl's act was deliberate although how she came to this conclusion was fuzzy. Why she was now alone in the world was only one aspect to the nagging question about what had driven Rokhl to kill herself. She was certain her mother had not been in a state of dementia when she wandered into traffic on Côte-des-Neiges. Her act was deliberate, and selfish. Hannah had to admit that in this respect, Rokhl had died the way she had lived, wrapped in her own world and catering to her own needs with not a thought as to how it would affect her only living relative. In a moment of resolve, Hannah decided to reach out to Cousin Sheryl and set-up a meeting after she returned from her trip. What did she have to lose?

Germany. About that, she had put no limits on playing out the myriad of possible situations arising from her negotiations, from seeing Max Mohr again and meeting the mysterious Heilemann. About Mohr, there were only two scenarios that continually unfolded in her imagination. The sparks that had emanated during their encounters, now fuelled by the few telephone conversations they shared, had left no doubt in her mind that she was in unknown territory. Things were stirring in her that had long gone dormant. When she let him, Mohr dominated her fantasies. She envisioned him leaning across a candlelit table, reaching for her hand, an image that often segued like a scene in a movie to one where his lean body reached out for her as they lay together. She wondered what he would be like in bed—passionate and urgent, or slow and sensual. She imagined the latter most and the sound of his low voice, so rich and mellifluous with its continental European lilt, rumbling in her ear. Would she have found him attractive if his English was thickly accented like that of Nazis in war movies or Colonel Klink?

She was drifting off but caught herself with a start. There was no time to sleep or daydream if she was going to get the duplex emptied. Placing her feet squarely on the floor, she pushed herself off the bed and headed to the closet where remnants of her childhood were living a lonely life. She found several pairs of dusty old sandals she thought she had tossed out years ago and which Rokhl probably retrieved from the garbage in the belief that fashions always come back. A multi-coloured wool poncho sagged on a bent metal hanger alongside a denim miniskirt that Hannah had lived in much to Barak's displeasure.

On the shelf above the clothes bar, Hannah found her high school yearbook embossed in silver with the words: Outremont High School, 1967. It lay beside two photo albums filled with Polaroids, and the four shoeboxes, one for each decade, stuffed with Rokhl's notes each neatly bundled with an elastic band. Hannah determined not to open the boxes or the albums but put them all in a Bay shopping bag she had found at the bottom of the closet. The shoebox for the 90s felt unusually heavy, but she decided not to investigate. Not today. There would be time enough to reminisce, she thought wearily.

CHAPTER TWENTY-TWO

*T*wo years into *the war I was not yet thirteen when we left the only home I had ever known, the one I would forever cherish. I don't remember how it felt when we learned that we were to vacate our apartment and leave anything we couldn't carry behind. I took photos, clothes, and my books especially the diary I had been keeping since Mameh left. When there was no one I could talk to, it was where I kept my deepest secrets and darkest fears. I was beginning to grow outwardly numb and kept my feelings to myself since Papa had enough to worry about.*

Oskar said the Nazis were forcing us to move to Podgórze to humiliate us and make us submissive, although Papa tried to assure me things weren't as bad as they looked. He said that but his eyes betrayed how he himself did not believe the words. Meanwhile by 1941, all the poor people who had lived in Podgórze were now living in Kazimierz.

"In our homes," Oskar said as his mouth twisted into a grim mask. "They are sitting on our furniture, cooking on our stoves, and eating off our tables while we are forced to live like rats crammed into a cage."

In those days Oskar was always angry. He and the others in Akiva were forever making plans on how to resist the Nazis. But without guns, I wondered, what could anyone do? In the end, moving didn't bother me so much. With half our furniture sold or bartered in exchange for food, our apartment had given off an aching echo whenever I entered. And then there were the strangers that Papa had brought home: a family of five from

Chrzanow who moved into the living room and another from Trzebina who took up residence in Papa's study where I had never been allowed to enter without an invitation. Papa said the 'visitors' only needed a temporary place to stay until they could find new accommodations but none of that mattered soon enough when we were all forced to move to a poorer area of Krakow. Suddenly, we were four families—twenty people—in a space that was a third the size of our old apartment. But there was one benefit: Oskar's family was among them. That made up for all the terrible things that had befallen us. Having Oskar close was almost enough to make me forget the smelly bathroom, the hallways with broken windows and the scratchy sound of rodents' feet scurrying around in the middle of the night. Us and the rats, we were living off crumbs. Meanwhile, Uncle Tadeusz had been given permission to keep open his pharmacy, 'Under the Eagle', and it was already located inside the ghetto. He no longer came for dinners, but I sometimes saw Papa go into the shop and stay a while. Whenever he spoke about Uncle, Papa's eyes would stare off into space as he pronounced Tadeusz Pankiewicz not only a good Pole but a decent man, a mensch.

One day walking home after standing for hours in the breadline, I was accosted by some soldiers. The three of them surrounded me laughing, taunting me, touching my hair.

"Is this your true colour?" one asked in German. He put his big hand on my head with fingers spread wide and gave my hair a hard tug. "Tell the truth; this is really a clown's wig," he said laughing. He pulled harder and harder until with one mighty tug he tore out a fistful of my hair.

"Well, it isn't a clown wig after all," he said triumphantly waving the handful of my hair at his cohorts. "It's copper wire. Maybe I can sell it and make a profit from this shitty posting."

For a moment, I stood frozen in shock and then the pain hit me like a hammer. I let out a wail as much from the agony as the sight of my hair flopping like a dead animal in the Nazi's fist. Hearing me, an old man came to my rescue, asking the soldiers politely to let me go, saying that I was only a child. They laughed, delighted at his chivalry, then one of them hit him with his rifle right across the face. He fell to his knees, and as they took turns kicking him, they forgot about me. I ran. I ran as if the world was on fire. I ran as fast as I could and did not turn around even when I heard the shot. I have heard that shot often in my dreams.

When he arrived home, Papa found me hunched in a corner, knees to my chest, my eyes vacant. When he saw the bloody bald spot on the side of my head, he began to scold me for not being careful enough out on the street. He forbade me to leave the apartment until he decided what must be done. When Oskar came home and saw me, he didn't need an explanation; atrocities were taking place every day in the ghetto. He said nothing but approached me tentatively and with the greatest tenderness, put his arms around me. "Don't cry," he said quietly.

But I wasn't going to cry. My head ached fiercely but my heart was full because in that moment, what I had yearned for became evident: Oskar cared for me.

The next evening, when Uncle Tadeusz learned of the assault, he had Papa bring me to the pharmacy where he gently administered an ointment on the raw patch of scalp that was now as prickly as cactus by a scabby layer. The treatment numbed the pain but not the memory. As he gently patted my head, Uncle spoke to Papa in a manner that seemed a continuation of an earlier conversation, one they have had many times before.

"I've told you, Shimon, you and Rokhl must leave Krakow. I have connections for papers, and safe house for you to ..."

"It is too dangerous ..." Papa interrupted nervously but Uncle Tadeusz raised his hand to stop the words he had clearly heard so many times before.

"Too dangerous?" he said, his face revealing a look of disbelief that suddenly alarmed me. "What do you call your life in the ghetto, working for the Germans? Rokhl never knows if you will come home or end up on a transport. You are living at the constant mercy of hooligans and murderers who need no reason to kill you other than you are a Jew. What do I have to do to convince you Shimon, that Poles—my own people—have turned against their one-time neighbours and friends in a frenzy of greed and malice? How much more proof do you need than Rokhl's close call?"

Papa looked defeated. He was once a man I believed to be strong, chivalrous, the protector of our family, of me and my mother. I thought of Oskar and his resolve, refusing to bow to the Nazis or to succumb to inaction, and in that moment, I realized that my father, as my mother had rightly understood, was too ineffectual to be a protector. I looked from Tadeusz to Papa and saw how my father was shrinking into his clothes. His hair had begun to thin and grey. When had this all happened?

Following Tadeusz's strong admonition, Papa turned to him, his eyes downcast, his hands limp at his side, and mumbled that Uncle was probably right.

"I have some Polish clients who have not forgotten me and have even offered to help should I need it. I will ..."

"No, no, Shimon, you mustn't trust anyone especially if they think you have money hidden away as all Jews must. They will bleed you dry and then turn you over to the SS."

Uncle Tadeusz was adamant that Papa not speak to anyone before checking with him first.

"Jews are being trapped by Poles who promise to get them out of the ghetto for a price and then, after collecting, hand them over for a reward to the Granatowa policja *or the Germans."*

I listened to all this as if trapped in a bad dream, one I finally understood there was no possibility of awakening from. It was like everything we were living. You survived the day, doing things you had to like stand in line for bread and then, you wondered when had you grown so accepting? I was not yet thirteen and I could see this. Why couldn't Papa?

☞ *The only time I felt alive was with Oskar. I hounded and begged him to bring me to Akiva so I too could be of use to the cause of resistance, so I would not end up like my father. After much nagging and with the help of some hair bleach, Oskar finally conceded that I could be of help. It was Uncle Tadeusz's idea. He said with my pretty face, blue eyes, and high cheekbones, I could easily pass for a Gentile if I dyed my hair blond. So, I did it. No more copper wiring to attract attention. It came with a bonus, something about the bleaching process, or it could have been my lack of protein, something made my hair lose its tight curls and instead, fall in soft waves just like Mameh's. What would she have said if she had seen me? Would have I been more appealing to her? Would she have loved me better?*

Dolek Liebeskind, the leader of the Akiva group, looked me over with a keen eye the day Oskar brought me to a meeting at their shelter on ulica Jozefinska, 13.

"What is this child doing here, Oskar?" There was no inflection in his tone.

"She wants to get involved. She's smart and quick."

Dolek turned to me, scanned my face, "And what is it you think you could do for the cause?"

"I could pass for Gentile and, if you taught me how, I could be a courier. I speak flawless German and I have no accent when I speak it or Polish. My father made sure of that. And I am not yet developed so I will attract no unwanted attention from soldiers."

At this last Dolek snorted, a sound that I would come to learn passed for laughter with him. Addressing Oskar, he said, "We will test her and if she is trustworthy, we will make use of her."

Turning to me he said, "This is not child's play, Blue Eyes. You will need all your talents to stay alive. Are you prepared?" Not believing there was any other option, I said yes.

The job I was given was the distribution of our underground newsletter, HeHaluc HaLohem, mostly to the other Zionist groups with whom we soon joined forces to work together with the Polish underground. It was easy for me to slip in and out of the ghetto if I attached myself to a work detail. Once outside the gate, I would stash my Jewish star under a rock and walk about like a free Christian girl. When Dolek deemed me trustworthy, I was given other things to deliver, usually identification papers to those who were already outside the ghetto but unable to travel. I wanted to procure papers for Papa. Dr. Szlapak said she could help. More people were being pushed into the ghetto which the Nazis kept shrinking in size. We were living on top of each other although with the many aktions, people continued to disappear, gathered up and sent to Belzec as slave labourers. Every day it seemed, the aktions grew worse with people being rounded up at random or simply shot in the street. Our lives became a lethal game in which we were forever losing because the rules were constantly changing. From our point of view, anyway. The teams collecting the dead with their carts could not keep up. I lived in terror that Papa would not come home but somehow, I feared nothing for myself convinced that I was invisible with my blonde hair and flat chest. No OD—the Jüdischer Ordnungsdienst, Jewish police or Nazi ever stopped me to ask why I wasn't wearing my armband. I still was not menstruating and so there was nothing about me for anyone to see but a gaunt face. Mostly I stayed off the streets, spending time with Oskar at Dr. Szlapak where she sheltered Jews. He didn't want to draw attention to his parents in the event he was captured. He was certain the OD were on to him. He called the Jewish police traitors, but I understood that sometimes you had to do what you could to keep your family alive. They weren't all bad.

One day, on my way to deliver some papers, I was stopped at the gate as I was leaving the ghetto. I had already taken off my armband. When I was asked where I was going, with eyes lowered, I said home and gave our old address. Then I looked the guard straight in the face. I said I had been sent by my father to make a delivery to Under the Eagle pharmacy. Impatiently, he waved me through the gate. I snuck back in later but when Dolek heard the story from Oskar, he said I needed to get out of the ghetto and could be working on the outside with the Polish partisans because with my looks he said I could easily pass. They were closing down the Akiva shelter on ulica Jozefinska as it was becoming too dangerous, but I refused to leave Podgórze. Papa had recently been relieved of his duties as a bookkeeper and was now leaving at dawn every day to work in some factory. How could I leave and abandon Papa? Or Oskar?

Then, Papa was gone. In a panic, I ran to Uncle Tadeusz to ask if he could make enquiries. He looked at me sadly but promised he would try. Since June there had been countless aktions *to 'resettle' people, sending them by cattle car to Belzec. My papa was among such a transport. He never returned and soon we began to hear that Belzec was not a slave labour camp like Plaszow but an extermination site. Still, I told myself, Papa is clever, he'll find a way to be of service, and stay alive. Nonetheless, Tadeusz said it was time to secure a new identity if I was going to live outside the ghetto, and that's how I became Anya Marya Cieski. Not long after, Oskar's parents and little brother were also taken away, and so the two of us now only had each other.*

Akiva had been causing some havoc attacking cafés and shops frequented by German officers. The reprisals were vicious and there was a sense that we were slowly losing our ability to fight. Everywhere we went we saw the dead and dying. Corpses littered the streets and little children like matchstick figures with hollowed, lifeless eyes begged for food no one had to share. Those of us who had chosen to resist were growing desperate. In November, Dolek gathered us together and said, before winter set in, it was time to stand our ground and fight if only so that one day we will deserve three little lines in the history books.

"We must do this if only to show them that Jewish youth did not go to the slaughter like sheep," he said as he broke apart a loaf of bread and gave each of us a piece.

"We have joined forces with Heshek Bauminger's group. We are now the Jewish Fighting Organization and have some weapons that have been smuggled in with the few we've managed to steal. Our contact with Warsaw, Tarnow, and Rzeszow has provided us with vital information and it is this: We must act now. This may be our last operation and this, our last supper, but we will not go quietly."

The target was a café called Cyganeria, a favourite with German officers and the SS. We blew it up, killed seven of the enemy and wounded many more. We were the first ghetto uprising, even before Warsaw. That's what the history books would say, if they were going to write about us at all.

↶ *They killed most of us, including my Oskar. I ran. I ran out of the ghetto with my false documents and never looked back, my breathing louder than the rifle shots.*

CHAPTER TWENTY-THREE

Dani carefully stacked the documents on Hannah's desk. She had taken it upon herself since the death of Hannah's mother to do as much as she could whenever her boss grew uncharacteristically distracted or pressured by falling behind in her work. Things had just begun to settle down when this trip to Germany put everything in flux again. Dani had asked Hannah point-blank why, if the Sonenshein parcel of land was located in Quebec, did Hannah have to go to Germany to make any kind of deal. Hannah tried to explain but when Dani's eyes glazed over, Hannah conceded that she too was unsure for the need of such a production. Both Dani and Hannah shared a distaste for unnecessary drama. But whether she understood it or not, Dani had to help her boss get it right. If the deal was concluded, they both were in for a big bonus that could swell Dani's savings substantially.

With or without the bonus, however, she knew she would put in the extra hours out of loyalty to Hannah, the woman who gave her a job when no one else would. Not once they learned she was straight out of rehab. For Hannah, Dani would walk on hot coals. After all her years working in real estate administration, Dani's experience was deemed worthless when viewed through the lens of a decade-long addiction and a dropped criminal charge for pilfering from her previous employer's petty cash. More than six years ago, Hannah had looked at Dani's work experience and not her record before giving Dani a job.

Dani double-checked the pile of documents pertaining to the Trois-Îles property one more time unsure whether she had everything Hannah needed. Something was missing she knew but she couldn't put her finger on what it could be. Hannah will know, she thought. Her boss had an uncanny ability to look at the totality of something and immediately see the missing components ... if her head was clear.

With each passing day—only 20 to go before the flight to Frankfurt —Hannah's anxiety increased exponentially. Only yesterday she received the cadaster for the Trois-Îles boundaries from Sonenshein's office and immediately realized that since the day Chaim purchased the plot from the farmer 50 years ago its boundaries had been neither reviewed nor surveyed. Understandable since Sonenshein apparently was being honest when he said that he never had any intentions of developing the land or selling it. But as the cadaster had never been updated, only God knew what regulations now governed its use. Was it still agricultural land or had it been re-zoned residential like so much else in that area? She was going to need an aerial photograph of the plot and a search of the land files in the regional office of the *Ministère des Ressources naturelles et de la Faune.*

She vaguely recalled that there was a regional park nearby and wondered if that somehow impacted the land's potential use. That raised the question of what Heilemann had in mind for the plot. It certainly wasn't her responsibility to educate Maximilian Mohr on what he needed to investigate and ascertain locally before making a deal with Sonenshein and yet inexplicably, she felt compelled to do so. Following his inspection, Mohr had seemed somewhat surprised at the ruggedness of the property and its distance to the closest village.

Depending on what Heilemann's intentions were, there were several steps Mohr would need to take before making the offer. If he was planning to build a resort, he needed to make an appointment with the town's mayor to ascertain whether he is allowed to build on the land, and then, get the permit to do so even before he made any offer. But Sonenshein had forewarned her about putting in too much work before she met with Mohr and Heilemann. When they last spoke, Hannah had bombarded Sonenshein with questions about what she needed to prepare and what he was expecting to come out of this trip and her negotiations.

"Take it easy. You are there as my agent and deputy but let them do the talking," Chaim counselled. "Reveal nothing until they ask a direct question. I know this trip is not the way we usually do business, but this is a unique case. And if Mohamed won't come to the mountain … you know that saying."

Nonetheless, being unprepared was counterintuitive to Hannah's modus operandi. Marilyn said she was always trying to make things stress-free for people but never herself. She shook her head. Lately it felt like Marilyn had taken up residence in a corner of her brain, tossing out cautionary comments the way her mother used to leave notes. Why was she so worried on Mohr's behalf anyway? Was it because she found him *sympatiche?* For some reason, she felt he would do the same for her if the tables were turned. Yet Sonenshein had made it clear that she was to play her cards close to the vest.

What he had revealed about Heilemann cast a dark shadow over an already baffling situation. When Sonenshein told her his story, Hannah could hardly believe it. Apparently, the German real estate mogul's father had unintentionally played a hand in Chaim's survival as a young boy. What Chaim owed to the son of his saviour was still unclear to Hannah but there was no doubt in her mind that, whatever the debt entailed, the payment of it was going to be made grudgingly. Sonenshein was a man who never forgot a favour—or a slight. Her respect for his prowess was tinged with a wariness about his methods.

Hannah momentarily considered her father's unlikely friendship with Chaim. They held such completely different social and political views that it was hard to understand how the relationship had survived for almost half a century. Barak had come from a well-to-do Vilna family, but his character was forged by his war experiences as a partisan and being among those that had liberated Auschwitz. Somehow, early on, he had become a devout socialist and a member of the Labor Zionist movement through the *Hashomer Hatzair* Zionist youth organization. With his last breath, Barak had been a firm believer in the sanctity and unassailability of workers' rights. Chaim, on the other hand, although born into a large and impoverished family in Chrzanow, a town near Krakow, made his fortune through shrewd investments and tough negotiations in every aspect involved in the building and marketing of properties. When war broke out, his father sent him on foot to Lodz to live with his uncle. It took him four nights walking as fast as he could and hiding during the day to get to Lodz, but when he arrived his uncle was already dead, shot by the Nazis without an argument in his elegant apartment simply because he refused to leave.

Homeless, Chaim briefly lived in the Rumkowski orphanage in the newly formed ghetto and then worked in various factories in whatever capacity he could. His wit and ability to adapt quickly kept him alive in the ghetto and from there, in Auschwitz and the subcamp, Sosnowiec where he became a runner between the factories, carrying messages. It was only luck and an encounter with Heilemann that he didn't die on the death march to Mauthausen.

Up until their last meeting, Hannah knew only the barest facts about Chaim's life before the war. When she was growing up and the adults got together, no one really talked about the war (not in front of the children, anyway) and at home, Barak only made passing references to his days as a partisan. Anyway, nobody in Montreal asked and no one wanted to hear the stories about the horrors of the war, that they survived at the cost of losing large portions or all of their families and childhood homes.

It was what Barak and Chaim most had in common, Hannah reasoned. She wasn't sure about what else had kept the friendship going. And she was not about to ask. On her last visit, she already learned more than she had wanted to know about Chaim. Trying to imagine what it must have been like scrabbling for your life in the ghetto and then in Auschwitz was beyond her ability to grasp. That he survived the initial selection by Mengele was a miracle in and of itself. He was 14 when he fell out of the teeming cattle car to stand in front of Mengele, the Angel of Death, and looked up to see the iron gates that proclaimed *Arbeit macht frei*—work sets you free. He took the message to heart and never stopped.

CHAPTER TWENTY-FOUR

Midair over the Atlantic, Hannah suffered a mild panic attack. She had been dozing with her head against the icy window and awoke with a start, certain she heard Rokhl softly calling her name. Eyes bleary, she shifted in her seat and rubbed at the kink in her neck and shoulders. Thank goodness she had taken Marilyn's advice and bought a neck pillow at the airport. She had also packed one of her knitted capes because, as her friend had wondered, who knew how well they washed those airline blankets? Settling in for the six-hour flight, she had wrapped herself up like a falafel. As she opened her eyes in the darkened cabin, her mother's voice once again called her name. She started in a panic and looked around despite knowing it was impossible; her imagination was playing tricks on her at 35,000 feet in the air.

Rokhl wasn't anywhere except in Hannah's dreams. There she was a sweeter, softer version of the woman who had raised her. Hannah recaptured the vision of standing in an elegant apartment, somewhere distinctly foreign, and her mother was holding her hand as one holds the hand of a young child. They were looking up at a man standing before them, a very proper looking gentleman with a large salt and pepper moustache in which Hannah could detect hints of coppery red. Her mother was talking to her and assuring Hannah that she wanted to meet this man because he was her grandfather. Hannah opened her mouth to say, '... but Zeyde Shimon is ...' The word 'dead' stopped her. And then she looked at her mother whose face held none of the pale gauntness with which she was familiar. Instead, Hannah saw a smooth countenance glowing with health. But she was thinking, 'You are also dead.' Yet the hand holding hers was warm and her mother said, '*Hannaleh,* this is your *Zeyde.* I always wanted you two to meet.'

It was at that moment in the dream that turbulence had jolted Hannah back to her reality. If she had not been in midair on Lufthansa flight #LH479, she would have struggled to exit the plane. Why on earth was she flying to Germany anyway, against the express wishes of her mother, now dead these three months? Because her client asked it of her? And what catastrophe awaited when she and Maximilian Mohr were once again thrown together. She was heading into the unknown, haunted by the knowledge that whatever little support system she had was now where she left it, back in Montreal.

Hannah closed her eyes once more. Despite the fear that Rokhl would materialize again, she needed to look rested when she arrived. Why had she agreed to have Mohr 'collect' her at Frankfurt airport? She could just as easily take a taxi to the hotel in Cologne, even if it was two hours away. After all, Chaim had given her carte blanche for this trip, possibly because there was some measure of guilt on his part. With eyes closed, she began drifting through a thick fog, groping her way to something, someplace that was both drawing her closer and at once repelling her.

A light tap on the shoulder brought her back into her seat. Her neighbour was pointing at the flight attendant offering a breakfast tray. Hannah smiled and shook her head but accepted a coffee that was surprisingly good. It revived her. A while later, the captain's voice floated over the speaker letting the passengers know, in German, English and French, that they would be starting their descent and arriving in Frankfurt on time at 06:55. Right on time. German precision, Hannah thought wryly. She passed her cup along when the trash trolley came by and closed her tray, reaching for the travel bag beneath her outstretched legs. From it, she pulled a small make-up case, her toothbrush and paste, and struggled out of her seat to get in line for the toilet.

⮑ Once through the gateway, Hannah stood a moment gathering her wits. Frankfurt International assaulted her with a cacophony of familiar sounds and slightly foreign smells. Part of her acknowledged that this was no different than other European airports she had travelled through—Heathrow, Charles de Gaulle, AIA in Athens—but the knowledge that she was in Germany somehow imbued the arrival with an air of expectation. The tension generated a slight headache and some grogginess, so when she walked through the passageway between sections and saw a Chasid in his prayer shawl and *tefillin*, Hannah thought she was hallucinating. Wait. Where was she? What was this man doing in Germany, openly practicing his religion? She couldn't take her eyes off him as he swayed to and fro, mumbling his morning prayer.

Unbidden, a soft snort escaped her lips; the irony was so blatant. And if Marilyn was there, she would have pronounced the encounter a 'sign' that Hannah was meant to return to Germany, the country in which she was born. Marilyn was all about reading the omens. The customs officer, checking her passport and seeing Germany as place of birth, he asked politely, "*Deutsch*? English?" "English, *bitte*," she replied, immediately regretting having sent a mixed signal. Unfazed, he asked her what the purpose of her visit was and how long she planned to stay in Germany. "Five days," she informed him, and he stamped her passport and waved for the person behind her to come forward.

Max was waiting, so Hannah hurried to the baggage section, passing elegant upscale shops displaying name brand bags and sweaters, shoes, and jewellery—Boss, Ferragamo, and Bulgari. It was so disorienting Hannah momentarily forgot where she was. The clatter of wheeled and dragged hand luggage brought her back to the moment and she picked up her pace as she remembered that someone was waiting for her. Thankfully, her bag was one of the first to circle the carousel and she headed through the door under the sign: Nothing to

Declare. Another omen? she wondered. As she walked through the doors, Hannah saw only the usual suspects waiting for family and friends. Then she caught sight of a full mane of silver, below it a smile and further down, a sign that read in bold letters: **H. Baran.** Self-consciously, she smiled and gave Max a little wave to acknowledge she had seen him. He walked to the edge of the rail against which those waiting were pressed and held out a single, long-stemmed red rose—like a promise.

CHAPTER TWENTY-FIVE

Max **had no** problem spotting Hannah and her froth of copper curls. The sight sparked a brief agitation in his chest. Max waved his sign and Hannah looked up with a smile that reached her eyes. They momentarily flickered when she spotted the rose. It suddenly occurred to Max that when viewed through the North American lens, a welcome rose could be misconstrued as something he had not intended. Or had he? Well, it was too late now. She was here and so was the rose. Before she reached him, he stole a moment to take in this inscrutable woman. He was impressed by how light she travelled—a large purse, a small tote, and compact suitcase. Her choice of travel fashion implied she was dressed for a skirmish in the military cut to her clothes: navy pants, a soft white blouse, and a wine-red army-style jacket that nipped her at the waist and ended at the hips. The look suited her long-limbed body and no-nonsense personality. When she was closer Hannah's free hand reached out for a business-like handshake. He clasped it in his, proffering the rose with the other.

"*Herzlich willkommen.* Welcome to Germany."

She smiled and he wondered again how she had this capacity to make him feel simultaneously drawn in and shut out.

"Thank you, Max, and thank you for taking the trouble to meet me at the airport. I do appreciate the gesture. I know it's quite a long drive from Cologne."

"Ach Quatsch! It's my pleasure ... really," he said releasing the rose and reaching for her bag. There was a slight hesitation on her part and for a moment, he thought she wouldn't let go but she did before the gesture might have become awkward. Suitcase in hand he walked Hannah through the airport to the car park, unlocked the passenger side door, and stowed her luggage in the boot of the M5. Hannah sat waiting with her eyes half closed. Max slid into the driver's seat, turned to her, momentarily struggling against a shameless desire to reach out for a handful of her mane.

"We're heading straight to your hotel as I imagine you want some time to freshen up before lunch. Is 1 p.m. suitable or would you prefer earlier?"

"Lunch?" Hannah said.

"Yes, lunch. I'm sure you haven't eaten much since you left Montreal."

"Why do you say that?"

"Oh? I'm honestly unsure how I know," he said with a chuckle. "But you seem to me to be someone who prefers decent food to what passes for a meal on transatlantic flights."

Hannah peered at him for a moment and gave him a smile. "That's quite an astute observation. What else do you think I like or dislike?"

"I think you don't like being examined and seem to be someone who values privacy, so if I am clever, I will say no more, say no more."

At this, Hannah laughed out loud. It was a high, light sound and Max, startled by her spontaneity, quickly joined in. They looked at each other, and for no reason, began to laugh again. "Wink, wink. Nudge, nudge, eh? So, you're a Monty Python aficionado?" as she raised the rose to take a whiff of its scent.

"This was very sweet of you. The rose, I mean. Thank you."

And in that moment, Max felt they may have turned a corner. He started the ignition, listening for the familiar thrum, and pulled out of the airport road onto the Autobahn. Within minutes he had manoeuvred the M5 into the left-hand lane and was hitting 200 kph. He heard her quick intake of breath. It gave him a little thrill of satisfaction that he could surprise Hannah Baran. Without taking his eyes from the road, he said, "Have I frightened you? North Americans are always shocked that Germans are allowed to drive so fast."

A moment passed before she answered. "A little warning may have been helpful but, no, you don't scare me ... I mean, you driving fast doesn't frighten me."

Max thought about exploring the Freudian slip but decided at this juncture it was wise to err on the side of caution. Five days was time enough to learn what he could about Hannah Baran and whether he had any effect on her.

"I've booked you into the Mercure Hotel Severinshof," he said. "It's one of my favourites—unpretentious, not too big, and with a lovely inner courtyard open to the sky. The added advantage is that it's close to everything if you're in the mood to explore my city."

"Do you live in the vicinity?" she asked.

"I do. It's a short drive to my place. But a bit of a drive to where we will meet with Ha-Gay Heilemann tomorrow afternoon. That will be at his Schloss, about an hour from here. Are you in accord with all of that?"

"Mmm."

He slid his eyes over to confirm that Hannah was holding her breath, so he eased his foot off the accelerator, dropping down to 180 kph to accommodate her. He signalled and moved into the middle lane. He heard the quiet exhalation. Hannah nodded yes to his earlier question never taking her eyes off the road.

"I always thought I had a lead foot," she finally said, "but by German standards, I can see I am a rank amateur. If I closed my eyes, however, I would never know how fast we were going."

Max laughed. "Germans have no problem with the Autobahn and the stretches without limits, but there are limits at various junctures. The problem is when we have non-Germans driving on our roads, taking the left lane, and then going only 140 or 150 when the left lane is for those going much faster."

"So, you like speed?"

"Mostly on the road ... for other things in life I like to take my time. I eat slowly and like to walk at a leisurely pace. Also, I like to take the time to get to know those people I find interesting."

"Hmm. Some people are not so willing to be known," Hannah said. "They may be curious about others but are not so eager to share anything about themselves. Which one are you?"

"The kind of man who has nothing to hide. You simply need to ask."

"Is that a fact? Then perhaps you can explain Herr Heilemann's interest in Trois-Îles. I've had a difficult time collating the information we might need to facilitate a sale and transfer something I always prepare for foreign buyers. But I have no idea what your client's intentions are for the property."

Max thought a moment, deciding whether candour would be of value.

"To be truthful," he said, "I have no clear indication as to what my client wants with the property. It is unlike any other acquisition I have transacted for him. Without revealing his plans to me, he has only authorized me to start negotiations. I don't think I am betraying any strategy by telling you that this is not Heilemann's usual modus operandi. That is why you are here, for which I am grateful on a personal level. But normally, I conduct all the business required to finalize a deal. Not this time. Honestly, I am a little baffled myself."

He gave Hannah a sidelong glance. She nodded.

"Yes, I'm also baffled at this unusual way of conducting business and saying so makes me feel a little guilty, like we're co-conspirators on some level. I guess we'll eventually learn what these two men are up to and, at that point, have to take up our position on opposite sides of the table."

"Well, before that happens," he said with a wry smile, "let's seat ourselves at a restaurant table over lunch this afternoon."

As he spoke, he pulled into the driveway of the hotel. He hopped out of the car and signalled the bellman to collect Hannah's luggage from the boot. At the Front Desk, he presented his Amex, ensured that the room had been readied for Hannah's early check-in, and handed her the key card. "I hope you like the room. I've had them put you on the top floor. It has a large balcony with a great view of Köln. Shall I collect you at 12:30? Are you OK with Italian?"

She nodded.

"There's a great restaurant very close by here; we can drive there in 5 minutes."

"Italian sounds just right. I'll be waiting downstairs in the lobby for you but if you don't mind, since the restaurant is that close, can we walk? I could really use the exercise."

Max gladly acceded and decided to head home to Rodenkirchen. It was so close and the office too far. Besides, he should tidy up. Just in case.

CHAPTER TWENTY-SIX

The suite Max had reserved was perfect and unlike any hotel room she had ever been in. A feeling of being 'at home' surprised her because Hannah had never been an easy traveller. The room was spacious yet spare, clean and orderly. The bed linens were white on white, and the sleek, black lacquered dresser was legless, attached directly to the wall. Over it, a large photograph offered a verdant splash of colour against the bright white wall. Up close, she identified the pattern as the centre of a plant with a swirling rosette of glossy, dark green leaves that spiralled into a nautilus-like centre. Hannah was drawn into the vortex of the photograph and after a few moments, became aware that there was warmth radiating off the floor. She smiled when she recognized that it was the same kind of bamboo flooring she had in her condo down to the built-in heating. There was a desk in high gloss white under the gently sloped ceiling which sported twin skylights positioned in such a way that she could imagine viewing the night sky while lying in the king-size bed. An ebony table with matching credenza were set to the side near a sliding glass door overlooking the courtyard and the café below. In the centre of the table an empty vase stood waiting to accommodate the rose Max had handed her at the airport. And off to the left, a clear glass wall provided a view of the spacious bathroom. Spying the shower Hannah decided that was the first thing she needed to do before settling in.

➤ By noon, she was washed, dressed, and had shot off a number of emails: to Dani about some afterthoughts she had on a bid; to Marilyn letting her know that she had arrived safely; and to the residential real estate agent handling the sale of her parents' duplex. She had promised the woman, Marina Farad, that she would let her do her job without interference but on the flight to Germany some things had occurred to her that she felt compelled to share. The impulse brought to mind Marilyn's inveterate desire to hang on to all the reins she had held in life and Hannah wondered, in the aftermath of Rokhl's death, if she hadn't started doing the same. Once again, Hannah considered whether she was completely losing control of her life.

If she were to make a list of successes and failures, she acknowledged that her list of accomplishments would amount to very little. She could claim to being a competent administrator, a successful agent with a capacity for getting people to trust her, and someone who was highly efficient at squirreling away money. The list of her failures far exceeded these successes. By her own admission, and corroborated by Albie, she sucked at marriage, especially at homemaking when it came to doing laundry and cooking. She failed to become a mother (although she wasn't sure that she had ever aspired to be one), and in the romance department, on a scale of one to ten, she rated at best a four, something all her long-gone romantic partners could attest to.

Worst of all, she had been unsuccessful in keeping her promise to Barak to take care of her mother, failing in her role as Rokhl's daughter. Why wasn't she enough for Rokhl to want to live? Thoughts of Rokhl led Hannah to reflect upon being in Germany. The image of the Chasid in Frankfurt's airport rose up time and again, and she considered whether she should share the moment with Marilyn. Her friend thought this journey to be idiocy although she had made the same argument to Marilyn as she had to Rokhl, that things most certainly must have changed in half a century.

What she couldn't shake, however, was the strange sense of familiarity Germany presented although it was impossible that she could remember any of it before the family left, maybe only truly remembering what Barak had shared in stories. Yet there was the ease in understanding the language—the words if not the structure—so like Yiddish, the mother tongue Barak had insisted they speak at home. She was able to puzzle out the meanings of some conversations by stringing words together. Street names and business signs were easily decipherable: *Schneider* was tailor; *Schuster*, shoemaker; *Bäcker*, baker. But some simply confused her by sounding familiar although with no relation to the Yiddish words they sounded like. *Schmuck* she learned from the little *Langenscheidt* German-English dictionary she had bought, meant jewellery. That was one she and Marilyn would have a good laugh over when she got home.

At 12:30 sharp, Hannah was in the lobby when Max Mohr arrived. The sight of him—first in the airport and now here—set off a flutter in her chest that was simultaneously frightening and arousing. His was an uncanny ability to tilt her off balance. He strode through the door, his head turned to share a word and a smile with the doorman, and upon spotting Hannah, a broad grin. She watched him approach. His gait loose-limbed and measured suggestive of a big cat leisurely ambling across the savannah. She turned her gaze down to her purse, pretending to retrieve something as a flush rose to her cheeks. Once out on the street, however, the cool October air of Cologne helped clear her head and sharpen her senses. Disorientation was natural since she had hardly slept during the flight.

Marilyn was right. It was time to cut herself some slack. The red shawl that had so faithfully served as her blanket on board was now doing double duty keeping the fall wind from chilling her tired body. She felt certain the walk would clear her head and, as a result, their lunch could be a pleasant and light affair before they suited up for battle tomorrow. Hannah quickly fell into stride beside Max as they turned left and left again delivering them to a broad avenue. Hannah looked up and stopped dead in her tracks. The street sign read Tel-Aviv-Strasse. Hannah's face made Max stop and ask if something was wrong. Hannah laughed, shaking her head, unable to reveal the questions that refused to be stilled: Where am I and what am I doing here?

⌐ Again, Max Mohr had divined what would please Hannah. The food and ambiance of the little Italian place set the stage for a pleasant tête-à-tête. Sitting in a corner of the restaurant, they fell into easy conversation exchanging the names of the musicians and music that had influenced their lives.

"And who is your favourite?" Hannah asked, taking a sip of rosé.

"Leonard Cohen, Bob Dylan, Paul Simon are in a three-way tie for that position."

"Leonard Cohen? Really? He's a Montrealer."

"Yes, I know," he said "I like Montreal. I saw him perform at the Deutschlandhalle in Berlin the fall of 1970 and there again in 1993. It is the poetry, like that of Dylan and Simon, that moves me."

"Hmm, I agree with you about Cohen and Simon, less so with Dylan but he is powerful."

From music they moved to movies and from there to travel, not as much about the places they had been but the long list of destinations they planned one day to see.

"Top of my list," Max said, "is Jasper National Park in the Canadian Rockies."

"It seems Canada is much on your mind. For me, I dream of touring New Zealand, but there are places I would return to."

They agreed that Provence and Ireland were on that list, magical places despite having a plethora of buildings that needed serious renovation if one was to buy some real estate. Both had read Peter Mayle's *A Year in Provence* and joked about how if they had been in charge of his home renovation, the title would have been, *A Month in Provence*. The third time the waiter came to ask if they would like more coffee, they finally realized that they had been in conversation for almost four hours, and were the last customers left as the staff waited to set-up for dinner.

"You must be tired," Max said once they were standing out on the street.

"I should be, but I've been having such a nice time, I haven't thought about it."

"Well, how about we catch a taxi and go have a glass of wine at the hotel bar?"

"I'd like that," Hannah said with a smile. "I really would."

CHAPTER TWENTY-SEVEN

From the moment they sat down in the hotel bar, Hannah sensed it was a mistake. What had happened to her customary caution? Clearly, the lack of sleep had erased it. In a reasonable scenario she should have graciously disentangled herself from Max Mohr and gone straight to her room. And to bed. Alone. Instead, here she was having a Pineau des Charentes, a fortified wine that would certainly do nothing to fortify her against Max Mohr's irresistible charms. As he spoke about his love of landscaping and how it led him into the field of architecture, Hannah leaned forward, and kept her eyes on his chin and the dimple there. She was enchanted by its movements, stretching, and returning to its original form like a fledgling attempting to fly and failing, only to settle back in the nest. In a trance-like state, she heard but half of that he was saying and then, the chin stopped moving. Looking up she saw him gazing at her with such intensity it pushed her back against her chair.

"What?" she asked.

"You are a very attractive woman, Hannah Baran," he said, looking suddenly as if he had come across something puzzling. "Why are you not married or at least in a relationship?"

"How do you know I'm not?" she said, sitting back and peering at him. She considered whether or not to be offended at this highly

156

personal question. Did it warrant a swift slap on the wrists? She came up with a third option to his question.

"Well, how is it that a man who is so handsome, seemingly full of vigour and clearly well-off appears to be equally alone? Or are you married? In a long-term relationship?"

Mohr chuckled and replied, "Touché. Well, I can see you're in no mood for personal questions, and I understand. Perhaps we should call it a night."

Hannah leaned in a little closer. "Was my question too direct?" Getting ready to rise, she said, "We should call it a night. After all, I still need to review some documents before we meet again."

"Hannah, I know you want to be prepared for tomorrow but bear in mind that this is just a preliminary meeting to bring both parties to the table to talk about the perimeters of an offer we have yet to make."

"With all due respect, Herr Mohr," Hannah said, straightening her back, "I didn't come across the Atlantic to have a pleasant chat about possibilities. I fully expect that I will be going back to Canada with a written offer that we have discussed and agreed upon."

An awkward silence followed. Hannah stood and took a last swallow of the Pineau. Max was immediately on his feet but at that moment, in the corner diagonally across from their table, a young man sat down at the piano and began to play a slow Latin rhythm. In tandem, they turned their eyes in the direction of the music.

"Before you go upstairs to your room, shall we have one dance?" Max asked, his hand outstretched.

Hannah's look of surprise was quickly replaced by such an obvious expression of dismay that Max winced and withdrew his outstretched hand. "Hannah, you look like I just asked you to take a walk on hot coals. I don't mean to upset you ..."

"I'm not upset," Hannah said. "I'm just sorry that I don't dance. I've never been much of a dancer and it's certainly not something I've done in a very long time and ..."

"But what do you mean that you don't dance? Everybody dances."

"Really? That may be true in your world but not where I come from. Few in my crowd dance much except those dances we did as teenagers like the Twist or the Cha-cha, this mostly at weddings and bar mitzvahs. I just haven't had enough occasions where I could dance … and certainly not this, whatever it is. The bottom line, Max, I really need to sleep. I think it's time I went to my room."

"Then I will release you without any further harassments but only if you promise that, before you go back to Canada, we will have an occasion to dance."

There was no harm in acceding, she thought. She could always, and most likely would, renege. As they said goodnight in the lobby, his parting words were, "A promise is a promise."

She nodded and stepped into the elevator. Her eyes were closing, and she desperately wanted to be in her nightgown and horizontal. From some corner of her brain, words began to float into her consciousness which she soon identified with a half-smile. The voice in her head was Leonard Cohen and he was singing "Dance Me to the End of Love":

> *Dance me to your beauty with a burning violin.*
> *Dance me through the panic till I'm gathered safely in.*
> *Lift me like an olive branch and be my homeward dove.*
> *Dance me to the end of love.*

CHAPTER TWENTY-EIGHT

I **saw it** *all—I witnessed the liquidation of the Krakow Ghetto. I saw how they herded the people like cattle, pushing them down streets, shooting into the crowd to create panic, people stumbling over bodies as they were steered to the train station where they were packed into cars meant for another kind of animal and the fittest were shipped to Plasznow slave camp, the others to Auschwitz-Birkenau. I was cowering inside the ghetto, trembling with fear but safe in Uncle Tadeusz's pharmacy along with others he was rescuing. I was luckier than most. I had false papers with which I could pass as a goya, and I was of value to the underground (or so I believed). When it grew quiet, I ran down the side streets where, on one, I found an open manhole cover. I slipped into the sewer and emerged covered in slime but safe on the other side of the ghetto wall with not a soul in sight.*

It was March of 1943. Spring was around the corner but that season promising rebirth brought no expectation of new life for those marked to die before their time. In my youth and stupidity, I was determined not to be counted among them. I had no home, no father, no mother, no Oskar—no one who loved me. All love was dead. I had been stripped of everything worth living for but was too stubborn to let go of life. As soon as I could I joined the ranks of the Battalion Zośka, the scouting battalion for the Armia Krajowa, the AK, those Poles who would eventually demonstrate how little they loved the Jews. My papers said I was Anya Marja

Cieski from Trzebina, Papa's hometown. He had cousins there we would visit on occasion, taking a promenade to the town square and stopping in at various shops to chat with his former classmates. As for the battalion, it was wise that I hid my true nature as well as my true colour. Thankfully, Tadeusz had supplied me with enough hair bleach to keep me blond. I did what I was told, kept to myself, and avoided getting close to anyone for fear that I would accidentally let something slip about my real identity. All of my caution came to gornisht *because I was caught with two other couriers carrying a satchel with false papers. I was beaten badly. There is no need for you to know more.*

As you know, Hannaleh, I did not die. Although later, I often wished I had. But life is relentless. We think we hold onto it but in truth, it holds on to us. All those millions of cells that make up our body and brain, when one dies another arises unbidden to replace it. Who asked for this life? Who wanted it when it was so full of loss and misery? There came a time when you were the only light that cut through the darkness but by then, I was no more able to touch you than I could the sun. I would have disintegrated.

CHAPTER TWENTY-NINE

Eyes closed Hannah could still envision the stars as they had appeared through the skylight the night before. No remnant of a dream remained with her upon waking for which she was thankful. She stretched sleepily and as she did, the goose-feather duvet enveloped her from head to foot. It reminded her of the *puchineh kohldreh* she had on her bed throughout her childhood. It had come with them from Germany, carried along with their other meagre belongings like the mismatched set of china, the manual meat-grinder and the cast iron pot she still had. What became of that childhood comforter? she wondered. So many things from her youth had disappeared, not only in reality but from memory as well. But here in Germany, little triggers seemed to be all around her.

When Hannah finally forced her eyes open, sun was streaming in through the transoms, spilling a buttery light over the room. A glance at the alarm by her bed had her sitting straight up. She had slept almost 12 hours uninterrupted. A quick calculation assured her it was only 2 a.m. back home so there was no rush to open her computer. Instead, she decided to do her yoga exercises before taking a shower. After all, it was hours before she had to be ready for the meeting with Heilemann and Mohr, and besides, she was feeling languorous for the first time in a while. She thought back to her lunch with Max. It had been a very long time since she had sat at a table opposite a man without checking her watch. Maybe it's something in the air, she thought. Maybe Europe moves at a slower pace. It had succeeded in surprising her on many levels. Yesterday, walking to the restaurant, she and Max passed some teenagers, two of them black, dressed as you would see teens in Canada or the US dressed in hip hop style with droopy pants, hoodies, and high-top runners. What startled Hannah was that as she passed the two black boys, they were speaking German! Their look was out of sync with what she was expecting, like the Chasid in the Frankfurt airport. She wished that Marilyn could have witnessed these two encounters; although surprising, they reinforced her belief that Germany was no longer the country their parents had known.

Her yoga completed, Hannah showered, dressed and as was her habit, put on a light application of make-up. She had never forgotten Rokhl's written advice about what too much make-up would do to her skin. She sat down at the immaculate white desk and opened her beloved IBM ThinkPad with more bells and whistles than she would ever know how to employ. She plugged in the cable and put in the password she had received with her key card. The speed at which she was connected startled her. Not only cars moved fast in Germany. Dani had written to confirm that she had carried out Hannah's instructions before leaving for the night but assured her that she would be up bright and early and online should Hannah need anything before the meeting.

Marilyn sent a brief note of caution: "Stay safe." Hannah had to laugh. Her friend was certain she had walked into a hornets' nest filled with stinging insects wearing swastikas on their wings. What did she imagine of Germany? The same as Rokhl apparently had—that it was a place of dire danger for any Jew to enter. It was not what Hannah had sensed at all and had never been one to see what good it did to tar an entire nation with the sins of the past. It was nothing she would ever admit in front of Barak, but she had had conversations along these lines with Marilyn years ago and finally gave up trying to find common ground. Marilyn hated all Germans who, she was certain, were still secretly harbouring WWII sentiments. Once, Hannah got her to concede that maybe they weren't all Nazis but, Marilyn maintained, they couldn't possibly be happy paying Jews blood money for the sins committed by their parents and grandparents over fifty years earlier.

"How would you like it," she asked, 'if our federal government suddenly decided that we had to pay reparations to the First Nations for stealing their lands and resources? You would not be thrilled because it's not you who perpetrated this wrong; you just happen to be benefitting from the wrong that was done. In short, the Germans will never have any reason to love the Jews."

Yes, the German question ... so many pitfalls for North American Jews. Long ago, Hannah had noted that it was the Jews who came after the war and never bought anything made in Germany—no cars or cameras or electronics. But the long-established Canadian Jews had no such problems. If they had the wealth, why should they deny themselves the best of everything—a BMW or a Leica or a Miele stove for the renovated kitchen? Then she realized that, without being conscious of it, she suffered from a similar ambiguity inasmuch as she would eat pork in a variety of forms but could not abide mixing dairy and meat.

The last email Hannah opened was from Chaim. It was short and to the point. He wrote: *Listen to Heilemann's offer. Reveal neither interest nor disinterest. Say little but make certain you learn his intentions. Call me after your meeting.* Chaim had never been so cryptic with his instructions, and this caused Hannah concern that her client was playing a dangerous form of brinksmanship; dangerous because as his proxy she did not know what was at stake. After all their years working together, she felt disrespected to be left out of the loop, in effect, expected to deliver the parcel without knowing the contents. At this juncture, with so many mysteries bearing down on her, she was not happy to have to juggle one more.

CHAPTER THIRTY

"**W**e'll be at the Schloss in another fifteen minutes," Max said, his eyes on the Autobahn and his hands firmly gripping the wheel. "Are there any last-minute questions that come to mind?"

All morning, he had been ruminating over how to best dispel the air of awkwardness between them. On the drive to the hotel, he had looked forward to seeing Hannah. A pulse throbbed in his neck when he first spied her walking through the front door. She smiled as she headed towards him and greeted him cordially, but he soon sensed an adjustment in her demeanour. The openness of yesterday afternoon had taken on a certain coolness in the daylight. He noted that she was dressed for serious business: a dark blue pantsuit over a white silk blouse tied in a loose bow at the neck. Beneath she wore a lime green vest that highlighted her trim figure in a bright vee.

They made small talk about how much she liked her suite, and what a large breakfast she had been offered, but as he headed onto the Autobahn, they fell silent. To Max, the quiet was unnatural, as if there were questions hanging in the air, waiting to be asked.

"Is something concerning you?" he finally asked.

Hannah took a moment.

"Will Frau Heilemann be joining us for lunch?"

Max sighed. He had been hoping for a more relevant question.

"Frau Heilemann died of breast cancer several years ago, leaving

Ha-Gay with five children ranging in age from 17 to 30, the two eldest are identical male twins and the remaining three are girls, well,
mostly women now."

"Are the eldest involved in the family business?"

"Yes, they are. In fact, they oversee the day-to-day functioning of
the properties allowing Ha-Gay to pursue opportunities to acquire new
properties for development."

"I see," Hannah said, "like the property he is planning for Trois-Îles?"

Max took a breath. She was clever, working him around to the
question she really wanted answered: What was Heilemann after?
He began to smile, turning his head only to find her peering closely
at his expression. The smile faded at the dispassionate look in her
eyes. This is not how he had hoped things would go with Hannah
Baran but Max, ever the pragmatist, knew that life rarely goes as
planned.

"I don't mean to be tedious, Hannah, but I've already explained—
and was sincere when I did so—that I have not been informed as to
Herr Heilemann's intentions for Trois-Îles, should we be successful in
acquiring it. I suspect that you are somehow also uninformed in the
same way. Back in June, you assured me that Chaim Sonenshein was
not in the least bit interested in selling his property yet here you are
five months later in Köln."

"Well," Hannah said, "you may be right. Neither of us has a real
grasp of what's at stake here, so we will just have to agree to be frenemies."

"What on earth," he asked, chuckling, "are frenemies?"

"Well, it's an oxymoron really, a contradiction in terms," Hannah
said. "It means a person with whom one is friendly despite a funda-
mental dislike or a rivalry. And I want to assure you there is no dislike
on my part ..."

"Or on mine ..." he said with a smile.

"But the simple fact of the matter is that we cannot get too congenial unless we conspire against our clients who have both left us in
the dark."

Max thought a moment. "I would never conspire against Ha-Gay
Heilemann."

"Nor I against Chaim Sonenshein so that settles it. We're frenemies until this is over and settled one way or the other."

Max stopped the car and Hannah looked around to see that they had arrived at the Schloss. Past the iron gates, the grounds stretched to the impressive doors of the Schloss. Max turned off the ignition.

"Well, this is certainly intimidating," she said with a little smile although Max noted that her features reflected no emotion. He opened his door but before he could come around to the passenger side, Hannah had already let herself out. She stood in the courtyard taking in the enormity of the property, the gleaming white stones of the Schloss against the expanse of a neon blue and cloudless sky. A welcome warmth radiated off the flagstones. Hannah shaded her eyes and looked up at the triple rows of tall windows and chortled softly.

"Something is amusing?" Max asked.

"My father had an expression in Yiddish to denote people who were wealthy. He would say they were *hoicheh fenster*."

"Tall windows?"

"Yes, but idiomatically it referred to wealthy people. If you had *hoicheh fenster*, you were among those who could afford that much sunshine and I guess the loss of heat that comes with having tall windows. That's what I'm seeing here through my father's eyes. Great wealth."

"The Schloss is certainly a draughty place and so I can see the rationale in the description." He paused before saying: "Well, are you ready, Mme Baran?"

"As I'll ever be," she said and followed Max to the massive front door.

"Hannah Baran, may I introduce Lothar," Max said as the door opened at the very moment they arrived. "Lothar is Herr Heilemann's major domo and he knows where all the best wine is buried."

The man towered over Hannah and even Max. He must be 6'4", she thought, and wondered idly how tall her father would have been had he not suffered starvation in his teens. Fleetingly, she acknowledged that being in Germany guaranteed that neither Rokhl nor Barak would ever be far from her thoughts. Lothar was almost a caricature of a major domo in his dress and manner; the dark suit and bowtie spoke of another era. With the fluid motion that comes with years of service, he led them through the main hall, an atrium three stories high, into a bright room surprisingly spare and modern in its décor. Two long carmine red leather couches and two contemporary pearl grey leather armchairs created an intimate setting around a large, polished slate coffee table, in the centre of which stood a massive bouquet of white lilies spilling over the sides of an elegant black Murano vase.

The effect was striking. And Hannah suspected she had been brought into an inner sanctum where business was not usually conducted. Only one painting hung on the walls. Some six feet high and four feet across, it was of a beautiful woman posed as in a Gainsborough portrait, her dark hair a fine web spun around a delicate face, her clothes soft and filmy only barely concealing a sensuous figure, and in the background, a range of snow-peaked mountains. Hannah silently took it all in thinking how different this room was to Chaim's private collection of portraits. Lothar broke into her thoughts asking whether she would prefer tea or coffee.

"Neither, *danke*," she said, "but I would be grateful for some sparkling water."

The major domo left the room as Hannah and Max seated themselves, she in an armchair and he on the sofa, to wait for Ha-Gay Heilemann.

"*Herzlich willkommen*." The booming voice arrived before the man. But when Hans-Georg Heilemann strode into the room, he headed straight for Hannah barely giving her time to rise gracefully. She somehow managed to have her hand outstretched before he reached her; his grip was bear-like. Without flinching, she simply exerted more pressure than she normally might have. A small smile crept across Heilemann's handsome face.

"Max," he said, turning to his agent, "you never mentioned how beautiful is this woman you've been dealing with."

Hannah proffered a small smile of acknowledgement but did not allow it to linger long. This kind of flip flattery was so commonplace she was inured to it. She was there to conduct business, not to engage in social repartee. Despite being accustomed to this form of banter, she found it particularly unpleasant coming from Heilemann. But if she had to, she could play the deflecting game.

"You have a magnificent property here, Herr Heilemann. This room is so lovely, made even more so by that stunning painting that seems to enhance the beauty of its surroundings." She turned to gaze at the portrait that loomed over them. "What a beautiful woman she is."

"Sadly, the correct term is 'was'. My late wife, Sophia, was beautiful but gone from us too soon," he said as if reciting words he had memorized for such occasions.

"I am so sorry for your loss," Hannah said, playing the game. "She looks to have been a formidable beauty."

"That she was, but from what I understand from Max, the same might be said of you."

Annoyed, Hannah's eyes shifted to Max standing silently by the couch, a chagrined look on his face by way of apology. He turned to his client who made a small gesture after which Max suggested that they sit down to lunch first and then address the business at hand.

"Conversation always comes more easily after a good meal and a full stomach."

In that remark, Hannah detected a cautionary note about what was to come, that digestion would be easier if their conversations were held after lunch rather than before. Business lunches were among her pet peeves. From the outset in her conversations with Max Mohr, she had tried to manoeuvre this appointment to take place either mid-morning or mid-afternoon, but to no avail. Ha-Gay Heilemann insisted that they meet over lunch, and here she was. Following orders.

Lunch was set at a table in the kitchen below a casement window that looked out on the vast grounds behind the manor. She was relieved not to be sitting in a formal dining room setting. The kitchen—although brushed steel and dark granite—was somehow conducive to an intimate lunch and the meal, with an earthy quality to it based on the inclusion of seasonal produce. They began with a savoury butternut squash and cider soup topped with tangy pomegranate seeds, followed by wine braised short ribs with roasted root vegetables and, for dessert, the best and lightest apple strudel Hannah had ever tasted.

Wine flowed. Despite being continually offered, however, she passed on the wine although Lothar kept Heilemann's glass full.

Throughout the lunch, the conversation was kept topical and light, devoid of politics or contentious issues. They talked about what a joke the panic had been over Y2K, the Russian crew reaching the International Space Station to begin the experiment of humans living in space, the widespread flooding in England and Wales, and bandied about opinions on whether Air France would ever reinstate the Concorde service after the devastating crash in Paris which had killed all the crew and passengers.

"I had been chastising myself for not taking the Concorde when I flew to Montreal," Max said, "but promised myself ... next time. Now there will likely never be a next time."

"You know, 96 of the 108 who died were Germans," Max said. Hannah nodded.

"A business associate of mine and his wife were on that flight," Heilemann said, shaking his head. "They were on their way to New York to board a ship, the MS Deutschland, for a cruise to Ecuador. He told me that he was reluctant to go but that his wife had talked him into the voyage because she worried that he worked too hard, and that all that hard work would eventually kill him." Heilemann chuckled. "Ironic, no? It is my opinion that hard work never killed anyone. That's what I tell my children when they complain that I am pushing them too far. If I had not been pushed by circumstances to apply myself, I would have ended up a poor slob—that's an acceptable term no, Frau Baran? Instead, I built an empire with my sweat, my wits, and a little luck. I think Sonenshein, your client, is like me, *ne?*"

A smile had affixed itself to Heilemann's face, but Hannah saw how it bypassed his eyes which remained trained on her. "Certainly, I can see some similarities," she responded. "Chaim Sonenshein is definitely entrepreneurial, a risk-taker and an innovator. In that respect, I would agree you two share certain traits."

As she spoke, Hannah was cautiously sorting her words, certain that Heilemann was working to set her up in some way. She determined to stop the chit-chat and cut to the chase.

"And of course, you both have something of an interest in an unprepossessing property in Trois-Îles although frankly your interest, Herr Heilemann, puzzles me. This property is not in a location that should, from your past purchases and business development, hold any interest for you. So, for what reason am I here?"

Heilemann's smile remained but Hannah could tell he was not happy with her directness. Max jumped in.

"Frau Baran, Hannah, is displaying the candour that I have come to admire."

Hannah held her gaze on Heilemann and her tongue.

"In Europe we like to approach discussions—negotiations—in a more, umm, circumspect manner. I know that this meeting is unusual for the parties concerned and perhaps I have been remiss in not setting some guidelines before we began."

The words struck Hannah like little blows. The colour rose in her cheeks as Barak's voice rang in her ears: *This is what comes of doing business with the enemy.* Before she could change her mind, she said, "I understand the German love of procedure, but I have come a long way and have but a short time in which to conduct any business should we decide to go forward. I told you last night, Herr Mohr, I don't dance. Either you want to make an offer on the property in question, and if so, you will need to advise me as to its purpose so I may make the necessary arrangements and prepare for your bid ..." And here Hannah stopped to take a dramatic breath, "... or if not, we are all simply wasting our time."

Heilemann rose from his seat and stepped away from the table. Max too got to his feet preparing to mediate whatever was coming next. He looked from his client to this impossible woman who was playing by her own set of rules.

"I fear you misunderstand the situation, Hannah Baran. I thought that Sonenshein might have revealed ... what shall I call it ... the dynamics of our deal. It seems he has left you in the dark."

Hannah's face flushed but before she could summon a response, Heilemann continued. "You see, Trois-Îles is already mine, technically, based on an agreement made between your client and my father after the war. You are here merely to facilitate the transaction—for want of a better word—and make it legal in the eyes of your regional government. And there is also a sum that will be paid and that must be agreed upon."

Hannah looked from one man to the other, her anger roiling so close beneath the surface that she could barely speak. At last, she said, "Herr Mohr, if you don't mind, I would like to go back to the hotel now, so if you would have Lothar kindly call a taxi, I will take my leave. I need to speak to my client before I continue."

"But of course, Frau Baran. No taxi. Lothar will drive you back to the hotel," Heilemann said. "Max, you will remain here with me."

CHAPTER THIRTY-ONE

I **did not** die after the beating but during those first days, I wished I could have as I lay in a tiny cell waiting for transport. With the Angel of Death always standing by my side, I would gladly have embraced his cold bones if it meant I could escape hell. That's what Auschwitz-Birkenau was. What else can you call it when all who entered there abandoned hope of leaving except through the chimney? And yet—this is so hard to understand, Hannaleh—something forced us to keep the body alive. Even when our minds were lost, our hands blindly sought a way out of the labyrinth. An indescribable force drove us to survive. There are no words to explain what or why. Do not wonder why I never shared any of this.

When the doors to the cattle car opened, someone pushed me hard. I tumbled out and scrambled to my feet and stood up quickly so as not to look weak. There was a sickly, sweet smell in the air but no time to think as I was pushed into a group separate from the other cars. A man who I came to know as *Der Todesengel*, Dr. Josef Mengele, was making a selection with his finger, pointing to the left or right. Behind him stood a woman who I later learned was usually by his side. I saw people beaten and herded into one of two groups—the fit and unfit (although I didn't know that at the time). As a political prisoner and a Pole, I was not marked for the gas chamber, not while I was still young, maybe useful.

Viciously prodded, I struggled to stay on my feet, stay conscious, when I heard an impossible sound. Above the shrieking of commands and the *barking of the dogs, I heard—music. An orchestra was playing. I thought I was hallucinating but then my eyes followed my ears and I saw them sitting by the entrance gate—a group of women, most no more than young girls—playing a German military march. Then something I never expected to see again in my life—my mother—sitting there playing her violin. I barely recognized her. One eye looked sealed shut and with an angry gash that ran the length of her once delicate face but there was no doubt. It was her—the woman who had borne me. Her one functioning eye was turned to her violin. She never knew I was there. Four years and two lifetimes had elapsed since I had last seen her. I made no move, no sound. I was well-trained. Reveal nothing, I had been taught. I stood there listening, not understanding how I had fallen into this nightmare.*

And then I heard a voice say, Der hier. *That one.*

A truncheon was jammed into my shoulder blades pushing me towards a stocky woman in uniform. Her hair was coiffed away from her face and her eyes were two black pebbles in an icy stream. Her well-shaped mouth was turned down at the corners. I didn't see all that then, but I had plenty of time to memorize those emotionless features in the year to follow.

She addressed me in German, saying, "You look healthy for a filthy Pole. Talk."

In perfect German, I replied, "Yes, Frau Kommandant, I can serve you faithfully."

Her face remained frozen in a sneer, revealing no reaction to my response but she pointed to someone and ordered them to get me processed.

"Bring her to me when she has been cleaned up and not smelling like a Polish whore."

They shaved my head, sprayed me with de-lousing powder, and gave me a striped uniform with a red triangle to distinguish me as a political prisoner and the letter P for Pole on it. Then they tattooed my left arm. 169036.

➤ It was my curse, my good luck, my misfortune, my affliction to have been chosen from the arrivals by SS-Lagerführerin Maria Mandl, the Beast of Auschwitz II. I became her slave who saw all but never spoke. Instead, I ingested what I saw the way some alchemists took venom to

prevent being poisoned. I swallowed the toxins, and my silence grew into a poison tree that sheltered me. I never spoke and never looked at Mandl directly. Those who did most often suffered a vicious, painful death. I was a shadow that stood by and watched The Beast select the women and children for the gas chambers. She had full control over us as Maria Mandl had no master in the Women's Camp except Auschwitz's commander, SS-Kommandant Rudolf Höss. I scrubbed her floors, her toilet, polished her boots, washed her clothes, her dishes, making everything German sauber, *all the while suffering her vitriol, kicks, punches, and cruelty like the others under her jackboots. At endless roll calls, the women were kept on their knees for hours (I was sometimes allowed to stand behind her) while the SS subordinates counted them over and over again. And all the while the orchestra played, like they did when the work details returned and had to step to the music or be beaten.*

↪ *One day, Mandl sent me with a message to find her favourite subordinate, SS Aufseherin Irma Grese, the one they called the Beautiful Beast. I could feel her eyes on me although mine were lowered. My view was of her shapely legs encased in perfectly shined, hobnailed boots. She sent me away with a flick of her rubber whip with which she often beat women who were weak or too attractive. Her vanity and brutal sadism were well-known. I was grateful that my breasts had not formed because when she found a young woman with beautiful breasts, she would strip and beat her across the chest until it was a mass of raw flesh. Sometimes she kicked them to death with those shiny boots. Once she made me stand watch as she brutally raped a young girl. I could not look but heard the screams and those screams joined the shots that echoed in my nightmares.*

One day I saw someone peering at me. Many women looked at me with hatred and fear. They thought I was chosen by the Beast for my willingness to accept cruelty. However, this woman looked like she knew me. Something about her reminded me of my cousin Fenia, the one from Warsaw. But I turned away as if I didn't see her in terror that she could inadvertently expose me as a Jew. I tried to convince myself it was my imagination. I was such an object of envy for those who thought I was in a place of privilege merely because I ate at least once a day, soup with a few beans floating in it, and bread that was usually not mouldy. I kept my eye on the others, the Jewish women that I was no longer one of, so many marched to the crematoria. The ones who remained, they feared Mandl, but they hated me and whispered as I passed—brudna dziwka and kurwa. And I deserved to be called bitch and whore. I had shut my mouth in order to survive.

There were a few times I spotted Fenia but I avoided her no longer in fear of being revealed as a Jew, but for having sold my soul in exchange for a piece of bread and a floating bean in my soup. My heart shrank when I saw Fenia but it hardened when I would watch my mother play. I never acknowledged her, and then one day, she too was gone and never came back. Yes, I knew the Shma, the prayer for the dead, but still I said nothing. I stayed silent beneath my poison tree.

➤ It was fall, awhile after the rumble of guns could be heard growing nearer, when suddenly the Beast was gone leaving me behind as if I was so worthless there was no need to kill me. I was 15, had not yet menstruated and weighed no more than a child. Irma Grese still remained and did not leave until just before the Russians came into the camp in January. By then there was no food, but there were many places to hide as the camp was being emptied out. If I kept moving, I could avoid being killed or taken on the death march. When Barak came riding through, my hair had grown out, but it was no longer red but a pale yellow-white. I weighed nothing. He lifted me up like I was a sack of feathers and carried me out of Auschwitz.

And the poison tree inside me stopped growing but never died.

CHAPTER THIRTY-TWO

Hannah's hands shook as she poured herself a glass of white wine. A few drops spilled on the glass of the coffee table, and she ran her finger over the spillage and brought it to her mouth. She needed every drop. Moments earlier, Room Service had wheeled in the bottle and a plate of celery and olives. Balefully, she looked at the snack, lifted the wine glass and moved to the bed where she plunked herself down on the edge so hard, she almost spilled her wine again. Steadying herself, she lifted the phone receiver and glanced at the digital readout on the clock radio. It was 5 p.m. in Cologne; 11 a.m. in Montreal. She called the hotel operator. Her foot tapped silently on the plush carpet as the operator connected her to Montreal and Chaim's private office number. While she waited, she once again considered how much Max was in on Heilemann's bombshell. It galled her that she had let her guard down when she knew full well that duplicity had been a very clear probability. What a fool she was to let emotions get in the way of business. It would not happen again.

Rose came on the line and upon hearing Hannah's voice, immediately transferred the call to her boss.

"So, how did it go?" Chaim asked foregoing any conversation about flights or weather.

"How do you think it went?" Hannah answered sharply, managing to keep her voice steady while the blood pounded in her ears. She felt the colour rising from her neck to her cheeks and didn't care if Chaim objected to her tone. For the moment, upsetting Chaim was not a concern. She was not going to tiptoe at the affront to her professionalism. Her humiliation at being blind-sided was bubbling like a lava lake. Nothing was going to take the edge off of this anger. Best to let it roll, let the Barak in her loose.

"I looked like an idiot when Heilemann announced that the land was already his. How could you have failed to mention that part of the story?"

"For good reason," Sonenshein said with a suppressed chuckle. "First of all, it's only partly true but I needed you to be genuinely surprised. Should I guess you were?"

"Yes, and I'm angry at being used as a pawn in this game you're playing with Heilemann. I don't like this, Chaim, and I think we need to think it through completely before we move forward. And by that, I mean that you give me the WHOLE story and all the details or I cannot—no—let me be clearer, I will not, continue."

"There's no reason to be upset, Hannah. You can trust me but I needed Heilemann to think he had the upper hand. Now he does. But he is not as fully informed as he believes himself to be. He has nothing but a 50-year-old verbal agreement and something like an I.O.U. that said Trois-Îles could be considered collateral."

Chaim paused and waited but Hannah maintained her silence; he knew her well enough to know he could eventually dampen her anger; years of dealing with three spoiled daughters had taught him that. Not that Hannah Baran was anything like his *shprintzeh Leahs*. Not one of them had ever worked a day in her life, nor had to. But Hannah was not built like that. She could have lived a more leisurely life, he knew, but she never sought the easy route. With a wry smile he recognised that was precisely why she was so valuable to him.

"Honestly, there is not that much more to add to the story I told you in my office," Chaim said. "Like I said, Heilemann's father saved my life. He kept me from starvation and from being shot during the death march from Sosnowiec to Bohemia. He was a cunning man, no fool. He understood that Germany was on the losing end of the war.

The Allies were closing in from all sides. But even when they knew that to be the reality, the SS were determined that no witnesses from the camps would survive. But Heilemann, a *Sturmscharführer* in the *Waffen-SS,* was a subordinate to Vaufel, the camp commandant, and he had a soft spot for me. Don't ask me why. Well, maybe because once, while working in the machine shop in Sosnowiec I made him something for Christmas because he was so depressed after receiving a letter from his wife that his parents had died in a bombing raid. From that time on, he treated me like a pesky pet. If he was in a good mood, I was patted; bad mood, he would beat me, but he never broke any bones. And he didn't starve me."

"Yes, you told me the story. I remember ..." Hannah allowed her irritation to slip into the receiver as if that would stop Chaim. But he continued, and hearing him tell the story again, she felt the familiar ache drilling deep into her belly, one that always arrived with the telling of war stories. Does he know? Was Chaim toying with her emotions? This old man, her client, her father's friend, he was a trickster at heart. A true real estate mogul who would shamelessly use any ploy to gain an advantage, even over someone who was on his side. Marilyn called it the 'survivor instinct', once acquired, she had claimed, survivors applied it to almost every aspect of life. It had been tattooed onto their genes.

"Yes, you know all that already ..." Chaim stopped, and Hannah couldn't tell whether it was to gather the nerve to tell the rest of the story, or for dramatic pause. That was the thing about dealing with a trickster, you could never be sure.

"But this is the part of the *geschichteh* I left out," Chaim said. "People were dropping like flies, lying by the side of the road dying of the cold, hunger and not caring whether they may be shot like a dog if the guards weren't too afraid to run out of ammunition. Most of us were the walking dead; we no longer cared. Heilemann kept me alive. Once in a while he slipped me a *shtickel* mouldy bread, a handful of sugar cubes. And each time he did, he would say, 'Remember that I am doing what I can to save you.' The other thing that kept me going was the sound of big guns in the distance—we didn't know whether they were American or Russian—but to us, to me, they sounded like hope. But when we arrived in Bohemia, we stopped hearing them and those of us left were crammed into cattle cars almost one on top of the other. Before we got on the train, Heilemann pulled me aside, and handed me a chunk of bread. 'Remember, if you live, and I live, you will need to tell them that I was a good man.' That day was the last time I would see Heilemann until more than a year later.

"In the cattle car, we had no food, no water. Another attempt to kill us, the witnesses now so close to being ghosts already. I had gobbled down Heilemann's bread but had saved some of the sugar cubes he gave me and would sneak them into my mouth, each time remembering Heilemann's words. After four days on the train—maybe less, maybe more—we arrived at Mauthausen. I would be optimistic to say that half of us were still alive but still, we were driven like the cattle we had become into the camp. Mauthausen was a piece of hell that the devil broke off and shoved up through a hole in the scorched earth. Sosnowiec was heaven by comparison. I will not tell you what I experienced or witnessed in those final days of the death camp. Then, one day not long after we arrived, all the SS disappeared. They were gone and we lay dazed, drifting, flattened like empty sacks. Maybe two days, maybe a week later, the American tanks arrived. It was the beginning of the end of that part of our nightmare. When they rolled into the camp, I weighed no more than 36 kilos, some 80 pounds but I was young. And alive. While I was learning to eat again, I made friends with some American soldiers, and they also fed me English. I always had a good head for languages. Before the war I spoke Yiddish, of course, but also an excellent Polish and German. In the camps, I had learned Russian and a little Hungarian. After I regained my strength, I landed in Pocking-Waldstadt, a large DP camp near Passau, close to the Austrian border. It so happened that some GIs recognized me and commandeered my services as a translator. All those other languages I knew became my ticket to freedom. Then one day, the Colonel summoned me. Three men who looked a little too well-fed to be locals had been caught hiding in the woods. The Colonel wanted me to help in an interrogation. 'Ask them who they are,' he instructed me. I didn't have to ask them. I recognized them immediately even without their uniforms. They were all SS and I said I knew them from Auschwitz, but that one—and I pointed to Heilemann—he saved my life, I said. Believe me, I didn't want to be his path to freedom, but it was a debt I owed and had to pay. Then I had to do it again. And again. Three times I had to testify that I had never seen him kill anyone. Life is strange. The tables had turned, the obligation had become his. One Jewish life was now worth three times that of an SS officer. In the end, I exacted a promise that if I ever needed anything, he could not refuse me. Seven years later, when I needed $5,000 to help buy the land in Trois-Îles, I found old Heilemann. He had done well for himself, and I called in his debt to me."

Hannah switched the phone from one ear to the next and with her free hand, poured another glass of wine. It was working to numb her anger and she was almost at the point where she was ready to let the conversation end. But no, he was not getting off with an unfinished story again. Sitting up, she suddenly asked, "But how does that explain Heilemann's son thinking he already owned the land?"

"Because I used it as collateral but ... there was never any indication as to when I had to repay the debt, so I didn't ... yet."

CHAPTER THIRTY-THREE

Max shoved his hands deep into his pockets and rummaged around as if the answer to this predicament with Heilemann could be extracted like a neatly folded handkerchief. It was not how he had anticipated this long-awaited meeting would go. It was certainly not meant to end like this. In truth, he was not sure why they had gathered at the Schloss in the first place. This deal had never made any sense to him. Heilemann keeping him in the dark made less sense. At a loss to say anything remotely diplomatic, Max finally broke his silence with what he knew would only come off sounding like a reproof.

"You might have told me before about this twist in the plot."

He and Ha-Gay were still standing at the front door of the Schloss watching Lothar drive off, direction Köln, with Hannah hunkered down in the back seat. Only a glint of copper curls in the rear window was visible as the car turned out of the driveway and onto the road. Beside Max, Ha-Gay stood with his head tilted back as if sniffing the air, an enigmatic smile twisting the corners of his mouth. Perhaps he's catching the scent of victory in the air, Max thought gloomily but having already taken one step over the boundary, he decided that the best course of action was silence. Patience was his only weapon in the struggle to understand what had just transpired. Heilemann's pronouncement had clearly upset Hannah but Max as well. He hated surprises. He hated this necessity to deceive, to mask his feelings, something at which he had had far too much practice. Yet, it had taken surprisingly little effort to ensure that his face remained devoid of any expression that might have been misinterpreted by either Hannah or Ha-Gay. It was his role, he knew, to be a facilitator in this process, so why did he suddenly feel abused?

With a tilt of his head toward the door, Heilemann indicated that they should head back to the salon.

"Before what?" Ha-Gay asked almost as an afterthought. In the large airy room, he headed to the liquor cabinet stocked with rows of alcoholic beverages worthy of any fine dining establishment. Ha-Gay's hand hovered over the bottles, a diviner trying to detect where the biggest treasure was to be found.

"Cognac? Brandy? Grappa? I also have some very fine Porto," he said.

"It's too early and I've already had two glasses of your fine wine. I still need to drive home. I'll have a vermouth on the rocks, but just a small one, please, I need to stay within the limit."

Heilemann shrugged indicating it made no difference to him what Max drank, and carefully poured the vermouth over ice and three skewered olives. For himself, he selected a snifter and poured himself a brandy from a baccarat decanter. Max sat nursing his drink for which he had only a faint desire. He'd learned his lesson about driving with more than the legal blood alcohol limit the hard way, after Nicole had told him she wanted a child and if not with him, then someone else. Trying to avoid thinking about the dilemma, he had had more than one too many and then was pulled over. This created a more immediate dilemma. His alcohol level was high enough that the *Polizei* insisted he leave his car on the spot where he had been stopped, and to find another way home. He received many demerit points, but the worst was the suspension of his licence for three months. Never again. He had been a fool to think he could maintain control then and was beginning to feel that in this situation too, he had little or no control. Max couldn't help but wonder if he was being played.

Gazing down, Ha-Gay cupped his snifter in his large, well-manicured hands and swirled the amber liquid. Thoughtfully, he lifted the glass to the sunlight which, penetrating the crystal, emblazoned the brandy. Slowly, he placed the glass under his nose and inhaled.

"Ah, ambrosia."

His drink still untouched Max waited for Ha-Gay to explain why he chose not to let him in on this choice tidbit. He could be patient although Heilemann had a reputation for knowing how to make people uncomfortable. The 'little people' he called them as if they had not quite finished being formed, had not yet grown to fully display the kind of mastery of life that he continued to exhibit with such self-confidence. These people were often suppliers, hotel staff, sometimes his children—all of whom he could make to feel somewhat diminished, derided. Max had never before experienced that side of him as Ha-Gay had always gone to great lengths to ensure that Max felt like an equal, a partner in one extended, prodigious adventure. So why these games? Had he not always proved himself reliable enough to be entrusted with a grand plan? By the manner in which Ha-Gay was responding it was becoming evident he was not yet willing to let Max in on the big picture. From the outset, this deal had felt like none other they had worked on together, and more and more, he could not dispel the suspicion that this latest development might not end well for him personally.

"Before what?" Ha-Gay suddenly repeated softly.

Max hesitated for a moment, his mind turning corners like a mouse in a maze. "I mean, could you not have shared this information with me before I met with Frau Baran in Montreal, before I led her to believe we were negotiating a different kind of deal?"

As he said this, Max recalled the look that had flashed across Hannah's face as she took her leave. He had immediately caught her meaning. She was deeply disappointed in him and, despite his innocence, he felt he deserved his fate, slipping several notches in her esteem. How could he blame her? She had been blindsided and, whether he was aware of the subterfuge or not, he was certainly complicit in the deception. Whatever may have been between him and Hannah was now surely set back, maybe gone for good.

Heilemann sat down but still offered no answer. He took another sip of his brandy and let it sit on his tongue before swallowing.

"I am at a loss," Max said, running a hand through his hair, "as to why there has been so much mystery around your intentions for this property when there is no discernible reason, I can determine, for your interest in developing it."

There, he thought, I've played my hand without any regard for how it will affect our relationship. He slowly rotated his glass of vermouth and glanced out the window at the fading light as it slipped into amber and crimson behind a row of poplars standing guard at the end of the driveway. He glanced up at Heilemann seemingly unfazed by the question, smiled his crooked smile, and gave Max a look that implied he may not want to hear the full story.

"Allow me a moment to savour how fortunate we are to be here," Ha-Gay said. "Well-fed, fashionably-clothed, beneath the roof of a fine structure—safe, sound, and prosperous. We have known no war and cannot know what unholy pacts we would make with the devil if our whole life hung in the balance." Ha-Gay paused and seemed to search for something in the snifter cradled in his palms.

"You never knew my father, did you Max? He was a practical man. He had to be as the third son of an impoverished Junker. He never said so, but I believe he was unloved—and worse—ignored as a child. Maybe that was why he was so indifferent to me even after I had made a name for myself. He may have been overlooked before the war but not after when he was the only son to come home on his own two feet. My father's two older brothers were heroes who came home in coffins. One was the first officer on a U-boat sunk by the British and the other fought alongside Rommel as a *Generalmajor* in the Afrika Korps. Yes, he died with great honour leading a division of the *Panzerarmee,* my father would say sheepishly. But that made my father the only Heilemann son to return from the war. He did not return covered in glory and medals but by default, he became the heir to the title and what was left of the land. Of this my grandfather never failed to remind him. He was alive but had remained so only as the result of deserting his men when the Russians drew too close to Auschwitz where he was a *Kommandant*. The Americans found him cowering in the Bavarian woods. I learned all this only after my grandfather's death, and then by sheer accident, I one day learned that my father had only managed that with the help of a wily Jew named Chaim Sonenshein."

CHAPTER THIRTY-FOUR

When she was young, Hannah had harboured a small, brown spider in the corner of her bedroom window. To ensure the spider remained undetected, she made certain to keep her room clean and tidy so Rokhl had no reason to enter. Not the best of housekeepers, Rokhl had smiled as she stood in the doorway, surveying Hannah's devotion to neatness. Although the web was small, Hannah's spider was efficient. It caught flies and mosquitoes, and once, a beautiful white moth. It pained Hannah to see the moth struggle throughout a fall afternoon but understood that everything must eat to live. Although she didn't actually think of the spider as her pet—it had no name—she felt an affinity with it and the doggedness of its constant attendance to its domain. What she had wanted was a real pet but Barak's response to her repeated requests was an unequivocal no.

"You are animal enough for us, a real *vilde chayeh*," he would say, not without a touch of affection. When the rule was tested, however, his response was vehement. She had brought home an adorable little black kitten that she and Marilyn had rescued from a gutter on Goyer. Barak had pointed at the animal as if it was some kind of demon and yelled, "Out! Get that thing out of this house. Your mother works hard enough taking care of you. She doesn't need to be cleaning up after a filthy cat."

Hannah had turned pleading eyes to Rokhl in the hope that maybe she would, just this once, contradict Barak's edict but Rokhl merely lowered her head and slid her eyes towards the kitchen, looking as forlorn as the orphaned cat. Hannah kept the kitten in a box under the front stoop and spent days canvassing everyone at school until she finally found a home for her stray. On that day, Rokhl had slipped a note into Hannah's raincoat. It read: *First take care of you and then you can help others.*

Curled up in the upholstered chair next to the window with Cologne neatly stretched out below, Hannah recalled the anguish of letting that kitten go. She had cried and cried until Barak in his fury had shouted, "Will you mourn like that for us when we're gone?"

It startled her to remember that accusation bringing, as it did, the realization that she had never again cried like that. Not for Barak. Not for Rokhl.

Her eyes half closed, Hannah lay her head back, and with her left arm kneaded the knot of muscles balled up under her hair. A sigh slowly escaped her lips. Years earlier, when Barak returned home after a stressful day in the factory, she used to massage his neck this way. He would say she had *goldeneh hent*, golden hands, that could make him feel instantly better. With something like surprise, it occurred to her that since Rokhl's death Barak hardly ever came to mind. But every day, her mother was always near, hovering in the background, ever present, ever silent.

Hannah lifted the glass, slowly rotated the stem to and fro. Shards of light shot through the fine crystal casting rainbows against the white walls. She took a small sip of wine and contemplated how each minor movement—or moment—can change what and how you see the world. Something to consider, she thought, as she turned the puzzle of Maximilian Mohr over in her mind. Her eyes closed. The wine was finally doing its duty.

When she opened them again it was to a glorious sunset invading her room, wantonly splashing searing bands of yellow across the walls. Slowly Hannah replayed and assessed the events of the day. They needed some perspective, and for some reason Rokhl's long-ago piece of advice—the one about taking care of herself first—came to mind. Was that how her mother had survived the war? Why didn't she know how Rokhl had survived? The story of her mother and the war always started with Barak finding her, lifting her emaciated body up, wrapping her in a blanket. His unit, the First Ukrainian Front, did not know he was a Jew, but he took a chance as a deserter when he slipped away with Rokhl. The brigade was marching to Berlin, but Barak took Rokhl and joined those who had been liberated, making their way in the opposite direction.

Hannah had never had the nerve to ask and now it was too late to do anything other than idly concoct scenarios and ultimately accept that she would never know. Best to release the desire into the cosmos, she thought wearily, in the heavens where so much of her history floated.

Resolved, she turned back to the matter at hand: the men who were complicating her life. It suddenly occurred to her that she was taking neither Max nor Chaim at their word. She ruminated on whether or not she was angry at Chaim Sonenshein. What did it profit her if she was? Would it soothe wounded pride? According to Chaim, that jab to her pride had been inflicted for a good cause although she did not yet see the logic. Nonetheless, in her experience, wounded pride heals soon enough. The bigger question was how to proceed with Max Mohr and his client.

When she left the Schloss, she had been deeply upset with Max for having mislead her although, in truth, she was angrier at herself for having been so open with him. Where Mohr was concerned, though, keeping her mind strictly on business was becoming more and more difficult the longer she knew him. When he trained those green eyes on her and ran his fingers through that thick mat of salt and pepper hair, a gesture she found irresistible, she would lose track of the topic at hand. Still, there was no denying that he had mislead her about this deal. And was she mislead or worse, betrayed?

Heilemann was clearly a piece of work—secure in his belief that he had Sonenshein—and as a result, Hannah—by the short hairs. The situation she found herself in rankled. The only remedy was to lay out her options. As a social worker, it was something she had learned to do whenever confronted by a difficult case. It surprised her that, of all her options, going back to Montreal on the next available flight was the one she dismissed first. There was something at stake here; something she was unable to name but of real import. She was going to stay and outwit not only Heilemann but Chaim as well. And then, there was Max Mohr. What she wanted from him was still a mystery but thinking about it made her fingertips itch.

CHAPTER THIRTY-FIVE

Focused on the road, Max took no notice of the sun's rays slipping through the trees like playful nymphs. Although crepuscule had always been his favourite time of day, the events of that afternoon were re-playing on a loop in his mind leaving him in no mood for beauty. Instead, he recalled the moment when what he thought he knew was suddenly deconstructed and reshaped into something wholly unfamil-iar. What worried him was how to explain to Hannah that he had no part in Heilemann's deception, and that he too had been blindsided. He was markedly uncertain how he felt about Ha-Gay's strategy.

After sharing his father's story, Ha-Gay had grown silent as if what he had related was everything Max needed to know. It wasn't. But Max was certain he had pushed the envelope as far as he could go for the moment. Anyway, Heilemann's father being a *Kommandant* in Auschwitz was not something Max would hold against Ha-Gay. His own father, Günter Nagel, probably had done much worse having joined the SS in its earliest stages. Committed and ambitious, young Günter had moved up the ranks especially after he caught the eye of the head of the SS, Heinrich Himmler. That was according to his sister Leni who was the only one who ever spoke of their father, although rarely. It was she who told him that their mother had changed Nagel to Mohr, her maiden name, to avoid repercussions. Mutti never mentioned his father at all. His grandmother, Omi Edda, if pressed explained that, when

Max was two and the twins ten, their father went on a short trip and never returned.

"Not a tear was shed by any of the women in this family," Oma said, straightening her apron. "And you were too young to remember him because he was away so often that you never missed him. Besides, you had all of us to spoil you."

She was right about that on both counts. Max had no recollection of the man who sired him although Leni and Eva confirmed that he had inherited his father's good looks. And that was where the resemblance ended, they assured him. The BMW sailed down the road as if on auto pilot, so Max was startled to inexplicably find himself not at his door but in front of the Mercure Severinshof. How had he arrived here at Hannah's hotel? It was not the destination he had set out for but this too, he wryly accepted, seemed to be following the erratic pattern the day had delivered.

In the gloom, he peered at his watch, an elegant Baume et Mercier Nicole had gifted him for Christmas when things were still good between them. It occurred to him, and not for the first time, that he had cared for her but, once she left, he never missed her. It was not too late, he reasoned, to call Hannah, invite her to dinner, and perhaps unravel some of the terrible knots that were plaguing this deal. The image of her in the back seat of Heilemann's car drifted into his memory—her rigid posture, the visible resolve to hold her head high—added to his unease at what had predicated her abrupt departure. Something else was niggling him, a small ache in his chest like a stitch that goes on too long. With a shrug, he eventually acknowledged it was not so much the business deal he was worried about but rather what Hannah might think of him now.

Hannah sat sprawled like a rag doll on the love seat. The bottle beside her was half empty. The wine had done its duty and dulled her anger, aided and abetted by the drama of the autumn sun slipping below the skyline. She was not normally a wine drinker, especially afflicted with a low tolerance for alcohol, but she recalled how after a hard day Barak would have a tumbler of Canadian Club before bed to help him sleep. Oh well, she thought, with this much wine, maybe sleeping will come easily and that might help bring some clarity in the morning. Her stomach felt hollow. It occurred to her that she should have ordered more than olives with the wine. But she knew the pang in her belly was not wholly related to hunger. Thoughts of Max made it worse. What a stinker he was! Leading her down the garden path only to blindside her when the opportunity presented itself. All of that Old World manner and continental charm. Smoke and mirrors to keep her off her game. And like the fool she was, she fell for it.

"That will not happen again," she said out loud, sitting up to pour herself another glass. As she moved it to her lips, the phone burred, startling her into nearly spilling some wine. Damn! She looked over at the bedside table and debated whether or not to answer it. She was not in the mood for Chaim again. What finally moved her out of the chair was the possibility that it wasn't her client.

"Hannah Baron," she said into the receiver.

"Ah, yah, good evening, Hanna. It's Max. Max Mohr."

"Yes, Max," she said working hard to keep her tone neutral. She was not going to allow her anger to surface. She waited. The silence between them was a little unsettling but she was a true redhead, Marilyn was fond of saying. When Max finally spoke, his voice was low, forcing Hannah to press the receiver closer to her ear.

"Hannah," he said, hesitatingly, "I'm not sure where to begin. I am truly sorry about this afternoon. I was totally unaware of the information that Heilemann revealed and from your reaction, it is clear that you were also not fully informed. I feel responsible somehow although, logically ... I, well ..."

"You were just following orders, right Max?" Hannah said. "I flew all this way to Germany at your invitation to negotiate a deal that is not a deal at all but some kind of game."

She waited for him to respond.

"Y'know, when we were kids, we played a game called Monkey in the Middle. I always hated that game."

Silent, Max shook his head. Peering balefully out at the hotel entrance, he determined not to let the bite of her words undermine his resolve to clarify his role. He let a moment pass before trying again.

"Hannah, I swear I knew nothing about this until Heilemann revealed it. Please, let's find a way to resolve this. I feel terrible. Listen, it's still early. Let's have dinner and try to make some order out of all this like the rational people we are."

Max waited but there was no sound emanating from the other end, not even breathing. He held his Blackberry up to make certain Hannah hadn't disconnected from the call. The glow indicated she was still on the line. Barely.

Hannah held the phone away from her head and in a bid to clear it leaned forward till her breasts lay pressed against her knees. It was not just the wine. Questions were buzzing in her head like trapped bees. What did he want from her? To be exonerated. To be relieved of any guilt. How could she trust that this man was telling the truth after the fiasco of this afternoon? She wasn't prepared to accept that Max had been as much in the dark as she was. For a moment, she wondered if they had both been played, then dismissed the notion. Her scepticism about what she knew of the ethics and truthfulness of realtors overruled the softer inclinations of her heart.

"Hannah, just have dinner with me," she heard him say over the buzz. "And if you prefer, we won't talk about this afternoon ..."

Resolutely, she rose from the bed and decided to play the hand she now held.

The silence over his Blackberry was palpable. Leaning against the steering wheel, Max held his breath until he heard a long sigh slip out from somewhere in the Hotel Severinshof. And he slowly eased himself back against the car seat.

"I'm not sure about dinner ..."

"Then let's have a drink," he said afraid to hear her turn him down.

"I'm way ahead of you in the drink department," Hannah said, allowing Max to entertain the hope that she was flirting with him a little. "You'll have to give me fifteen minutes to make myself presentable."

Max smiled. She *was* flirting with him. The tightness in his chest loosened.

"Deal, I'll meet you in the hotel dining room in 15 minutes. You'll recognize me by the look of relief on my face."

In her hotel room, staring into the bathroom mirror, Hannah practiced a seductive smile then applied her lipstick, a shade of soft ginger.

"I don't think there is really anything we can do to prepare for what's coming next," Hannah said. Despite Max's promise that they would not talk business, they were talking business and the awkwardness of their situation. "We're just going to have to keep on our toes and hope that we are not put into a set of circumstances where we're forced to take up arms against each other."

"To be honest," Max said with a sly smile, "I would rather take you *into* my arms … to dance, of course."

"As I've told you before, dancing is not in my repertoire."

"I find that hard to believe, Hannah, a beautiful woman like you? Why, you're built to dance. Tall, slim, graceful in how you move …"

Much to her chagrin, a deep blush coloured her cheeks. She quickly looked away so as not to betray her embarrassment.

"I mean it," Max said, reaching out across the table and taking her hand in his. There was no resistance against the move. He turned her hand palm up and wondered aloud at how small it looked lying there cupped in his own.

"Hannah, you must know that there is something else between us than this crazy land deal."

She looked up at him to see mirrored there the same look of surprise she was feeling. And they both laughed.

"I had no idea I was going to say that but now that I have, I am very relieved. I read by your expression that I have some hope that you may feel the same way. So, what are we going to do about it?"

CHAPTER THIRTY-SIX

Perhaps the mistake was deciding against dinner, opting for a drink instead. It began with a glass of chardonnay for her and a single malt for him. Just as they were about to order another round—against Hannah's better judgement—the piano man from the night before sat down to begin his set with Titanic's theme song *The Heart Will Go On*. Hannah burst out laughing. Puzzled, Max asked what she found so funny.

"I came halfway around the world," she said, "and can't escape that Celine Dion song. For some reason, I really wasn't expecting to hear echoes of it here in Germany."

"You can't blame us. Her music is everywhere ever since the movie became such a monster hit. Besides, she's enormously popular in Europe. We seem to like things from Canada, like her and Leonard Cohen and ..." he said, lowering his head and shooting a look over his brows to gauge the effect of the unspoken compliment.

The response was not what Max expected. Sticking out her tongue, Hannah blew him a raspberry. The look on his face had her doubled over with laughter. It only took a second for him to join in. When the medley ended, the piano man began to play a Latin rhythm that had Max on his feet, standing by her chair and offering an outstretched hand. Without hesitation, Hannah rose, steadied herself against the table, and followed Max to the dance floor. There, he put her right hand in his left palm and her other hand on his shoulder while his hand slipped around her waist.

"Just relax. Hannah, look at me—not down; let me lead you," he said as he began to move with a languorous, easy motion.

The wine was clearly working its magic because all Hannah felt like doing was letting go. It only took a moment for her to find that in fact she could dance. No thinking. No planning her next move. Just this marvellous sensation of being a sail turned into the wind, and Max, the mast around which she moved with ease. After the tempo changed, they continued to dance, the rhythm and the light in Max's eyes lifting her, whirling her, freeing her from everything but the moment. Every suspicion that had jangled her nerves earlier in the evening was now neatly folded away.

"Let's stop," she finally said, needing to catch her breath.

Max pulled her to him and leaned in so close a current ran through her. Her eyes closed as she awaited the longed-for kiss but instead, he placed his lips over her ear and whispered, "I knew you were made to dance."

There was a tightness in her chest as she moved her head to the side until at last his lips came to rest on hers. For a moment nothing existed but the sensation of falling. But his arms tightened around her and pulled her to his chest while his lips and tongue consumed her, gently sucking, probing, enveloping, sending fiery sensations straight to her extremities. In that moment, Hannah was standing on the moon watching herself being devoured by a man she barely knew yet hoped would never let her go. A thought flashed through her brain that, if Max Mohr did release her, she would fall and keep falling forever.

When they finally separated, neither said a word. Hannah put her hand in Max's and led him to the elevator where they entered and stood side-by-side looking straight ahead. In her hotel room, it was if they had been swept up by a rogue wave. They came together, lips, arms, chests, groin, and slowly undressed. Naked, they stood facing each other. Hannah who had never allowed a man to see her naked unless in the dark now remained still in the moonlight as Max caressed her first with his eyes, and then, with his fingertips sliding them down her arms and up over her breasts, skimming her thighs and buttocks, moving up her back where he stopped. At the nape of her neck, he slipped his hand under the thick bramble of tightly curled hair, clutched a handful, and gently tugged. Hannah's knees buckled. As she swayed, Max lifted her up and laid her gently on the bed beneath him. She ran her hands down his back and let them rest on his buttocks as he kissed her neck and then licked a nipple, his tongue circling it until her back arched and she moaned. A deep sigh escaped her lips as he entered her. She was a sail again, turned masterfully this way and that to catch the wind, to ride the waves. When she finally reached shore, she came to rest yearning to sail out once again. Had she ever before experienced this feeling of being so alive and safe?

CHAPTER THIRTY-SEVEN

he poison tree *inside me stopped growing but never died. In those first days with Barak, it continued to feed me while we made our way from Poland moving towards Germany and the American zone where he said we could find safety. Of all the allies, he trusted them the most although, he admitted, that wasn't saying much. We travelled over 900 kilometres, by night and hiding during the day to avoid coming in contact with those Russisheh hint as Barak called them because those dogs would certainly tear him to pieces if they learned he had deserted. Barak made it clear, although we spoke little or not at all, that we had to get away from the eastern front or he would be shot and what would happen to me, he said, would make me wish I had died in Auschwitz.*

I never questioned how Barak came to choose me, why he carried me away from death, and nursed me until I was strong enough to walk. I never questioned why because he held me as I slept and asked for nothing. One day he brought me clothes to replace the filthy prison camp uniform I had been living in. Where he found a dress, I do not know and did not ask but the first chance I had I burned everything except the red triangle. That I sewed onto the underside of the kerchief I wore over my hair which, to my eyes, was no longer my hair. My face, too, was no longer mine. It belonged to the creature I had become shaped by demonic forces. The war had carved life into it, into my cheekbones and chin although it was death that had altered my eyes. As I examined myself in the broken mirror Barak found on the road, it surprised me to see how much I had changed. Watching me examine myself, Barak grunted softly and said in Russian, "You are beautiful." Beauty was not what I saw so I said nothing.

We walked and walked and walked. Eventually, we slipped out of Poland, a country that had ceased forever to be my home and headed south and west. In Czechoslovakia we were finally able to travel by day and sometimes, would beg a ride in an oxcart or a farm wagon. We were making our way to Prague where Barak had a relative he hoped to find. There was no reason for him to go back to Vilna. But along the way, we heard that Czech partisans and the Soviets were still battling the Germans in the Czech capital. That changed Barak's mind and our course.

To circumvent the fighting, we headed south through the countryside around Brno. Just past it, we came upon a road with a long, staggering stream, people still wearing their concentration camp uniforms, or bundled in many layers of clothing. Every once in a while, a transport came by and as many as could would cram into the back of the truck. But Barak and I always chose to stay on the road. It seemed the only small thing we had control over. I was glad to avoid large crowds, afraid someone from the camp might see me, remember me. I knew there were those who thought me an accomplice to Mandl, thought I helped her pick out victims. I knew this by the way the other women shunned me, feared me. Me! Hiding behind my red triangle. Me! Hiding behind my identity as the Polish partisan, Anya Marja Cieski. Me who lived in terror that someone might recognize me and shout Yid! Yid! We had been walking for weeks, rarely speaking to anyone, or even each other. Barak spoke to me in Polish and so that's how I would answer him.

One night, Barak called out in his sleep a jumble of words in Yiddish, among them Mameh. I shook him and without thinking, assured him in Yiddish 'es is gut, es is gut', it's OK, you're safe. Hearing this, Barak bolted upright and looked at me with bewilderment. "Du redst yidish?" 'How is it you speak Yiddish?' he repeated in Polish. I didn't understand what he meant. I also didn't understand how he came to be speaking Yiddish. Was he a Jew? I thought he was a Russian who finally had had enough of the war. Did he not know I was a Jew? Who did he think I was? Why was it me he chose to carry off? As I was sorting out these questions, Barak grabbed me by the shoulders and shook me.

"Bist du eine Yideneh?"

I nodded my head, "Ja," and said, "Ja! Ick bin Rokhl."

The name sounded foreign to my own ears. No one had called me by that name since Oskar died. And until that moment, Barak had had no name for me but Devushka, Russian for girl. It is understandable. I mean his confusion about who I was, what I was. It was the badge I was wearing, the inverted red triangle. It was not a yellow star. More to the point, I was not as completely emaciated as the other inmates Barak had seen when he entered the camp. None of the men were prepared for what they found. I am still shamed when I remember that I had only suffered a few weeks without eating, in those weeks before the liberation, before Barak lifted me up and carried me away. Me. Rokhl.

I don't know how to describe the look on Barak's face when he learned I was a Jew. Admitting I was felt unnerving because it was not how I thought of myself anymore. Not then. I really didn't know what I was. Once I would have said I am a Pole but that was no longer true. Once I had been a daughter and that, too, was no longer so. As for being a Jew, well that was what the others had labelled me, so they had permission to starve, beat, or kill me according to their whims. But not before they took away everything that made me human. So, I wondered, what part of me was Jewish? I have no idea but the look of relief on Barak's face made me happy to be one. Maybe it was in that brief moment of joy. That look which deadened the power of the poison tree. The only other time he looked like that was when ... No, there is so much more you must know first.

CHAPTER THIRTY-EIGHT

Warm breath on the back of her neck unexpectedly woke Hannah from a disturbing dream. Her lips were dry. She licked them gingerly and discovered they were also a little swollen. As she turned onto her back the previous night came flooding back. Suddenly, she was aware that she was not alone in the bed. The memory of what had been set in motion between her and Max last night—or was it this morning?—momentarily delivered a strange mixture of anxiety and pleasure. What had she been thinking? An image floated through her mind, the vague recollection of a dream. If she kept her eyes closed maybe she could retrieve it. A series of disjointed images fluttered behind her closed lids, the last one of Rokhl standing alone on a road as something was moving Hannah away from her. Was she on the back of a truck leaving Rokhl by herself in the middle of nowhere? In the dream, she had tried to call out but was unable to make any sound. The final image was of her mother, standing immobile, a distant pinpoint on the road.

Max, laying beside her, began to stir, his hand reaching out came to rest on her shoulder. She lay stock still fearful of waking him before she knew what she was going to say or do. How did she end up in this situation? Despite its seriousness, Hannah realized she was smiling. Whatever got into her? An impertinent answer presented itself. Max is what got into her. That was indisputable, and despite all the incredible complications that suddenly presented themselves, Hannah couldn't keep from smiling. The smile grew until it became an irrepressible giggling that bubbled up from somewhere that, notwithstanding a real effort to restrain it, she was unable to muffle.

Stretching like a cat, Max woke and, with a clear sense of entitlement, pulled Hannah into his arms, stifling her laughter. They lay there, nose to nose, examining each other's faces, memorizing details. Eventually, Max's hand slid up Hannah's back to the nape of her neck where he grabbed a handful of copper strands and tugged gently. The kiss that followed lost none of the intensity from the night before. If anything, their lust had increased.

A half hour later, as Hannah lay with her head on Max's chest, he said, "I hadn't realized how long it has been since I felt anything like this."

"Like what?" Hannah asked quietly, uncertain whether she wanted the answer.

"Alive. Engaged. Tender. And full of desire. You have bewitched me, Hannah Baran. I have not felt this way since ... well ..."—he hesitated for a moment—"... for a very long time."

Hannah sat up in the bed the better to look at Max as he confessed to what she aroused in him because her first instinct was to disbelieve every word. The previous afternoon in the Schloss flashed through her mind but she shook her curls to clear it away and stay focused on the moment. There was something delicious in feeling the skin of this man warming her. She didn't know how long it had been since Max had had sex but for her, she quickly calculated, it had been six years.

➢ Ages ago, Marilyn had tried pushing her into online dating, citing all the people she knew or had heard about who had found their mate through J-Date, e-Harmony, and even Lavalife. But in all that time, Hannah had had no urge to meet anyone, no desire to go through the excruciating exercise of the awkward first encounter, the contorted conversation in search of a subject. She did not miss being held or petted or kissed and yet, since last night, Hannah was unable to imagine never again being touched by Max. It was as if she had been waiting all her life for this encounter—to be seen, caressed, sheltered. Could it be she had been waiting for Max? In one night, he had opened a door she had kept so tightly sealed she had somehow forgotten it existed. Was that the door Albie said she had slammed in his face after they married, the one that left him out in the cold? That's what he had called her, a cold woman, an ice queen.

That's not what Max was saying about her now. His words were floating to her through a fog of emotion, and she was having difficulty making out what he was saying. What really penetrated the haze was how astonished he was at the heat she roused in him, what a passionate woman she was. So much candour all at once was unnerving, unaccustomed as Hannah was to open admiration. It was nothing like winning Best Flaubert Agent of the Year. That kind of admiration she could handle, something she had worked for and achieved. This was entirely different because it was about who she was, not what she'd done. It reminded her to be cautious.

Neither Barak nor Rokhl had believed in praise. As a child, their lack of condemnation became the equivalent of being told she had done well. And those times were few and far between no matter how many excellent report cards she brought home. If she received 95% on an exam, Barak would ask why not 100? Who was this man suddenly filling her with compliments and bravado? Could she trust him? Or was this just his way of circumventing her defenses and undermining her determination to represent Chaim Sonenshein successfully? One thing was certain, for Barak and Rokhl, he was the enemy. So, what did that make him in her eyes? Until she knew for sure, she burrowed her face into the warmth of his chest and said nothing. Unwilling to leave the comfort of the hotel room, Max had ordered an elaborate breakfast of soft-boiled eggs, with three types of ham, a variety of cheeses, a basket full of seed-encrusted rolls, and a bottle of *sekt*. Once the waiter had transferred the food from the cart to the breakfast table Hannah's eyes grew wide at the sight of the spread.

"We can't eat all this," she said. "You can't possibly think we could."

"Well, I'm ravenous," Max said. "I need to replenish my strength if I'm even going to make it through the day. I'm not as resilient, or as robust as I once was."

"Thank God!" Hannah said, laughing. "And what do you expect to do with that bottle of sparkling wine you ordered? It's 8:30 in the morning!"

"This is a fine, dry *sekt,* the equivalent to Spanish *cava* or French champagne although not quite so highly regarded. I am accustomed to drinking it on special occasions, and this is most certainly one of those. Won't you have a little bit just to mark this momentous coming together?"

Hannah winced remembering how easily she had slipped into another persona with the help of some wine the evening before.

"I think I had too much last night ..."

"Then a little ... what do you call it? Hair of the dog is just the thing." And without waiting for an answer, he expertly poured the bubbly into her glass but only halfway, although giving himself twice as much.

"Here is to us. *Prost,*" Max said, lifting his glass to her.

"*L'chaim,*" Hannah replied.

CHAPTER THIRTY-NINE

Chaim called mid-afternoon several hours after Max had gathered himself up and departed, but not without leaving Hannah with one last passionate kiss and the promise to call later about their dinner plans. The few hours she spent alone did nothing to quell the anxiety assailing her about these new and treacherous waters. She had only herself to blame for this predicament. In her wildest dreams and at this stage in her life, Hannah had never imagined that she would become so entangled with a man. And a German—one representing a potential buyer who, it now seemed, was not a buyer at all but a dangerous adversary who believed he was entitled to land he didn't own.

By the time Chaim called, Hannah had a pounding headache. Without any preamble, Chaim began laying out the next steps for Hannah to take. She was to tell Heilemann that her client has decided against selling the property, and as there was never any documentation supporting the allegation that Heilemann already owns the land, there could be no legal standing for his claim. Furthermore, in the matter of the $5,000 loan for which, incidentally, there was also no documentation except for a receipt of a 45-year-old bank transfer, he considered this to be a debt of honour and Chaim Sonenshein always paid his debts. She was to say that he would have his accountants calculate the interest owed, calibrated at the going rate of each year since the loan was made, and Heilemann could expect the full amount to be remitted before the end of the year. Without a world of apology, Chaim turned Hannah's world on its head.

"Just to let you know," he said, "that over the past few months, there have been some developments I was unaware of when we were first contacted by Heilemann. It seems the provincial government hasn't stirred up enough trouble because now they are proposing a law to conserve certain areas from overdevelopment. Some of that particular Trois-Îles property would be affected. You know I haven't built anything there since the fifties, and then, it was only a few summer cottages for the family. Now the government is working to prevent any future development in order to protect what they call wetlands. Wetlands, *nu?* And I always just called it The Swamp. Anyway ..." Chaim paused as if trying to remember where he was going with this piece of information. "You know this land has always been special to me, and since I have no desire to see any further development on it anyway, I have decided to donate the land to something called the Nature Conservancy of Canada. I'm told they do good work and in return, I'll get a nice fat tax receipt."

The pounding in Hannah's head was now on the scale of ten taiko drummers going at the skins full force. She closed her eyes and waited to find a way to interrupt.

"Okay, Chaim," she said, finally finding an opening. "I'm to tell Max Mohr and Heilemann that we are no longer interested in the game and we're taking our ball and going home? Do I have that right?"

"I can see I caught you in a good humour today." Chaim's dig missed its mark but listening to him chuckle at her expense only served to raise Hannah's ire up two notches. Her head was on the verge of exploding. Just as she was about to channel Barak with a cutting remark, she stopped. In the moment it took her to inhale slowly, she slipped through some invisible barrier into a place where everything was weighted differently, and she conceded. Given the way her life had been unfolding in the last few months, this was no longer a battle worth fighting.

From the start, the trip to Germany had been cursed, setting off a cascade of events that began with that fight with Rokhl, and that led her to this moment in time. And to Max. There was no point in letting pride or revenge veer her off the path. What if she had been played as a pawn? The important thing was that Chaim had designated a role for her and she had fulfilled it. Now it was time to broaden her vistas, look around her, find out what were the other invisible and uncontrolled forces impacting her life. If not now, when? It was time to let go.

Chaim continued, oblivious to Hannah's lack of response: "After you have informed Maximilian Mohr of all this, feel free to return home. Your work in Germany is done."

"Thank you, Chaim, I will do as you ask and inform the potential buyers that the property is off the table and of your intention to pay back the loan. Whatever Heilemann may think, he really has no recourse. Am I right?"

"You are correct," Chaim said before adding: "And I owe you a big dinner when you get back."

"Well, right now I'm not sure when that will be. Since I'm here, I was thinking that I would go visit the town where I was born, to Landsberg am Lech ..."

"Well, if you're that close, you should definitely do that and also explore Munich, maybe even Cologne. There is much to see in Germany. I myself love Berlin, a very unusual city. Take your time, Hannah. I'll cover your hotel bills for another week. My way of saying I appreciate the work you've done. You're the best, *Maidel.*"

And that was as close as Hannah was going to get to an apology from Chaim Sonenshein. She lay down to relieve the pounding in her head, falling asleep secure in the knowledge the call from Max would wake her.

CHAPTER FORTY

When Barak and *I reached the American Zone, the straggling line had become a ragtag, endless caravan of Jewish refugees. Out of habit, we stuck together for safety although there were some whose skills as gonifs and collaborators had been honed in the ghettos and the camps. I was one of them, a collaborator, that's what others believed. I lived in a cloud of fear that I could come across someone who recognized me—the constant companion of the Beast. So, I kept my head down and spoke little or not at all. Every night when we stopped, we heard stories from those who had returned home only to find the world they had known gone forever. Their parents, their siblings, their possessions, the history of Jews in their town all erased. When they returned, some were chased out by the Poles who had taken over their possessions and would now never give them back. But on a good night, you could hear the excitement when someone learned they had located a sibling, an aunt, an old friend or a true miracle, a parent. Sometimes while walking, I thought I saw my father in the way some man held his shoulders or had a familiar profile. In that moment, my heart would leap, and I would be ready to call out until the person turned and I saw the face and understood again that my father was gone forever.*

By now, Barak and I had had intimate relations. I feel shame to share this with you, Hannaleh, but where I am right now, far away on the other side, shame does not exist, only the faint echoes of a life. Intimacy was the only way we seemed able to express any feeling for each other. After sex, I would cling to Barak as if I was drowning. So many images would be floating around in my head, my life swimming before my eyes. During the day, I followed him like a shadow and let him do all the talking necessary to get registered with the International Red Cross, the United Nations Refugee people and the Jewish Immigrant Aid Service.

I did not bother to make a list of missing relatives. I told the officials they were all dead. Besides, I barely remembered the life I had before the war began. Each of my parents had two brothers. Although I remembered the names of my father's brothers because we saw them often in Krakow, I knew very little about the Wachsbergs of Warsaw, my mother's side of the family. I only remembered one cousin, Fenia, because she was around my age and had always been nice to me. And hers was the only name that the Red Cross contacted me about. She had survived two years in Auschwitz III, they said, and was now in a DP camp near Passau, not far from Mauthausen. I told the woman at the Red Cross we were not related.

When I got the news, I panicked. My worst fear was being realized, that Fenia had in fact been the woman I saw in Auschwitz, and I didn't want to see her. I didn't want to be seen. How could I explain how I came to stand at Maria Mandl's side? How could I convince her or anyone that I had no choice but to remain silent as I watched hundreds of women beaten, dehumanized, and murdered, or I too would have been dead. My fear of exposure was so deep, I buried my past with the ashes of my parents and kept everything to myself.

Barak and I married in Landsberg in a ceremony that took no more than 15 minutes. He had been placed in a vocational program that trained young men with no formal education how to become tailors. It seemed your father was not a man cut out to do the fine work of pushing a needle through fabric, but he was very talented at cutting through a pile of cloth. He was a man who knew how to plough into things. As for me, I spent my time standing in line for rations and trying to cook on the communal stove always making sure to avoid the other women. Most of them understood how to leave alone a person who was uncomfortable speaking.

It was just before my 17th birthday when I suddenly began gaining weight, rounder from all the food that seemed so plentiful. My cheeks were growing rounder too and Barak teased me saying I would soon become like a fat Polish housewife. But I knew he didn't mean it in a bad way because he said it with a smile. Then one morning, I threw up. And the next morning, and the morning after that. I stopped eating and one of the braver women asked me what month I was in. I looked at her as if she was speaking a foreign language. She wasn't. I had had only sporadic periods before and after Auschwitz and no one to explain to me how a woman's body worked. I had not been paying any attention to this particular bodily function, relieved not to have to worry about washing bloody rags.

When I told Barak what I suspected, he immediately ran out to buy a bottle of schnapps in celebration. He also insisted I go to the doctor at the camp clinic. I was terrified. No man other than Barak had touched me in a very long time, not since the man who tattooed me at Auschwitz. I didn't trust the doctors in the DP camp because they weren't Jewish. How did I know what they had done during the war? There were terrible stories that every now and then I would overhear about what some doctors did under the Nazis. Stories about abortions and babies starved to death after being taken from their mothers who were slave labourers. But Barak went with me, and the doctor was gentle. He told me I was three months pregnant, and everything seemed to be in good order with the baby. He told me to be sure to eat properly and often.

After that, Barak went crazy. He ran around doing odd jobs, bartering work for food so that there was never a moment I could possibly go hungry. One night, with unusual shyness, he asked if it was a boy could we name the baby after his younger brother, Srulek. He didn't bother considering what we should name a girl, he so wanted a boy. He showed me a pair of baby shoes in a beautiful soft, blue leather that he had purchased at a very good price for his baby boy.

And his wish was answered—we had a son. He was a beautiful boy, born with not too much fuss and a head of black hair like Barak. A perfectly healthy baby when he was born yet he didn't live long enough to have his bris. He died when he was only six days old. He wasn't the only baby to die. Too many babies were dying in Landsberg. One day the Americans arrested the nice doctor.

The war may have been over, but they were still killing us.

CHAPTER FORTY-ONE

After careful deliberation, Max decided on a quiet little bistro for dinner with Hannah. He had hopes for the evening despite knowing better than to expect a happy resolution from an impossible situation. There was no question that what was going on between them had some obstacles to overcome. Recognizing that what was growing was still fragile, he decided that close scrutiny might endanger the relationship from moving forward. He opted to give it a little more time. He headed to the hotel to pick-up Hannah, driving to Dire Straits on the CD. The irony of the lyrics made him smile as it offered up advice for the moment.

> *Why worry? / There should be laughter after pain / There should be sunshine after rain / These things have always been the same / So why worry now ...*

Only one grey cloud hovered over his thoughts: the possibility that Hannah had re-evaluated their evening together. An inexplicable change of attitude was not out of the question. It had occurred before. In fact, almost every time they had shared a wonderful encounter. The next time they met, Hannah had withdrawn like a frightened animal retreating into her burrow. One step forward, two steps back. Remembering the previous night, however, Max could not help but believe this time it would be different. Did she feel as transformed as he did? He was suddenly a wanderer in a barren land who comes upon a verdant valley so lush in possibilities, one could imagine making a home there. That's what Hannah felt like—home. So, what if they came from very different backgrounds? We cannot forever let our pasts define us, he thought. She was the one, he acknowledged, for whom he would make any sacrifice.

How he had arrived at this remarkable moment was baffling, but the big question that kept popping up was whether she felt the same way or not. He could not recall whether he had experienced the same with Nadya. Probably, but one can never be sure what they remember of their youth. Is it the truth or something we wished had been true? After all, age does teach patience and alters the ego's priorities. His only regrets about Nadya were directly tied to the loss of Alexander, his beautiful boy, but he had no regrets about putting an end to his tempestuous marriage. Nadya was—and still remains—a bitter woman with a sharp, lacerating tongue. He had never known such meanness, certainly not from the women who had raised him—his grandmother and the twins, Leni and Eva.

True, he had been a little prince as Nadya had so angrily pointed out. As the only male in his family, he had been treated with kid gloves throughout his childhood. But there was no call for her to have wreaked such revenge after they divorced, vowing that he would never see his son again. Poor Alexander. Like father like son. Alex had grown up never knowing Max. And it was too late now to try and reach out. Alex must be 17. All those lost years. He shook his head to rid himself of the sadness. To stave off more unpleasant thoughts, Max hit replay and this time sang along to *Why Worry*.

☞ The bistro Max chose for dinner, located off of *Brüsseler Platz*, was an intimate affair of only eight tables, tucked away on a side street of the *Belgisches Viertel*. Family-run by transplanted Persians, the husband was the chef and the wife served as both maître d' and sommelier. Hannah seemed charmed by the area although she was surprisingly quiet. Since collecting her at the hotel, Max had noted a certain wariness about her that oddly excited him. He couldn't take his eyes off her even though it seemed to make her uneasy.

"Please stop that," she finally said. He noted she had taken to absentmindedly rolling the linen napkin around her end of the table.

"What?"

"Please stop looking at me so … so …"

"I'm sorry. So what?" Max said with a crooked smile.

"So intently. You're making me very uncomfortable, Max. I'm not accustomed to being scrutinized so openly."

"I'm not scrutinizing you. I am simply enjoying the moment, being here with you, taking in the beautiful scene."

"That's very sweet, but …"

"Or should I try being more discreet? Maybe I should be stealing furtive glances like a thief trying not to be caught out."

Hannah smiled. She appeared from Max's vantage point to relax a little more once she began to smooth out the napkin before laying it in her lap. As the main course arrived, Hannah asked about the district and how it came to be called the Belgian Quartier. Max said he wasn't sure although he thought it had something to do with the Franco-Prussian War in the late 1800s. What he did know, however, was that he had missed an opportunity to buy a property in the area when flats and commercial buildings were going at bargain prices, just before the hip restaurants, galleries and funky clothing shops started to move in.

"They say hindsight is 20/20 vision," Hannah said as the waitress put down her plate of *Khoresh Bademjan,* lamb and eggplant stew. "But you must certainly have many opportunities to get in on deals when Heilemann is scouting a location, do you not?"

"That sort of thing would make me uncomfortable especially as Ha-Gay always manages to buy up all the available properties surrounding an asset. If I were to avail myself, I would be taking advantage of privileged information and probably would be, how do you say … stepping on his toes?"

"Umm. But has he never offered you an opportunity like that?"

Hannah asked, gingerly dipping into her stew. "Why would he not want you to prosper a little further beyond what you earn in commissions? Or are you on retainer?"

Max peered at her over his saffron lamb kebabs. "I'm on retainer," he said, suddenly wary. This was not a subject he thought appropriate. Talking about their respective clients would ruin the evening. He especially didn't want to remind Hannah of their unfinished business, not while he was sitting so close that he was able to catch a whiff of her intoxicating perfume rising from the dampened skin beneath her hair.

He reached across the table and took her left hand in his, lifting her arm to his nose to nuzzle her wrist. A disconcerting swarm of thoughts was buzzing round Hannah's head like distressed bees—Chaim's precise instructions on how to end the negotiations; the tender confessions Max made the night before; the echo of Rokhl's voice calling her a child for not understanding the great danger that being in Germany posed; Heilemann's smug smile when he dropped his bombshell.

All these recollections were set off by Max's lips brushing her wrist. Those lips sent a powerful electrical charge racing through her. She slowly withdrew her hand from his. Beneath lowered lids, she looked at this man who had turned her topsy-turvy world right side up again and was suddenly overwhelmed by a surge of terror. Their situation was hopeless. How was she going to tell him that the Trois-Îles deal was off, and that soon she would be going back to Canada? Yet how could she leave him now that there was a chance she did not have to be alone ever again?

"What has happened, Hannah? You look like you've just seen a ghost." From across the table, Max took hold of both her hands. "These are like ice. What's wrong? Tell me."

His green eyes settled on her like a warm blanket and for the moment, Hannah felt safe. What to tell him?

"Since I'm here in Germany," she said, "and don't know when the opportunity will present itself again ..."

At this, Max cocked his head and pursed his lips as if she was talking nonsense.

"Don't look at me like that, Max. No one knows what tomorrow brings. Anyway, as I have the weekend to myself and can forget about business, I've decided to visit the town where I was born."

"Yes, wonderful!" he said, brightening. "I remember you were born in Landsberg am Lech."

Hannah nodded.

"Tell me again, how is it you are not German? And how can you know for sure?"

"I know because my best friend, Marilyn, who was also born in a Displaced Persons camp, tried to get a German birth certificate several years ago. What she learned was that these camps were a kind of a no-man's land. Those born there were not issued birth certificates because, like Marilyn, being born in a camp in the American zone, administered by the United Nations department for refugees, we weren't technically on German soil.

"At the time, Marilyn thought we might be EU citizens, but it seems German law stipulates that you must be born of German parents. I was most certainly not. But had she been born outside the camp, in a town like I was, you would receive a birth certificate but no citizenship."

"Well, I guess that's *logisch*. With so many refugees gathered into Germany, it would make sense."

"Yes ... sense," Hannah said a little too quickly, anxious to keep their conversation on the one track she felt she could navigate without being derailed.

"Anyway, I want to see where my parents lived when the war ended. We only left Germany after I was born in late 1950. They had been in the DP camp for almost five years by then. I just want to see the town. I don't really know very much about that time in their lives. My father would talk about the war and how he met my mother, but almost never anything about the time after the war."

Max was still holding Hannah's hands in his. When she began to draw them away, he pulled them back towards his chest. He squeezed them a little until she looked up at his face.

"May I drive you? I could be of help since not everyone speaks

English and I know you don't speak German," he said, trying to lighten her mood with a theatrical wink.

It worked. Whatever had been keeping Hannah tied to the ground, suddenly came loose, and set her free. She was weightless for the first time in months.

"Yes, yes ... I would like that," she said, rising from her chair to lean across the table; she planted a kiss gently on his lips.

CHAPTER FORTY-TWO

Whatever hold reality *had on me when Barak found me was now buried in an unmarked grave beside my unnamed son. I faded into the shadows and wandered through each day like a ghost. I doubt that the women around me marked little difference in my behaviour. If I had been withdrawn before, I seemed the same. No one asked what happened to the child I had been carrying. Barak was the only one to see the agony crushing my heart as I lay whimpering in our bed every night. I did not know a body could manufacture so many tears. There was a deep well inside me from which water poured without end. I did not know I could grieve more for a soul I had held for only six days than a father I had loved my entire life. Barak dealt with the death of our son in his customary bull-like fashion. He put his head down and weighed into it plodding to the atelier every day, and every night, returning to the barracks that we shared with three other families separated by nothing more than a piece of plywood for privacy. If they heard my sobs, they said nothing because who did not have a deep well of tears in that camp, at that time? We were all sharp bits of broken families, lost towns and cultures, worlds that after the war lived only in memory. Each of us lay trapped in the black caves, looking for a splinter of light to follow, a hope to hang on to. Until my baby died, I had not realized what I had invested in that little flickering flame. When it went out, I wrapped myself in a shroud.*

It was Barak who saved me a second time. Although maybe that wasn't his intent. Maybe he only wanted me to stop crying and the only way he seemed able to do that was to hold me, pet me, kiss me. Eventually, being a man, that led to other things, and as I mentioned before, it seemed to be the one way in which we were able to communicate. It was some two years later when I began to throw up morning after morning. This time, I knew what was happening, but I was not going to make the same mistake twice. I would not invest in hope. You were growing in me, Hannaleh, but I was not convinced that you were mine. After all, if you were not mine, no one, nothing could take you away from me. Yet still, there were things I had to do. I told Barak I had to give birth in town, away from the DP clinic, although by now, all births had been taking place at the DP hospital, Sankt Ottilien, a former monastery. When that closed, I drove Barak crazy until he agreed to find the money for a proper hospital. He never told me how he did it, but it may be that he had some black-market dealings with the Germans. I did not want to know.

You were born in the Klinikum Landsberg and arriving, like your brother before you, without much fuss. You were a healthy, beautiful girl for whom we had been too afraid to choose a name in advance. After a week, we decided to name you for Barak's mother as I would not hear of naming you for mine. Barak stayed with me during the three days I re-mained in the hospital. He held you and sang to you when I would not. I was so frightened that, if I held you too long, I would never let go of you. Feeding you became our only contact. When you took my breast and I held you, I would skim my hand over your perfect skull where your little crown of reddish gold hair formed a halo especially when the sun came through the window. You rarely cried although you always made a little squeak when I took you from my breast and gave you back to Barak. It was like a note of surprise, not too loud so as not to suggest that you were displeased, only startled that I did not hold you longer. But I gave you back to Barak because I knew he would keep you safe. Understand, I could not hold on to you, Hannaleh, because you were not mine. And if you were not mine, I could never lose you. In this way, our life began to take the shape it would follow. You learned that crying would not bring you comfort. Not from me.

I refused to leave the barracks with you unless Barak was with us. I was that afraid. Before you were born, I got it into my head that we had to redouble our efforts to get out of Germany. We applied to many countries, telling whatever lies were needed to be accepted. For Australia, Uruguay, and Argentina, I was a seamstress and Barak, a farmer. For the United States, he was a bricklayer and for Canada, your father listed himself as a cutter and that was how we came to this country six months after you were born. We did not choose Canada. Canada chose us and we were grateful. We were latecomers. The heaviest flow of Jews had been between '47 and '49 so in a way we were lucky. The systems were already well-established and immediately Barak got a job in a factory cutting coats. Then JIAS found a relative of Barak's from Vilna, a distant cousin by marriage who had immigrated in the 1920s and was now a widow.

Ida Blustein had a large apartment at the eastern, less fashionable end of Outremont with a large bedroom off the kitchen that she rented to us for a small sum. She was kind to me although her Litvakesche yiddish was foreign to my ears. It was my excuse for continuing to be so silent. What also worked well was that, in having no grandchildren, Ida immediately fell in love with you and would hold you for hours on end while you slept. I was silently grateful although she believed my act was that of a big heart—my way of showing gratitude. Maybe because she wanted to have you to herself, she encouraged me to take the free English language classes at the Beth Moishe synagogue down the street. I went for two years. This was where I learned how to read and write in English. Maybe I knew that one day I might tell you who I was and how I came to be such a poor mother. You know, I tried to help you by sharing what I knew or understood of life through my notes. It was more than I ever got from my own mother.

CHAPTER FORTY-THREE

As they neared Landsberg, Max mentioned that the road they were on was known as the *Romantische Straße,* the Romantic Route. It came four hours into their leisurely drive during which Hannah found herself coolly disconnected from everything but the fleeting scenery. The comment brought a sardonic smile to her lips at the suggestion that her town of birth was located along some dreamy-eyed setting in Germany. Before leaving, Max had warned that the drive could be some five hours, but Hanna had said she was fine with that. A three-day weekend was her due although hovering in the back of her mind was the hope that somewhere along the way, when they were both perfectly at ease, she would find an opening to break the news to Max vis-à-vis Chaim's about-face on the land deal. For now, however, she contented herself with being a passenger in a car with a clear destination.

For much of the drive, swaths of silence hung lightly between them. Max was clearly enjoying the open and uncrowded road and, for her part, Hannah was experiencing an unfamiliar calm watching the greenery blend into a long, lush line of trees. The names of familiar towns flashed by as they glided down the Autobahn—Frankfurt, Heidelberg, Karlsruhe came and went; this made her wonder how the Germans had managed to conceal such extensive population and countless structures behind an unending wall of greenery. All that was evident were the signs declaring their proximity and those indicating *Einfahrt* and *Ausfahrt*.

"It's a testament to our love of nature," Max had said when she asked where all those municipalities were hiding. What truly surprised her though was the complete lack of roadkill anywhere.

"How is that possible with so many cars flying along at such incredible speeds?" she asked.

In the stretches of no limits when she dared to look, she would catch the speedometer sitting at 220 kph without the slightest indication that the BMW was actually flying. Max shrugged as he dutifully kept his eyes trained on the road.

"Are there no wild animals left crossing the highways? Does German efficiency remove them as they drop or do you all drive so fast that when you hit them, they soar through the air at such a rate that friction causes them to evaporate?"

Max burst out laughing and promised he would investigate whether there was any factual or some scientific basis to her theory. Around Stuttgart, the landscape began to undulate reminding Hannah of the gentle slopes of the lower Laurentians, but somehow with all the wildness tamed. Here and there a vineyard ribbed the hillsides in perfect rolling rows and on occasion, a schloss emerged like a crown on a mountaintop.

⌒ Arriving in Landsberg at last, Max pulled the car into a garage from which they exited into the late afternoon sun. A pedestrian tunnel brought them right into the town's main square. Hannah looked around and was more charmed than she had expected. Landsberg am Lech was picture-perfect and storybook pretty. Ice cream-coloured buildings, immaculately maintained, nuzzled up against each other, their peaked roofs jutting upward into a clear blue sky as if shouting 'Hallelujah!' The buildings edging the river were rewarded with an untainted reflection of their façades. In that moment, what she saw had such a fairy tale quality, Hannah half expected to see people parading down the street in *lederhosen* and *dirndls*. Max remained quiet, giving her a moment to take it all in. As she stood there, he stretched out his hand. She placed her palm in his and he led her down to the river and over to a small waterfall.

"I know it's not Niagara," Max said, "but you have to admit it is pretty."

"It's all pretty," Hannah said, trying to remember why she had wanted to come here. What was the point of this journey? She could no longer recall what she expected to find. She held tight to Max's hand; his cool fingers wrapped around hers. As a child, when she listened to Barak's stories about the DP camp, she had envisioned naked trees and the ground barren and brown, not these luscious shapes and shades, the sunshine warm on her face.

"Are you disappointed, Hannah?" Max asked. "Is this not what you expected? I thought you knew something about this town when you decided to come here."

"What I know about Landsberg comes from only one source, my father, and he had nothing complimentary to say about it or its people. This visit was not on my radar as you know. I'm not sure what has brought me here." Hannah examined her hands as if the answer was somehow at her fingertips. "I don't remember much of what my father had to say except this one thing every time he told me his story. He said that, when Hitler was imprisoned here for treason, sometime in the twenties, he wrote *Mein Kampf* in his Landsberg prison cell."

"It was 1924," Max said.

"Really? How do know that exact date?"

"Before the war," he said, "I was told, my father would lead groups of Hitler Youth to Landsberg as a sort of pilgrimage ..."

Hannah stopped walking and looked at Max in astonishment. She would never have had the nerve to ask Max about his father or his family. But this? How could he just blurt that out as if it held no significance to her, to them?

"Your father?" She could not stop herself from sounding accusatory.

The tone told Max he may have accidentally fallen into a black hole from which escape was unlikely. Perhaps a quick explanation might remedy the situation. He chose to be straightforward about the family's dark history. He sensed this could be cathartic or catastrophic yet, he felt no guilt for a past he had not been a part of.

"My father," he said quietly, "was an officer in the SS, a fairly high ranking one." As he told Hannah this, Max kept his eyes focused on some distant point so as not to lose his nerve. "He joined early on just as Hitler was making his mark and, I was told, never lost faith in the ambitions of the Nazi party. He led those young boys and girls to Landsberg to what he called the birthplace of the ideology of National-Socialism."

When Hannah slipped her hand from his, he finally looked at her. He knew he had to hasten to repair the damage that this unvarnished truth could inflict.

"This is all I know and only because my sister Leni told me. I never knew my father, Hannah. Even now I don't know what he looked like because he and my mother divorced when I was two and my Omi removed every photograph there was of him. Omi loathed my father. So did my sisters according to Leni, though Eva never said a word for or against him. It eventually came out that my father 'relocated' to Argentina and started another family. I really can't remember who told me this. Once I thought I might do some research on him but then decided against it. I saw no point. He had nothing to do with me so why stir the pot. I am not my father."

"Had nothing to do with you," Hannah repeated softly, tasting the bitterness of the words. Max tried to gauge how much damage this information had wreaked. Hannah had taken a few steps back, looking at him as if they had just met. As if he was some curious stranger who had mysteriously appeared by her side.

"Hannah, please don't look at me like that."

"How else can I look at you? I have no idea who you are and where you come from, no more than I have any idea where I come from."

"Hannah, I am the same person I was five minutes ago. I am not my father. Don't you understand that if we allow the past to be the path to the future we will forever be walking in circles. What happened under the Nazis was beyond despicable, horrifying and the root of evil.

If I live to be 100, I will never understand the cruelty, the methodical destruction, the inhumanity towards a people who have contributed so much not only to Germany, but to the world. I repeat, Hannah, I am not my father."

"Of course, you're not your father. If you were, how could I be here, how could I be feeling as I do towards you? But ... but ... I am *my* father's daughter."

"You must know that I am in love with you. I am not falling. I have arrived here, in love, and I want you to understand that I have never felt this way about anyone before. I am past 50 and no longer impulsive or foolish. I realize now how little I know of anything, but I know this: I do love you."

Before she could say another word, he enveloped her in a deep hug, putting one hand on her head to draw it towards his chest. For the second time that day, despite her better judgement, Hannah inexplicably surrendered to the moment.

CHAPTER FORTY-FOUR

The next morning, down in the breakfast room, Max was making an effort at conversation.

"Did you know that for the past fifteen years Landsberg has been a *Europäische Holocaust-Gedenkstätte?*"

"A what?" Hannah said a little too sharply. "What on earth does that mean?"

She was unable to stop thinking about Max's family history and beyond that was disturbed that she was in Landsberg without knowing why she had followed a crazy impulse to see the town where she was born. She had woken with a start when she sensed she was alone in the bed. Max and his clothes were gone. Hannah panicked, then gave in to anger. What was this incomprehensible attachment she had to Max Mohr? She who had fended so long for herself with no man to act as a compass could now barely be alone in a hotel room. Crazy thoughts, what Barak called *misheganah gedanken,* suddenly ran rampant in her head. Why did he leave her without a word? Had she been a fool to trust him? Why had she not told anyone that she was going to Landsberg? She could die here, and no one would know but her murderer.

When Max returned minutes later with two steaming café au lait from the lobby bar, Hannah simultaneously experienced anger and a wave of relief although she was mortified at how quickly she had lost it. Was she becoming unhinged? How much longer could she tell herself that she was suffering the after-effects of a terrible loss? When she saw the tentative smile on Max's face, she chose not to reassure him that everything was okay. Everything was not okay. She was falling in love with the son of a Nazi. In the hotel's Breakfast Room, Max chose to sidestep the irritation in Hannah's voice. He recognized that they were learning about each other every day but had a long way to go. As he slathered his bread with a healthy glob of butter, he explained that *Holocaust-Gedenkstätte* translates as a place of Holocaust remembrance.

"Really? How is it they didn't remember for the previous 40 years?" Hannah asked cutting him off. "What took them so long?"

Max looked up in surprise and at a loss for a response, ran his hands through his hair, a gesture Hannah recognized as a sign that he was feeling uneasy. At the moment, she didn't care. This trip to Landsberg was likely a big mistake. However, if asked, she would have been hard put to verbalize what she had expected of the weekend in the town of her birth, and in the company of Max Mohr.

"Hannah, I thought you would be pleased to learn that the place where you were born has acknowledged the horrors that were perpetrated here. I thought …"

Hannah waved her hand as if shooing away a pesky fly. She wanted him to stop because, if he continued, she didn't know if she could suppress the terrible words bubbling up inside her, words she knew that belonged in Barak's mouth, not her own. Her voice quivered as she forced herself to quietly explain that this was not why she had come to Landsberg.

"What happened in this town before and after the war doesn't interest me. This is just the place where I happen to have been born. In the Klinikum Landsberg. That's all I know. My parents were not from this town. My mother was not in a camp here or even near here. She was in Auschwitz, and my father was a partisan, a Russian soldier who liberated her. I was only born here because this is where my parents ended up after fleeing from the advancing Soviets. My father was an army deserter. He had been passing as a Gentile but knew that he could not keep up the charade once the fighting ended. The reason I came here was to ... I don't know ... get an idea of where they—we—had lived when they started out. In retrospect, I don't think that was very sound reasoning."

"Your mother was in Auschwitz? Truly?" Max said looking unnerved. "And she survived? But that's remarkable. Can you tell me about it?"

"No, I can't because I know nothing except that she was there and that my father rescued her. That's all I know. My mother did not ... she never told me ... she never spoke ..."

"I understand. She did not want to relive her experiences," Max said trying to fill in the words Hannah seemed unable to find.

"No," Hannah said softly, "I mean she never spoke at all. My mother was very ... I don't know what you would call it. Withdrawn, maybe. She was probably clinically depressed but, since she refused to see a psychiatrist, there is no way of knowing for sure. I have no idea how my grandparents died and nothing about their backgrounds. I know that my mother was an only child. And that I learned from my father who did most of the talking in our family. He talked about his life—about his hometown of Vilna, and the horror of the ghetto, about the death of his parents and his younger brother, about joining the partisans, and how he came to rescue my mother. I guess that I'm not that different from you when it comes to knowing my history, except I had no grandmother and no siblings who might have been able to fill in the gaping holes of my story. But it's also true that neither one of us knows who our parents were before the war and how that shaped their lives forever. And since they—our parents—shaped our lives, well, it's as if we're standing in a doorway but there's nothing behind us. Like we came from nowhere. But, of course, *you* could always ask your sisters ... if you really wanted to know. It wasn't like that for my friends." She rolled her napkin. "Growing up, whenever my friends' parents got together, they would share their war stories. That's all they ever talked about the older they grew. But not my mother. And because we had no living relatives—or so I thought until recently—there was no one to ask."

"So, your parents are gone?" Max asked.

"Yes, both gone. My father died of cancer more than two years ago. And my mother ... well, my mother ... she ..."

Hannah stopped, confused as to why she was suddenly blurting all this out. And to Max of all people. As she considered this, she felt something on her cheek and lifted her napkin to dab at her face. When she brought it to her lap, she was surprised to find dark gashes on the white linen, splotches of smudged mascara. She took a gulp of air to find her voice, but it was gone. Gone like her mother who had slipped into some deep cave and disappeared forever. Max moved his chair around next to Hannah's and stretched his arm around her shoulder pulling her close. She tried to wrench away but he held her fast.

"My mother, Rokhl, killed herself in August of this year. She killed herself because I told her I was coming to Germany."

Why was she telling Max this? In that moment, she hated him. Her mother was dead, and it was all her fault. No, it was his fault. Or was it no one's fault?

"I don't know what I'm doing here. I don't know how I could love you. How you could love me. This is all so hopeless."

As he gathered her closer, she buried her face in his neck, and he placed his palm against her cheek to shield her from prying eyes.

☞ Leaving the hotel, they walked hand in hand, each lost in their thoughts. As he sorted through what the morning had delivered, Max was finding it difficult to determine from which angle, if any, he could broach the subject of her mother's suicide. He was conflicted by his desire to ease Hannah's anguish but also to understand how you could survive Auschwitz and, 55 years later, take your own life. Then, there was that other part of him that wanted to pretend this entire morning never happened. The thought raised the spectre of Nadya, her eyes narrowed and her forefinger waggling, as she heaped scorn on him. She was lambasting him for his inability to be moved by emotions, accusing him of resorting to logic as his approach to every problem. Nadya had claimed it was unnatural how he never lost his temper, or his cool. The accusation was accurate, but it didn't mean that he was unfeeling. Holding Hannah in the restaurant earlier, there had been a physical ache in his chest. He found it almost unbearable to sense how her body shuddered with the power of pent-up tears. He felt the heat of her sadness rising against his neck and could taste the sorrow lodged in her throat. Perhaps, with age, his defenses had been lowered or grown thin. In fact, where Hannah was concerned, he realized that whatever defenses he had were somehow gone for the first time since he was a child.

CHAPTER FORTY-FIVE

On Sunday, they awoke to the tolling of church bells from several directions. Reluctant to open her eyes, Hannah was hanging on to the scattered images of a dream. Marilyn always said that, if you described your dreams before opening your eyes, there was a better chance of recalling them. Hannah reached out and Max's voice rumbled in her ear. "Ah, the princess awakens, and I didn't even have to kiss her."

His breath on her cheek sent a small shiver down the side of her body.

"Wait." Her voice was husky with sleep. "I want to tell you about a dream I had. You were in it. It was like a movie. We were sitting in a taverna in Greece somewhere, listening to a man playing a bouzouki. You were listening closely, but I was anxious to leave because I was supposed to meet someone at a museum or a library ... I think it was a library, and I didn't want to be late."

"Amazing. How did you know I happen to love bouzouki music?"

"Shh! Let me get this out or I'll lose it. You were so involved in the music I didn't want to make you leave so I said that I would head to the library, and you could meet me there afterwards. I was anxious not to be late for my date. I think it was with my father. I'm not sure. Outside the taverna, the sun was blinding. I could barely see where I was headed. I seemed to be going on instinct. Two men passed me on the street. They were dressed in neat clothing, but they were very skinny, so skinny that their jackets looked like they were on hangers, not shoulders. I wondered if they were homeless but the way they walked it seemed as if they had somewhere to be. I finally arrived at the library and was sad to see such an elegant old building in a terrible state of disrepair. When I went up to the counter where I was supposed to meet my father, the librarian asked if I was *Hannaleh* ... that's what my father sometimes called me. I was surprised and answered yes, thinking my father had left a message, but the librarian handed me a book and said, 'This was left here for you by a woman named Rokhl.'"

Hannah grew still and Max waited for her to clarify what she thought it all meant. When she held her silence, Max asked, "So Rokhl is your mother?"

"Yes."

"Is that how the dream ended?"

"Mmm, I awoke to the sound of the bells."

"Wow. Like you said, very cinematic. I dream but I never remember any of them with such clarity."

"I don't usually recall them that clearly either, but the images were so real that I was surprised to awake and find myself here, in bed ... and with you."

"I hope that was a happy surprise," Max said, as Hannah's hand came to rest on his cheek. "Because I am a very happy man, Hannah Baran, all because of you, happier than I have been in a very long time." He gazed down at her, the strands of her hair fanned out and in bright relief against the white pillow.

"Do you remember that Jim Croce song?" he asked. "The one about time in a bottle. That's what I wish for us, to make this moment last a very long time."

Hannah turned towards Max and tucked herself into the crook of his arm. It never failed to amaze her how easily she fit into that space as if it had been carved out precisely to match her measurements. She nuzzled his shoulder, clinging to the moment sensing it was unsustainable. Finally, fully awake, she found herself wondering whether they would ever be able to bottle time, to keep themselves separated from a world so much more complicated than this guileless moment. For the moment, she was luxuriating in the warm breath on her ear. A hand was moving down her back but before reaching her buttocks, it began to slip tantalizingly upwards again. She turned her face into the soft hair on Max's chest and lightly licked a nipple. The desired effect was realized. Max pulled her to him tighter, his hands in the furrow at the back of her thighs. He slipped into her like a sloop with the wind at its back coming home to a familiar bay.

It was their last dinner before driving back to Cologne the following morning. Hannah knew she could not delay much longer. Once in Cologne, Max would have to turn to the business at hand, which left no choice. She had to inform him of Chaim's decision before they returned. Max had ordered a bottle of *sekt* to mark the end of a wonderful weekend although Hannah continued to protest that she was not accustomed to drinking so much. Max had laughed and asked her to define what she considered 'so much.'

"Two glasses of anything," she said. Max laughed again saying that was a point on which they greatly differed but likely could reconcile in the future. He looked up at her smiling broadly but with an intense gaze that was becoming familiar. It always made her slightly uncomfortable identifying it as the look of a man who was besotted. Never before had she been the focus of so much adoration, neither as a child nor as a grown woman. Following their main course and her second glass of *sekt,* Hannah could delay no longer and finally came out with it.

"I've heard from Chaim Sonenshein and I'm afraid you are not going to be happy with what he has asked me to relay."

Max looked at her quizzically but with an expression that said nothing could make him unhappy at that moment making what she had to tell him all the more difficult.

"Mr. Sonenshein has decided not to sell Trois-Îles. In fact, he may be saving Heilemann a great deal of trouble because the provincial government of Quebec is making noise about creating a law for the protection of wetlands and that would affect at least half of the property's acreage."

Max leaned back in his chair and took another slow sip of the bubbly. Eyes on the tablecloth, Hannah hurriedly continued on. "Sonenshein wanted me to explain that as there was never any documentation supporting the allegation that Heilemann has a right to the land, he doesn't have a legal premise for any kind of claim. But, in the matter of the $5,000 loan for which, incidentally, there was also no documentation except for a 45-year-old bank transfer receipt, he considered this a debt of honour and, I am quoting here, 'Chaim Sonenshein always pays his debts.' The interest owed will be calculated, calibrated at the going rate of each year since the loan was made, and Heilemann can expect the full amount to be remitted before the end of this year."

When Hannah finally looked up, she was stunned by the brilliance of the smile creasing Max's cheeks. He looked like a man who just learned he was holding a winning lotto ticket.

"What are you smiling about? Didn't you hear what I said?" she asked, tucking her hair behind her ears as if to better capture what Max was about to say. But he just continued to smile broadly. Clearly frustrated, she leaned towards him over the table.

"All of this work—our work—has been for nothing. Almost half a year of going back and forth. Do you want to hear the best? Sonenshein is going to donate the land to the Nature Conservancy of Canada, an act so foreign to his nature I couldn't be more surprised if I had found him dressed in a tutu and dancing the Waltz of the Fairies."

Max burst out laughing at the image.

"You clearly think this is amusing but for me, this has been some kind of crazy exercise and totally incomprehensible. And you, you're laughing?"

He reached for Hannah's hands, which she quickly withdrew, annoyed that she had been obsessing over how badly Max was going to take this news only to determine from his reaction that he was clearly delighted that the deal had disappeared into thin air. Slowly, he leaned back in his chair.

"First of all," he said, "this deal is far from a waste of my time as it brought me to you. And you to me, here in Germany. Secondly, and most importantly, I was very disquieted about how Ha-Gay had set-up a trap for you without informing me that he was going to. And truthfully, I was taken aback at the sordidness of this so-called debt. Here in Germany, we all have skeletons in our closet—a father like mine, an uncle or grandfather who benefitted from slave labour, or someone who, at the very least, lacked the courage to raise their voice. There are those who got away with thieving or worse, murder. It disturbed me that Ha-Gay seemed to be proud of his ruse. It will now forever colour my work with him. But to be honest, I have lost no commission as I work on a retainer, and I have gained the joy of getting to know and falling in love with a beautiful woman, one with whom I want to spend much more time. Chaim Sonenshein has provided the best possible way out for me ... and for you, too. Don't you see? We are no longer on opposing sides."

Once again, Max reached for Hannah's hands and this time, she met him halfway.

"Now tell me, Hannah, where do we go from here?"

CHAPTER FORTY-SIX

Where could they go from here? She had no idea. Theirs was an impossible set of circumstances, and this trip to Landsberg she now realized had been ill-conceived. What could the future hold for them? A line from the movie, *Fiddler on the Roof,* kept running through her head. Although Tevye had grudgingly made concessions for his eldest daughter who chose the man she wished to marry and then the middle daughter who also chose her own husband, a man rebelling against tradition, his third daughter had gone too far because she wanted to marry a Russian gentile. "A bird can love a fish," Tevye said balefully, "but where would they make their home?"

How could Hannah love Max, knowing that her parents were certainly spinning in their graves because their only child had not just become entangled with a *goy* but more gallingly with a German, a man whose Nazi father, an SS officer, had no doubt delighted in killing Jews? And how long could they remain together if they had nowhere to make a home, if the weight of history was always pressing at their back and dragging on them like the chains of Marley's ghost? She was fifty years of age, not old but no spring chicken. Did he imagine she would move to Cologne? Was he thinking she could just pull up roots and change her whole life? And yet, when she thought about it, she had to acknowledge that her whole life had, in fact, already changed without her having chosen any of the paths that it could meander down.

Rokhl's death. The trip to Germany. Max.

These were all things that happened beyond her control. She had always believed she had no choice as to the family and circumstances she had been born into but that she always had a choice as to how she dealt with those exigencies of life. Being faced with that clear choice was terrifying although, she realized, for the first time in her life she had no one to whom she owed duty or commitment. Her father was gone. Her mother was gone leaving behind the most enigmatic message she had ever written: *I am not her.* When Hannah looked around her, all that remained was an ominous landscape shrouded in fog and filled with flitting shadows. When she called out, the echo of her own voice came back to laugh at her loneliness and ask mockingly, 'Now what'?

Every once in a while, during the drive back to Cologne, Max stole a glance at Hannah sitting deep in thought, the only wrinkle on her unlined face being the crease between her brows. He knew she was turning his question over, the one about what was next for them. He had posed it in a moment of elation and had no regrets although he knew the responsibility to come up with an answer was as much his as hers. As in a business negotiation, the core issue was whether they could find some common ground on which to meet, and work from there towards a satisfactory solution.

Max was not so besotted as to overlook the many obstacles they faced as a couple, the greatest being how to sustain a long-distance romance. To begin with, there could be no pressure to change their work circumstances as they both had successful careers which were challenging, particularly where their principal clients were concerned. Max had no expectation that Hannah would walk away from the solid reputation it had taken her years to establish or give up the lucrative position she held with the Flaubert agency. As for his work with Heilemann, it would continue as before, filled with challenges but with none of the upheaval this Trois-Îles deal had raised. Thoughts of Ha-Gay led Max to contemplate how he was going to convey Hannah's news—the final turn of events in this whole silly saga.

Something was niggling at him, a level of disappointment in his client after seeing a side of him that he would have preferred not to know. The admiration in which he had always held Ha-Gay had been diminished. A certain regret came with that thought but he pushed it aside to once again ponder how to move forward with this woman he was now determined not to lose. Maybe he should ask Leni for some advice, he thought. Since his Omi died, he was closest to Leni and trusted her judgement. Unlike Eva, Leni was a good and thoughtful listener. Perhaps she and Hannah should meet. It would give Leni a chance to get to know her a little. It might help her formulate some advice as to how to avoid making the same mistakes he had made with Nadya and Nicole. Never again in his life did he want to see the look of despair that he had found in their eyes at one time or another.

"Hannah?" he asked breaking the silence. "Would you like to meet my sister Leni? She's the one I am closest to. She lives in Porz-Zündorf, a suburb of Köln, just about a half hour away from my place. You did intend to stay the week. Right? We could go there on Tuesday or Wednesday."

"Your sister?" Hannah seemed to be rising out of a trance. "Umm ... sure, I guess. That would be nice. I was thinking of flying back to Montreal on Saturday to have a day to get some rest before I go back to the office. Tuesday or Wednesday is fine, whenever it suits her."

"*Wunderbar*, I will speak to Leni after I drop you off. What kind of food are you in the mood for dinner tonight?"

Hannah remained silent so long that Max was about to repeat the question when she finally responded.

"If you don't mind, Max, I'd like to spend the evening alone ..."

"Is everything OK?" He turned to look at her, a crease furrowing his brow.

"Yes, yes, of course, it is, but I have a lot to sort out. Plus, I want to call the office, connect with Danielle, have her re-arrange my flight back to Montreal. I just need a little time to myself. This trip has been such a whirlwind so far I can barely catch my breath."

"Yes, you take my breath away, too," he said in an effort to lighten the mood. He turned to her and was confronted by a wan smile, so hurriedly he said, "But I understand what you're saying although I was enjoying being breathless for the first time in a long time."

Much to her surprise, Hannah began to cry. She turned away from Max who slowed the car and pulled over to park next to a wooded area. He reached out, over the console to put his arm around Hannah but she withdrew, huddling against the car door where she remained a few moments weeping silently. Max sat back in his seat and remained quiet until Hannah was ready to speak.

"I'm sorry, Max, this is so out of character for me," she said, fumbling in her purse for a handkerchief. "I've been here less than a week and it feels as if my whole life has been turned inside out. Left is right; back is front. I never imagined I would feel about anyone the way I feel about you but there are things I have not told you about that I must deal with. Important things. And I want to tell you, but I cannot just blurt them out, blubbering like a baby. I want to be calm and rational when I share how my life has been in upheaval these last few months. I know this all sounds crazy, but I grew up with a father who was always bellowing, and a mother always silent and remote. It's just the way my life has always been."

She stopped and blew her nose.

Max touched her arm and smiled gently. He waited until Hannah appeared to have collected herself and said, "Whatever you think you must do, I will wait. It feels like I've waited my whole life to meet you so I'm prepared to wait a little longer, as long as I must, until you are comfortable and happy and ready to tell me what you need to. Whatever I can do to ensure that safe place, please let me know. And if there is nothing I can do, I will wait until you're ready." Then, with a smile that flashed his dimple: "Are we good, as the Americans like to say?"

"You are an unusual man, Maximilian Mohr. We are good."

CHAPTER FORTY-SEVEN

On Tuesday, Max parked the M5 on a narrow street edged by *fachwerk* houses, their diagonal beams of dark wood bright against white plaster walls. From there he led Hannah down to *die Groov*, the park running alongside the Rhine. The towering, century-old trees were beginning to lose their leaves, carpeting the path they walked along. In the distance, cruise ships and barges stacked high with containers glided silently down the river. The area, full of pubs and restaurants, was alive with boisterous chatter.

"We're close to where Leni lives but I thought you would enjoy a little walk to give you a chance to see how lovely this part of Köln is."

He took her hand as they continued, and she revelled in how good it felt to walk hand-in-hand with Max. When she was little, Barak would lead her by the hand but neither her mother nor Albie had believed in displays of intimacy, her mother not at all and Albie not in public. Leni lived on the top floor of an elegant, three-story building that overlooked the river. She rang them in and as they climbed the stairs to her flat, Hannah admired the expansive and airy apartment with floor to ceiling windows visible from the entrance and offering a magnificent view of the water and forest beyond. Waiting for them at the top of the stairs, Leni reached out and hugged Max hard, then turned to Hannah and hugged her as well leaving a whiff of jasmine when she let go. Slightly abashed, Hannah handed Leni the bouquet she had purchased in Cologne. She took the flowers to the kitchen. Hannah followed Leni, tall with an athletic build and a tawny complexion offset by a head of thick silver hair worn loose and straight to the collarbone. A pair of blue-grey eyes glistened above high cheekbones that had smiled at Hannah with an open and welcoming expression. In her early sixties, with that smile, despite her hair colour, Leni could have easily passed as a decade younger.

"*Willkommen,* Hannah, I am so happy to meet you. Please come in and sit down. Max, you're looking well, *fit wie ein Turnschuh.* Make yourself useful. There's a bottle of *sekt* on the sideboard. *Bitte,* pour us each a glass."

Max saluted his sister and went to fulfill his duties saying, "As you can see, Leni can be a very bossy woman, but I love her enough to accept my role as her humble servant."

Leni laughed and turned her attention back to Hannah who was surveying the explosion of colour from the abstract art hung around the room.

"What marvellous paintings," Hannah said. "I'm not usually a fan of abstract but these are so intriguing. Are they all by the same artist?"

"Did Max put you up to this?" Leni asked, narrowing her eyes and wagging her finger at Max who was returning with three glasses brimming with *sekt.*

"Put her up to what?" Max asked Leni. "Absolutely not."

Turning to Hannah, he explained that his sister was the artist of all the works but considered herself an amateur and not very good. Leni looked momentarily flustered but after thanking Hannah for the compliment swiftly changed the subject. Leni raised her glass: "*Prost.* I am so glad that we were able to meet."

Hannah took a small sip of the bubbly having already learnt that to empty the glass too quickly only led to an immediate refill. She looked at Leni and Max, spotting the familial similarities in their facial bone structure, cleft chin, and excellent posture, sitting with their backs straight. They had a particular way of leaning from the hip when putting their glasses down on the coffee table.

"So, Hannah, this is your first time in Germany?"

"Well, not exactly," she replied, plunging in as she had rehearsed earlier that morning. She knew this question was inevitable and had decided just to lay it all out without knowing what Max may or may not have already told Leni.

"My parents were refugees; my father was Belorussian and my mother Polish. They lived in a displaced persons camp in Landsberg, and I was born there but we left almost immediately after and moved to Canada, to Montreal where I now live."

"Oh," Leni said, her eyes shifting to Max and back to Hannah. "I have never been to Canada. Is it as cold as we hear on the news every winter?"

Hannah laughed, relieved to move on from family history to the safety of discussing the weather. "Not in summer, it isn't. We have all the extremes possible in Quebec. It can be minus 30 Celsius in January and plus 30 C in July. In between we have a beautiful spring that usually does not last long enough. One minute there is snow on the ground and the next, the trees are bursting with leaves and flowers are popping up out of the ground. We stay green from May to September and then we get the fall colours right about now. In fact, your canvases remind me of autumn in my province. It's a time when the trees display a profusion of red, yellow, gold and orange, then by late November, we usually have our first snowfall."

"You are describing a land of extremes, *ja?*"

"Yes," Hannah said. "Maybe that's why we're such a peaceful nation. When you spend so much time fighting the elements, who has the time or energy to fight with your neighbours?"

Surprised at her facility with English, Hannah complimented Leni who explained she had acquired the language working as a nanny for a British family stationed in Cologne after the war. Leni maintained she had been well-trained for the position having dealt with Max's incorrigible behaviour as a young boy. Max made a face at his sister.

"He was a little imp in a house with three adoring women—four if you count the few times in the week my mother was awake or at home, and we all coddled him. Our *Omi,* my mother's mother, was really the one who raised us even before our father left. When he went to Argentina without us, only my mother was sad to see him go, something none of us understood. It was clear that *Omi* had always despised my father. And he tolerated her only to keep peace in the house because he barely lived there anyway during our childhood. *Ja*, Eva and I were born just after the war started. *Vati* was gone most of the war and we were almost 10 when *der Bengel* was born in 1948."

"Bengel?"

"Leni!" Max protested, then turning to Hannah with a pained smile to explain. "That's the nickname with which my sisters would unjustly scold me."

"Unjustly? How can you say that? You were a little terror who always had us doing your bidding," she said with a sly smile and a wink. "But to be honest, Hannah, if he was like that it was our fault. We spoiled him too much."

"Enough about me," Max said but Hannah waved him away, wanting more. As an only child she craved stories about siblings and how they irritated each other. Oh, how she had longed for a baby brother and once, while young, had asked Rokhl if she could have one. The look of anguish on her mother's silent face ensured she never asked again.

There was something in the way Leni was telling her these stories that suggested to Hannah she had been prepped by Max; that he wanted her to know about the warmth in their relationship despite his father's background, wanted her to know how he had been raised. Clearly, it was a history he could not recall from his own perspective. As a result, the afternoon was filled with a kind of intimacy that created a longing in Hannah akin to what she had felt so many times growing up, times when she had wished she could belong to Marilyn's loud and loving family. When Max turned on the living room lamp, they suddenly realized that it was time for their evening meal. Leni suggested the Argentinian steakhouse, Max's favourite.

↝ On the way back to Cologne, Max asked if perhaps Hannah would like to see his flat instead of going back to the hotel, but she averred, saying it had been quite a full day.

"How about tomorrow?" she suggested and when he went silent added that she would prefer to have him spend the night with her at the hotel. He quickly agreed.

When they entered the room, the message light on Hannah's phone was blinking. She was expecting a call from Danielle with information on her revised flight booking. Hannah noted the reservation number on Lufthansa but there were another two messages waiting. The second was from Danielle again, this time to let Hannah know that her cousin in New Jersey, Sheryl Shapiro, had called to say that she planned to fly to Montreal with a friend to attend a family bar mitzvah in mid-November, asking if Hannah would be available to meet with her then. With something bordering on excitement, Hannah made a note and saved the message. The last message was from Marilyn and, because it was long distance, she'd kept it brief.

"Where the hell are you? Call me."

CHAPTER FORTY-EIGHT

"**W**here are you, Hannah? Why haven't you kept in touch like you said you would?"

When they finally connected Marilyn's voice was high-pitched and grating, the force of the questions straightening Hannah's back. Her friend had not wasted so much as a moment to say 'Hello ... how are you?' but had immediately leapt in on the attack. It was a tactic Barak used to employ and it took her by surprise that Marilyn was using it now.

Hannah quietly replied that she was still in Germany as she had told Marilyn she would be and that she had not called because there was a lot going on. The information, rather than calming her friend, seemed to upset Marilyn.

"You told me that you were going to Germany for four days and it's been almost a week without a word. What is going on there that you're so busy you don't remember to keep in touch as you promised? I was worried; you could have been dead!"

"Really, Marilyn, don't be so dramatic. I'm not one of your daughters."

"Is it that Mohr guy?" Marilyn said lowering her voice. "Is he the one keeping you busy?"

The question was so blatant yet right on the mark that Hannah had the unpleasant sensation Marilyn had been spying on her. The strong note of disapproval set off warning signals. Normally Hannah would have happily shared all her news—about the unforeseen ending to the real estate deal, the blooming love affair with Max, the visit to Landsberg—but Marilyn's verbal assault pushed her into a protective silence. In this situation, she would not provide additional ammunition to stock Marilyn's anger arsenal. Instead, she deflected the attack by sharing that she was going to meet her second cousin, Sheryl Shapiro, in November.

"What second cousin?" Marilyn asked, her voice wavering with news of yet another unknown.

"I told you about the phone call I received last month from a woman in New Jersey who said our mothers were first cousins." Being met with silence, Hannah rushed on. "Honestly, Marilyn, I thought I told you. I guess with all that has been going on since Rokhl ... well, since my mother ..." Hannah was unable to say the words, 'killed herself'. "Since her death, I've lost track of the things I've told you or sometimes forgot that I meant to. I'm really sorry if I worried you, Marilyn. I'm coming home next Saturday, and with a head full of things to sort out. I can't talk about it now so please, don't ask me. But we'll talk about it when I get home. I can tell you one thing for certain, for the first time in a long time, I am seeing choices about the directions I want to take, and there's no one I have to answer to before I decide. I am also realizing that there is more of my life behind me than ahead and so I have to figure out how to make the most of what I have left."

"Well," Marilyn finally said after a sufficiently dramatic pause, "I guess that you are more like Rokhl than you thought. Just a well of deep secrets but, don't forget, we have always relied on each other's counsel when making important decisions."

Hannah agreed with a sigh, decoding the secret message Marilyn was sending: I'm the only one you can trust.

"What was that all about?" Max asked as he reached to pull Hannah towards him.

"Just my best friend doing what she thinks is in my better interest."

Hannah leaned in to kiss Max lightly on the lips, but he was having none of that. He wanted more and, in moments, so did Hannah.

↝ Early the next morning, Leni called Max to say she was coming into town later to do some shopping and suggested they have lunch. The call came as no surprise; he knew that Leni would get in touch when she figured out that Hannah was not a casual affair.

"Meet me at the Excelsior. I'll treat you to a lavish lunch at the *Hanse Stube*. I just got a very nice dividend cheque." She laughed at his protesting groan. "Don't be so macho. I'm your sister and I like to share a treat with you when I so rarely can. And to see you twice in one week, *ja, prima!*"

The restaurant was as elegant as Max remembered as his last visit was not a happy one, since it was here that Nicole and he had argued over whether he would ever father another child. He wondered if Leni remembered that story and if that was why she had chosen this particular restaurant from so many others available in Köln. She spotted him as he walked in and waved from a booth in a corner of the room. Dressed in a caramel-coloured cashmere turtleneck with a chunky Berber necklace he had gifted her years ago, his sister was unquestionably the most elegant woman in the room. He leaned in and kissed her warmly on both cheeks.

"You look wonderful as usual," Max said, sliding into the booth across from Leni.

"Save your charm for where it matters," she responded with a sly smile. "Use it on Hannah." A glass of chardonnay in her hand, she said she had taken the liberty of ordering him a *Kölsch*. Leni knew what he liked. When the server appeared with the beer, they quickly ordered their lunch.

"*Prost*, dear brother," Leni said, raising her glass again. "I drink to a happy future for you." Taking a sip, she looked intently at Max who was waiting patiently for the barrage of questions he knew to be coming.

"She is lovely, your Hannah—" she said.

"She's not my Hannah ... not yet anyway, but I very much want her to be, Leni. I have never before felt so sure of my feelings for a woman."

"That is evident in the way you look at her. It's almost as if you want to inhale her. And I think she may feel the same way about you

246

but probably is not ready to admit it yet. What do you think could hold her back?"

Max took a long haul on his beer and shook his head slowly. He had only a few theories. He supposed, he said, it could be concern about how they would be able to sustain a long-distance romance or the fact that she was businesswoman who had fought long and hard for a position that he might end up suggesting she abandon. Also, she had been married briefly, Max told Leni, and that had not ended well but luckily, he added, there were no children.

"What about her parents and siblings?" Leni asked.

"She was an only child. Both her parents are dead, her mother just within the last few months, I believe."

"And they were *jüdisch*. Hannah is Jewish, *ja?*"

"What has that got to do with anything, Leni? You know I left the church after Nadya absconded with Alexander. You and I do not practice any religion; a Tannenbaum at Christmas is the full extent of it so what has Hannah being Jewish have to do with anything?"

Leni slowly shook her head as she cast a baleful eye at her brother. He looked at her with that open, earnest expression he had as a young boy when he had asked her why no one ever talked about *Vati*. He wanted to know where he had gone, and why?

"Don't you think that our father being a Nazi, an SS command-ant, may give Hannah something to wonder about? If she is *jüdisch*, born in a refugee camp, does it not mean her parents were Holocaust survivors? Are you so naïve? Even at 52 years of age, do you not im-agine that, for some people, history is not something you read in a book, but is inculcated in their bones, their DNA?" She leaned back in her chair and combed her fingers through her silver hair.

"Being born after the war, you have no idea what Eva and I lived through. I came out of it determined never to be poor and starving again because that's what we were in 1945 as the war was ending. Eva and I scavenged for food along with gangs of other children. *Omi* sold her jewellery and *Mutti's* fur coat and fancy dresses so that we would have bread and cheese on the table. When *Vati* finally came home it was better for a while. According to *Omi* he seemed to have a secret source of funds but, after you were born and the Allies began arresting former commandants, *Vati* said he had to go away for a while, and that was the last we saw of him."

"Why have you never told me any of this before, Leni? I am no longer a child. I have a right to know."

"You were our hope, Maximilian, for all of us, our hope for the future, a fresh start so we could forget about the rallies, the marching boots, the nastiness that seemed to spread like a virus. We wanted to forget about the people lying broken on the street after some run-in with the brown shirts. Or how we were taught to love Hitler. *Omi* made sure that we didn't. She fought with *Mutti* about it. When you were born, we wanted to believe there was a future. And then we learned that our father was a wanted war criminal for countless acts of murder and profiteering in the Lodz Ghetto. Why did we not tell you that? Because it had all happened before you were born so why should you carry the mark of Cain? We changed our name back to *Mutti's* maiden name, to *Omi's* last name, and we made a new life."

Max leaned back and, like Leni had done, ran his hand through his hair. His face was a landscape shadowed by storm clouds.

"So, you're saying what? That this somehow has an impact on my relationship and my future with Hannah? If I didn't know about my own history, how would this affect Hannah?"

"Because, dear brother, it is not what she knows of our history that you should be concerned about. It is what she knows of her own that may open an impassable gulf."

CHAPTER FORTY-NINE

Max lay on his side, his head propped up on his right hand, gazing down at Hannah sleeping beside him. In the light filtering through the jalousies, he memorized the curve of her jaw and the way her thick lashes formed two dark crescent moons against cheeks pale as night clouds. He reached out to touch a coil of hair scrunched on the pillow. He had awoken with a start at first light, his head buzzing with the realization that they had only one more day before Hannah left for Montreal. After all the time they had spent together, he still had no idea when they would meet again. Neither seemed to have the courage to broach the subject of what future their relationship might hold yet he knew that, having found this woman who challenged him, infuriated, and fascinated him, he could not lose her. Hannah stirred and moaned in her sleep. He put his hand on her shoulder and she grew calm. Max lay back on the pillow replaying his conversation with Leni and her reaction after he had suggested that she might be over-analyzing Hannah. She accused him of being naïve.

"Why had you wanted me to meet Hannah if not so that I could tell you what I thought about her, about whether you have a future together?" she had asked.

He had protested and made a joke of it saying that he simply wanted her to advise him on how not to make a mess of this relationship. At this, she had shrugged her shoulders and ordered another glass of chardonnay as if to imply that her part was done, and it was high time he stopped fooling himself. Was he doing that? he wondered. Was he falling back on old patterns? Hannah was waking and turned towards him nuzzling into his shoulder, their arms and legs so intertwined he could not tell where he ended, and she began. He ran his hand over her hair again and again, loving the way the curls sprung back beneath his fingers.

"You'll never straighten my hair that way," she said, a taunting laughter in her voice.

A moment of regret gripped him as he realized he would have given anything to father a child with this woman. He hugged her so hard she protested.

⮑ Hannah was slow to open her eyes and survey the room, the bedroom of Max's apartment. Yesterday, she had finally agreed to dinner at his flat. If he had asked her why she twice turned down his invitation, she would have been hard put to come up with a reasonable answer. She was glad she had finally accepted as both the meal and the apartment were surprisingly pleasant. Max lived on the top floor of an attractive three-story building on Rurstrasse, a lovely tree-lined street in an area that appeared to highly value trees. There was a tranquil botanical garden mere blocks away, he told her, someplace he often strolled through when he needed to let his mind solve problems without any deep-thinking intruding on the process. It was a place where he could let go, he said. Hannah thought of the view from her living room window and how she often stood staring out onto Montreal's downtown skyline as a way of arriving at a moment of calm. Not exactly the same, she had to admit.

Max's apartment was an eclectic mix of modern furnishings and antiques which, although not her style, proved to be very pleasing to the eye. There was a lacquered Italian contemporary breakfront which somehow mixed well with African sculptures and masks. A startling orange leather sofa was surprisingly softened juxtaposed between two tall palms next to a half wall of windows. He had also done some interesting things with lighting so that the entire effect of the living and dining area was calming. The candlelight dinner had been a simple but impressive three course affair: a fresh green salad of mâche with a honey lemon dressing, chicken roasted in a lemon garlic Dijon sauce, and *Bratkartoffeln,* fried potatoes. For dessert, Max had brought out a *Schwarzwälder* torte with a candle in it.

"What's that for?" Hannah asked, eyeing the torte with trepidation. She had eaten more than her fill of the incredibly savoury chicken.

"It is your one-week anniversary of being in Germany and, to my mind, a cause for celebration," he said. "I believe that the course of your life can change in a minute, but sometimes it takes a week." He draped his arm around her shoulders. "I hope you feel the same way. And if you do, I hope we can talk about what comes next because you never did answer my question."

Hannah kissed him lightly on the cheek and drew closer to the candle. A sense of composure descended on her from some surprising place she had not known existed. For the first time, she knew what she had to tell Max.

"OK, I will blow out the candle and make a wish for our future."

Her words hit the mark. Max's grin stretched from ear to ear, and the deepening of his dimples emphasized his happiness. Hannah snuffed the candle easily and took Max by the hand, leading him to the couch where she sat down facing him. And then she told him everything. What it was like growing up with a mother who was unable to show affection or communicate in any normal way, and a father who was bellicose and bossy. She had never heard the words 'I love you' from either although she never doubted that they did in fact love her. She described growing up an only child without family, how she felt when Barak died, and the horror of Rokhl's disappearance, how she blamed herself. Haltingly, she described what she went through to finally learn that her mother had killed herself. That took the longest to recount and, several times, she had to put her hand on Max's chest to keep him from comforting her. She explained how she was still processing what happened and what it meant to her life now that she was all alone.

At this last confession, Max enveloped her in his arms and said she could choose not to be alone ever again but, once more, Hannah gently pushed him away asking him to allow her to finish because this was probably one of the hardest things she had ever set out to do.

"Sharing is not my forte," she said thinking of Marilyn and her friend's justifiable anger. "But I want you to know this story so you will understand that I am, for the first time in my life, examining the paths open to me. That's hard to do when you have no real understanding about the forces that have impacted your life, when you don't know where you come from, and the chronicle of your life is incomplete."

Hannah sighed.

"When we were in Landsberg, I realized that I was looking for something magical to happen. I hoped it would suddenly become apparent who I am and where I came from, maybe more specifically, *who* I came from. It was there in the town where I was born—and later, meeting Leni—that I realized I know nothing of my history except what my father told me. But why should I believe him? He told me we had no living relatives, and it turns out I have a cousin in New Jersey I knew nothing about. But my mother knew, and she kept it from me. Why would she do that? I have so many questions and very few possibilities for answers because, well ... everybody is dead."

Hannah stopped as if she had just come across a hidden cave and was afraid to enter. The words that had come pouring out were as close as she had ever come to acknowledging her deepest fears. She turned to Max.

"I love you," she said, "and you have no idea how long it has been that I have said that to anyone. Or felt about anyone the way I do about you. I can't explain how or why but I trust you to do me no harm. I was never so sure of anyone as I am of you. And that is why I must ask you to understand that I must find out whatever I can about where I am and where I want to go. I need to go home. I have to meet this cousin, my only living relative, and learn what she knows about my past, if anything. As a social worker, I worked with Holocaust survivors and studied their files never once thinking to look up my own parents. I don't know why I didn't. Maybe I was afraid of what I would learn. There were questions I never asked my father although he always seemed prepared to share stories about the war, but his stories were always the same. Maybe I was afraid to open an old wound, too scared to dig up something that was best left buried ..."

Hannah stopped, suddenly out of steam. She looked up with an expression that that's all there is. She saw Max was nodding his head, a pained look written across his face as if her words had struck a nerve. They sat like that in silence for several minutes. Max had to accept that Leni had been right about the situation, but he had no way to explain to Hannah that he understood what she was saying.

Finally, he took her hands in his, kissed the palms and said, "I trust you, too, Hannah, and leave in your beautiful hands our fate. I believe you will find a way back to me and I will wait for however long it takes because I believe in you and what we feel for each other. A month ago, if you would have asked me whether I believed that love could conquer all, I would have laughed. I am still unsure about love, but I am very sure about you. You will find a way for us to be together. I believe it."

CHAPTER FIFTY

To avoid a stopover in Munich, Max drove Hannah two hours to Frankfurt so she could catch a direct flight home. It was a sombre journey, Hannah silently reviewing the twists and turns over eight days in Germany. It felt like she had been away from Montreal for a month. She had come to Cologne to make a real estate deal and, despite the deal evaporating like water on a July sidewalk, she was leaving with more than she ever expected possible. In a little more than a week, she had said things she never imagined herself uttering, discovered roads leading back to and away from a life she had so carefully constructed. It had, in some ways, been handed to her as a fait accompli, the circumstances of which she had never before questioned.

Hannah had made only three of what she considered the biggest decisions in her life—to marry Albie, to leave social work to become a real estate broker, and to go to Germany against her mother's wishes. It was like entering an alternate universe when Max appeared. He was not only a catalyst who lifted her from the known patterns of her life; he had demonstrated that he loved her whole-heartedly. What did that mean? she wondered, as they headed to the airport at a suspiciously slower pace than they had left it? Whole-hearted. She had never really understood the meaning of that word. From early on, she had been taught to measure life in teaspoons when she could have been using cups all along. Max revealed to her one other important thing:

how to trust. It was a lesson she often found herself unable to hold in good faith. Doubt crept into her ear like an annoying insect, making unpleasant noises in her head.

⌒⌐ Max also remained quiet during the drive. Once at the airport, he parked the M5 in the cavernous garage, took Hannah's bag out of the trunk, opened the passenger side door, and walked Hannah to the counter where she picked up her ticket and checked a bag. Max was focusing on executing each action with methodical precision meant to hold him together. He wasn't at all sure it was working. He was attempting to memorize every small detail of their last moments together like a squirrel storing nuts for the winter. He noted that Hannah's choice of attire was the same smart business attire he had seen her in when she arrived. Yet there was something different in her appearance—in the relaxed line of her jaw, the slope of her shoulders as she stood beside him, and the glistening in her striking violet-blue eyes. Although they had not determined when they would see each other again, they had voiced a commitment that it would be in the not-too-distant future. Finally, at the gate, they stood side-by-side, silently holding hands. When it came time for her to pass through, Max kissed Hannah lightly on the lips and whispered *Auf Wiedersehen. Bis bald.* Let it be soon. He stood rooted to the spot, watching her disappear, and remained unmoving for some time after she was gone.

⌒⌐ In line at security, Hannah did not turn around for fear that, if she saw Max one more time, she would make a spectacle of herself. Instead, she walked through the process mechanically. She thought about her call with Marilyn the day before to let her know when she was arriving. Despite her best efforts to dissuade her, Marilyn insisted that she would pick her up at Dorval. And there she was waiting for Hannah as she came through the gate. Marilyn wrapped her arms around her friend and pulled her into her ample bosom to convey how happy she was to see her home, safe and sound. Hannah surrendered to her friend's affection, knowing that what was to come might not be as warm. During the eight-hour flight, Hannah had settled on how she would deal with the inevitable barrage of questions Marilyn was certain to fire at her.

"You look different," Marilyn said, holding her friend at arm's length. "But really wonderful."

Hannah took the compliment with a smile and quickly changed the subject, asking after Marilyn, her girls, and Bram, and what the weather had been like over the past week. Stepping outside, the air was crisper than in Germany, Hannah observed, as they walked to the car. Once on Highway 20, Marilyn sat back in the driver's seat, a little more relaxed after negotiating the Dorval Circle, one of Montreal's many complicated interchanges.

"So, are you going to tell me how the deal with that German real estate mogul went? Did you get what you wanted? Was that Mohr guy a tough negotiator?"

Hannah couldn't help but smile at Marilyn's obvious approach to the information she was after.

"It went well for Sonenshein is all I can tell you. In fact, it turned out to be pretty much of a done deal by the time I arrived. As for Max Mohr, well, he turned out to be a pushover although we didn't really have a lot of opportunity to negotiate."

"Really?" Marilyn quickly swivelled her eyes off the road ahead to catch a glimpse of Hannah's face. It always held some hint of turmoil roiling beneath the surface. Marilyn believed she would know when her friend was withholding but this time, what she saw was a look of utter calm. She had been right in her first observation. Hannah did look different in a way that Marilyn, after a lifetime of knowing her, was suddenly unable to put her finger on.

"Should we stop for a bite of something before I take you home?" she asked. "You don't usually eat on planes if I recall correctly."

"Yes. That would be great. How about Robichaud & LaFortune? I love their Mexican," Hannah replied with more enthusiasm than Marilyn expected.

Yes, something was definitely different.

Once seated, they gave the server their orders, which included a margarita for Hannah. Marilyn laced her fingers and folded her hands on the table in front of her like the good teacher she had been, waiting for her star pupil to recite what she had learned. It was clear to Marilyn that there was no need for her to ask questions or pry; Hannah was going to share as much as she wanted and not an iota more. Until the food arrived, they made small talk about Bram rising in the ranks at the Canadian Jewish Congress. Hannah hungrily dug into the guacamole with cumin and took a long sip of her margarita, then smiled broadly at Marilyn.

"So, this is the story and, if you want to hear all of it, I'm going to ask you not to interrupt or I will lose my nerve and won't be able to continue."

Marilyn nodded in agreement, ran fingers across her lips to zip her mouth, folded her hands again and leaned in. Hannah began to describe what had happened from her first meeting with Max to the supper at the Ritz, and to how she felt so disoriented when he picked her up at the airport in Cologne. Seeing the look of disbelief in Marilyn's eyes, she tried to explain how she had found Max so intriguing from the outset, so different than any of the other men she had known. But, she explained, due to their business negotiations she had not initially allowed herself to do anything more than focus on the land deal. Max and everything about him had been shoved into some dark recess of her brain after Rokhl's death but, when the meeting in Germany was finally re-scheduled, something shifted for her. She spoke in an almost dream-like state as if telling herself the story. Doors were appearing where none had been visible before, she said. Whether to walk through them or not became a daily dilemma. She told Marilyn about going to Landsberg and the realization that she had no idea what she was looking for because she knew so little of her own history. Finally, Marilyn could not hold her tongue a minute longer.

"Did you sleep with him?" Marilyn asked, her eyes fixed on Hannah's face. She didn't really need an answer. She already knew.

"I did. Because I love him, and he loves me."

"Of course, he loves you," Marilyn said leaning back in her chair. "Why wouldn't he love you? You are a beautiful, accomplished, self-sufficient woman. If you'd let them, men would be forever sitting at your feet. But since your divorce, you've kept them at bay until they all gave up. My question is how can you love him? He is only one generation from those who robbed, raped, starved, and murdered our families. How could you betray them by loving him? A German?"

With this last question, Marilyn's voice had grown louder and several women at the surrounding tables turned to look at the two of them.

"I love Max. And would continue to do so, no matter if he was a different colour or nationality. He is a kind, intelligent, thoughtful man. A gentle man in every possible definition of that word."

Marilyn was shaking her head, her face betraying the effort she was making to mask her fury.

"You're a fool, Hannah, if you think this can work out well. This is some kind of schoolgirl infatuation brought on by the tragedy you have been through. Believe me, I know you. You will come to your senses in no time."

Something in Marilyn's tone and her accusation that Hannah was only experiencing a schoolgirl crush inflamed her cheeks. It was Rokhl's accusation on the last night they were together, yelling at her: *Du bist eine narish kindt.* And here was Marilyn also accusing her of being a silly child. Hannah rose from the table and without a word, went to the cash to pay their bill. When she returned, she batted away Marilyn's hand as she tried to repay her portion. In a voice tight with control Hannah asked to be taken home. She said she was tired and needed to get to bed.

CHAPTER FIFTY-ONE

Monday was insanely busy. During Hannah's first day back at her desk, Danielle kept running into her office carrying another contract for review, another surveyor's report, another bid. The only moment of respite in the entire day came around noon when Max called, their first opportunity to talk since she had left Germany. He wanted to know how she was feeling, was she jetlagged? Unspoken but clear was the question: Are you missing me?

"The flight was easy, and I am feeling fine. But I'm unhappy about a fight I had with my oldest friend, the one who picked me up at Dorval."

Max asked what it was about, but Hannah was vague, saying only that it was a serious difference in point of view although not fatal; they would work it out. "But I awoke this morning thinking about how was it that Marilyn and I became so angry so fast? Although I'm very surprised that I'm not more upset. I can't explain it, but I have this feeling that, if I just let things take their natural course, everything will get resolved somehow. This is a new philosophy I'm adopting."

Max chuckled as she hoped he would. Hannah had fudged the answer. When Marilyn met Max—and that was inevitable—she would feel differently about him, see him for what he was: a man who loved her dearest friend.

"May I give you a wake-up call tomorrow?" Max asked.

"Of course, it's OK," she answered, but as soon as they signed off, she wondered if this daily contact would make it more difficult for her to sort out her feelings. Doubt was forever poking her in the ribs. She shook the thought from her head and turned back to the files piled on her desk.

↪ By the end of the day, jetlagged and too exhausted to make the trek down Atwater, Hannah hailed a cab and returned to the apartment. When she got home, as she was putting her keys away in her purse, Hannah found a paper note she had shoved into it. She had forgotten; the message Danielle had passed on to her about Sheryl Shapiro's visit to Montreal. Time had become so fluid lately that Hannah was surprised that her cousin's visit was coming up the following week. As she had requested, Dani had called Sheryl to arrange for a day during her visit to spend with Hannah, and Sheryl had responded that in fact, she had arranged to fly back two days after the *simcha* to give her time to get to know her new cousin. Hannah put the message slip on her desk to tag it in her agenda.

It occurred to her that perhaps she should make a list of what she knew about her mother's background—as brief as that would be—to rundown with Sheryl who might be able to add something to their shared history. What would she put on that list? What could she, knowing so little? She drifted off thinking of her mother's notes untouched, unread, and mostly, forgotten.

CHAPTER FIFTY-TWO

Meeting her first-ever cousin made Hannah as jumpy as a teenager on a blind date. Sheryl Shapiro called as soon as she arrived in Montreal to confirm the time and place for their get-together. She was staying with friends in Côte Saint-Luc. Hannah offered to pick her up and suggested that they have a get-to-know-you lunch, then head over to Hannah's condo for an afternoon of exchanging stories. *To the extent that I have anything worth sharing,* Hannah thought anxiously. As she drove up to the neat bungalow on Mackle Road, she spotted a woman standing on the porch, craning her neck for the blue Subaru she had been told to look for. A shiver ran down her arms and spine when Sheryl finally came into full view.

If there had been any doubt that they were related, the sight of her new cousin erased it. Petite and compactly built, Hannah was looking at a twin to Rokhl, but with red hair like her own. It suddenly occurred to Hannah that her mother may have once been a redhead although she had only ever known Rokhl with hair the colour of freshly fallen snow. Pulling up to the curb, Hannah stepped out of the car and suddenly felt awkward as she stood looming over her diminutive cousin. Without hesitation, Sheryl reached up and gathered her cousin into a surprisingly strong embrace, then took a step back to fully examine this woman she had longed to meet.

"So, let me look at you, Cousin," she said, her arms stretched out.

She made no effort to hide her glistening eyes. "I can't tell you how excited I am to be here. To meet you at last. I just know my mother, Fenia, is in *Gan Eden* looking down and *qvelling* to see us together."

Hannah remained frozen to the curb, overcome by her cousin's emotional display. A moment later, without thinking, she returned Sheryl's hug.

"We have a lot to talk about," Hannah said, "Come. Let's get off the street and into a restaurant. I don't know about you, but I need a glass of celebratory wine."

⇝ They drove to Old Montreal, to one of Hannah's favourite haunts, La Cheminée. Along the way, Sheryl had kept up a steady stream of chatter about how she had wangled an invitation to the bar mitzvah of her friend's grandson, the surprisingly short flight from Newark, and how much she liked the little she had seen of Montreal on this first visit. Hannah caught the implication that she hoped there would be occasion for more.

"Ooh ... it's so lovely," Sheryl exclaimed as they drove down rue St. Paul. "I feel like I'm in another world here." They parked the car and entered the restaurant to a cry of delight from the owner.

"*Ah, Mme Baran, c'est un grand plaisir vous revoir.*"

"It's lovely to see you again, too, Henri. It's been too long. I'd like to introduce you to my cousin from *les États-Unis,* Sheryl Shapiro."

"*Enchanté, Madame, et bienvenue,*" Henri said with a slight dip of his polished bald head.

He led them to the reserved table near the window. Sitting down, Sheryl was beaming from ear-to-ear. They gave Henri their drink orders and, as he bustled away, the two women fell momentarily silent, the weight of the myriad of questions they had been saving pushing their way to the surface. When their wine arrived, they ceremoniously clinked glasses and smiled across the table.

"Well, where do we begin?" Sheryl asked, sipping at her chardonnay.

"Why don't you start? Tell me about your mother, Fenia," Hannah said lowering her gaze when she saw Sheryl's eyes well up. There was a tinge of guilt as Hannah thought about how few tears she had shed for Rokhl.

"My mother Fenia was a remarkable woman, one who was truly *feyig,* as my father used to say. There wasn't anything she couldn't turn her hand to. She sewed and knitted and had a wonderful fashion sense. She had a natural affinity for math, which I sadly did not inherit as she did all the books for my father's insurance agency for years; he didn't trust anyone else. She was also a marvellous cook, homemaker, and a talented musician. She played the piano daily until just before she died. And she sang as she played. Sometimes, I can hear the sound of my mother's high, clear voice in my dreams."

Once again Sheryl's eyes were swimming.

"It sounds like your mother was a wonderfully happy person. You are fortunate to have had her in your life," Hannah said, tamping down her envy.

"Yes, she was, mostly. But there was another side to her, a deep sadness that started to show more as she grew older especially after she was diagnosed with ovarian cancer. It was around then she started talking more and more about the war, and her long dead family. Her parents and two brothers were in the Warsaw Ghetto, but my grandfather had managed to get her out before the uprising in '43. For some reason he was certain she could fend for herself, so he paid off a Jewish policeman to help my mother slip out of the ghetto and onto the Polish side. She managed to stay hidden in the countryside, foraging for food for almost a year. Around the end of 1943, however, she was caught and immediately put on a transport to Auschwitz."

"Auschwitz? She was in Auschwitz? But my mother was there, too … although she never spoke of it," Hannah said, then seeing the look of anticipation on Sheryl's face, added, "She didn't speak very much at all about anything—never about her childhood, never about the war. Everything I know about those times I learned from my father's stories."

Sheryl shifted in her chair. "It may have been that speaking of the war raised memories for her that were too painful."

"Maybe," Hannah said, unconvinced.

"My mother was young," Sheryl said, "and in relatively good physical condition and resourceful. So, she survived. Barely. What kept her alive was hope. She said she never let go of the belief that she would find her family again, despite having heard the rumours that the Ghetto had been razed to the ground. She had little hope that her parents had survived but her brothers were young and part of the resistance. She idolized them and was certain they would somehow survive. That hope grew when she saw her aunt—your grandmother, Liba —playing the violin in the camp orchestra. She saw her every dawn as she left the camp on work details and when she came home half dead at—"

"What? Wait! My grandmother?" Hannah was thunderstruck. "She was at Auschwitz, too?"

Hannah's hand reached across the table for Sheryl's arm, her eyes as large as saucers.

"I'm sorry to interrupt but you must tell me about my grandmother. My own mother never spoke of her. Not a word. All I know is her name."

Sheryl took Hannah's hand in hers and held it like a wounded bird.

"According to my mother, Rokhl would have had good reason never to speak of Tante Liba. My mother told me that at the outset of the war your grandmother abandoned her daughter and husband —your grandfather—in Krakow and fled to her family in Warsaw. Tante Liba was a talented musician but a heartless woman by all accounts. My mother said your grandmother had no love for her own child, sharp words from a woman who I never knew to have anything bad to say against anyone. My mother liked your grandfather though. She said he was a good man who clearly adored not only his wife but his daughter."

"My grandmother played the violin?" Hannah's mind was on its hands and knees crawling through a mine field. Whatever she was expecting from her encounter with Sheryl, this was already more than she had bargained for.

"Yes, your grandmother was very accomplished. Our great-grandfather and your great-uncle were also gifted musically but both became highly respected doctors in Warsaw. My mother said that Tante Liba arrived back in her native city expecting to find the world as she had left it on the day she married and moved away to Krakow. But that world was already gone. I'm sure you know your history, Hannah. The first targets of the Germans were academics, professionals, the intelligentsia. A few months after Liba returned, things grew worse daily. First the family had to share their home with relatives including my mother's family—"

"Wait," Hannah said, a tremor in her voice, "you have to draw the lines for me. Remind me how we are related?"

"Oh, I'm sorry. I thought you knew. Well, my grandfather, Moritz, and your grandmother, Liba, were brother and sister. "Liba was younger, very beautiful and talented and, my mother said, apparently indulged growing up. That did not serve her well in the end. Moritz—"

"Your grandfather?" Hannah said.

"Right. He was an architect and, when the uprising in the ghetto began, he and his sons, my uncles, helped the partisans navigate the underground city."

Hannah raised her hand as if in surrender just as the main course arrived. The women momentarily glanced at their plates, smiled at the waiter and looked at one another as if to signal that the story should continue between bites.

"My mother, Fenia, was one of three children—the middle child between two brothers—but she was the only one to survive the war and that haunted her."

"Can you tell me more about my grandfather Shimon?" Hannah asked, softly.

"Not much more," Sheryl said. "My mother only saw him a few times after your parents married. She seemed to have liked him and was a little envious of your mother who, she said, was like a little grown-up, always beautifully dressed, very seriously chatting with the adults, very anxious to impress and please."

"Mmm," Hannah said, trying to imagine her mother as anything but a cipher. She wondered what happened to that young girl that would still her tongue for the rest of her life. "And when your mother saw my grandmother in the orchestra?"

"It was some time after my mother arrived at Auschwitz, maybe a month, before she even recognized her aunt. She clearly had violent encounters and the evidence was on her face. Although it took her some time to recognize Tante Liba, it somehow gave her hope that perhaps there were others of her family still alive. And she tried, as much as was possible, to seek her out in the women's compound."

Hannah's knife and fork hovered over her plate, her back rigid against the seat as Sheryl laid out a small slice of her history. She leaned forward and, in a voice, barely above a whisper said, "Why don't we eat our food before it grows stone cold? This story has waited so long, it can wait a little longer." And she lowered her cutlery. "*Bon appétit,* dear cousin. I can't thank you enough for making this journey and sharing this story with me."

Sheryl nodded her head. Despite their intentions, they ate in silence, each lost in thought.

As the waiter cleared their plates Sheryl said, "That was absolutely delicious."

"Are you up for dessert?" Hannah asked. "They make a killer *crème brûlée* Ricardo with vanilla and rum. Or would you prefer your alcohol in a glass?"

"Oh no." Sheryl was laughing and shook her carefully coiffed head. "The chardonnay was enough for now. No dessert, but I'd love a coffee. Do they have Americano?"

"Here we call that an *espresso allongée* ... elongated. Yes, they have it."

Coffees ordered, the two women leaned back in their chairs and smiled at one another like co-conspirators. For Hannah, what Sheryl had shared was the key to a secret code, the existence of which had been a lifelong mystery. Suddenly, it unlocked a door behind which Rokhl stood. It also introduced her to a haughty grandmother who abandoned her family in the time of their direst needs. She wondered if Rokhl's coldness had been learned at her mother's knee.

"Did your mother ever talk to my grandmother?"

"No," Sheryl said. "Tante Liba just disappeared one day, replaced by another violinist. My mother understood she was gone for good. That was around the time that she thought she saw your mother. Mameh said it was hard to be sure that it was actually her. The woman looked like Rokhl but her hair had been her most outstanding feature. Of course, most heads were shaved and often covered by rags to keep the scalp warm. But there was something else. The woman was standing next to Mandl, the commandant they called The Beast, looking like her aide. And like I told you on the phone, my mother noticed that she was wearing a red triangle not a yellow star."

"What?" Hannah asked sitting up. "What do you mean a red triangle?"

"The red triangle was how the Nazis distinguished political prisoners, mostly Poles. It's what led my mother to believe that she was mistaken, that the woman with Mandl could not be her cousin."

Hannah cleared her throat, hesitating a moment. "When you come to the condo after lunch," she said, her eyes fixed on the tablecloth, "I want to show you something I found while cleaning out my parents' home last September. But please, finish this story. It has opened up a world I have been shut out of for my whole life."

Sheryl gave her a curious look but continued. "Shortly after the sighting, my mother was shipped to Monowitz as a slave labourer in the synthetic rubber plant. She survived the work there and the death march that led her to Bergen-Belsen. When the war ended, it's not clear to me how but she managed to get back to Warsaw only to find everything she had ever known was gone. Along the way, she met my father. They fell in love, or in need, I am still not sure which. I was born in Flossenbürg and we immigrated to the States in 1949. I was just a year old. And that's my story."

Sheryl looked up to find Hannah's face frozen, expressionless. "What's the matter, Hannah? I can see I have distressed you. I'm so sorry."

Hannah shook her head slowly, softly, and somehow found her voice. "I have never realized how utterly bereft I am of my own history. You have given me a great gift, Sheryl, a piece of a puzzle that helps me envision some of the landscape that was part of my mother's life and, if not a window, at least a peephole on who she was before the war."

CHAPTER FIFTY-THREE

The days had been inordinately busy since her return from Germany and Sheryl's subsequent visit. It had been like this for weeks. It seemed the only moments of tranquillity were Max's morning wake-up calls. Unbidden, thoughts of him accompanied her throughout the day, but Hannah had come to realize that she was missing Max less and less as the memory of their time together grew faint, like an old photo. Still, she relished the intimacy of the morning calls and the unspoken but clear question that hung in the air between them: *Are you missing me?* So, each conversation served to rekindle the flame, if only for that moment. Hot and cold. That's the way Hannah was running, unable to settle on what the future might hold for this impossible romance.

One morning, Max asked how things were going with Marilyn. Hannah, who had mentioned they had a falling out upon her return to Montreal, confessed that they were still not talking.

"I guess what happened between us was surprising for both of us. I never before challenged her mixture of love and intimidation. Anyway, when I thought about it, I realized I'm not too upset by the situation."

One Friday, at the end of a gruelling week, Hannah grabbed a cab back to the apartment. When she got home, she shed her clothes, washed her face and put on her sweats, then stood by the living room window letting exhaustion wash over her. It was already two weeks since Sheryl had returned to New Jersey. She left with a promise to stay in touch on a regular basis and had already sent Hannah the URL of some websites that might be helpful in researching the family history. More and more information has been uncovered every year, she said. It was something Sheryl had decided to delve into more deeply just as her mother fell ill.

The idea of research was not tempting to Hannah but something Sheryl had said echoed in her brain.

"At birth," she said, "we're handed a suitcase that someone else has packed and we carry it without thinking until one day, usually in middle age when we have acquired so much baggage of our own, we realize how heavy it is and we start to wonder what the hell is inside."

The weight of Rokhl's story was so light yet ever-present. She ought to write down everything she knew, Hannah thought, as Sheryl had suggested. She could supplement the story with a list of ... what could she call them ... hints or clues Rokhl may have left in her notes? Her shoulders sagged with the thought. Was she really ready for the work of researching her mother's tragic past? The sharp edges of Rokhl's death, the way she had abandoned Hannah, the mystery she left behind, had become a little dulled with the passing months. Hannah thought back to when she had shown Sheryl the red felt triangle she had found, the black threads that once bound it to cloth, still dangling from its edges.

"Another key to my mother's story with no lock to open," she had said. Sheryl held the cloth gently, turned it over in her hand, rubbing the worn felt with her thumb as if trying to divine its significance, its source.

"Where do you think your mother got this?" Sheryl asked. Hannah shrugged, feeling as lost as a child in the woods.

"And why would she have kept it? It must have held some significance. If I recall correctly, at Auschwitz it identified a Polish political prisoner."

Hannah shrugged again, burning with shame over her ignorance.

It was just one more piece of the puzzle to add to the Rokhl enigma but with no guiding overview to lead to any kind of conclusions, logical or otherwise. At least Sheryl had put questions to her mother while she was alive, not waited until it was too late to ever ask.

⌐ Maybe it was high time to tackle the notes that she had so carefully stashed away in shoeboxes over the decades. Since the big clean-up before selling the duplex, the boxes had taken up residence in a corner of her condo locker, like children hiding from the Boogie Man.

The shoeboxes were the last thought she had as she drifted off that night and, in the morning, half asleep, snatches of notes flashed through Hannah's memory like fireflies winking bright for a moment before fading to black. The phone jangling dispelled all thoughts of the notes. Mornings now began with Max whispering into her ear, caressing her with his voice and his longing. There was something new this morning. Would she come to Germany for *Weihnachten* to spend the Christmas season with him and his sisters?

"Maybe," she said. "What's the hurry? It's only early November, Max."

But he persisted, exacting a promise that she would give him a decision by the following week because he wanted to send her the Lufthansa ticket as a Christmas present. After they had said lingering goodbyes, Hannah had a flash of memory, of sitting at breakfast with Max, the table laden with cheeses, meats, soft boiled eggs, and a variety of rolls. It was not the food he ate, Max only consumed small portions but chose what he ate with a sense of equality, and intention. She liked that about Max, the way he stayed in the moment, savouring the pleasure of what he was doing, while he was doing it. Rising from the bed, Hannah drew the shades to find a world scrubbed clean by the first snowfall of the season. Flakes as fat as cotton puffs drifted past her window in a gentle, balletic dance. It cheered her to see the landscape as inviting as a clean page on the first day of school, no erasures or cross outs marring its perfection.

Over her second cup of coffee, Hannah created a list of Rokhl's family facts gleaned in her conversation with Sheryl. The brevity was disheartening. It was time to retrieve the shoeboxes. Dressed in her sweats, she headed to the condo locker, a series of rooms off the indoor garage. When packing the notes away months ago, Hannah had wrapped the old shoeboxes in plastic to guard against moisture. She selected the fourth box the one marked: The Nineties. Once again, she was surprised at its heft. The weight of it momentarily drained her of ambition, and she sat down on a container of kitchenware to compose herself. She stared at the cache and sighed. What was so pressing, she suddenly wondered? Rokhl was now dead more than five months. What was not lost would still be there when she was ready to take on the task, so why now when there were so many other things complicating her life? She thought of Max and the tempting possibility of being with him, if only for a short time. In that moment, she decided she would travel to Germany in December. The past wasn't going anywhere. Rokhl's story would still be there when she was ready for it. Yes, that was a good decision. For now, she could live with that.

Hannah rose and reached up to replace the shoebox alongside the others, but something stayed her movement. Her arms remained outstretched, frozen in place. As if in a trance, she sat back down and brought the box to her lap. Removing the lid, her breath caught in her throat. There was Rokhl's familiar script swimming into view. Not on a pile of notes but filling an entire page, sitting atop a sheaf of papers held together with two broad elastic bands. Hannah could not avert her eyes. The words reached out to her like a pair of open arms.

If you are reading this, Hannaleh, I have gone to the other world, to where my beloved Papa has been waiting so long to greet me. Perhaps I can finally rest now. I have failed you in so many ways, I know. Yet, I cannot abandon you forever and take my story with me. It is your story, too.

—The Beginning—

Acknowledgements

In 2004, I started writing this novel. The following year, I travelled to my birthplace in Passau, Germany, to do some research. That visit, thanks to my dear friend, Jane Hawtin, turned into the award-winning documentary, "My Mother, the Nazi Midwife and Me." That sent me in another direction for the next eight years. In short, this novel was ready for its bar mitzvah by the time it was completed. It might still be lying in a drawer if not for the love, encouragement, sharp eyes, and profound kindness of the many people who have read and commented on it. My gratitude for their contributions goes to the ever-vigilant Elise Moser who read it twice, to Jane Hawtin who asked germane questions, to Marilyn Cooperman, Francine Desjardins, Anna Fuerstenberg, the inimitable Lori Schubert, and the eagle-eyed Liz Ulin; to Anat Bar-Cohen, Esther Safran Foer, and Michlean Amir in the US; the thoughtful David Homel sitting on his porch in Outremont, and the inspiring Susan Doherty. In 2019 I attended Can Serrat, a transformative artists' retreat in Spain. I will always be grateful for the people I met and the space and time it afforded me. For her perseverance and methodical editing, I am most grateful to have had Sonia Di Placido in my corner. And most of all, for his devotion, his reassurance, his patience, proofreading skills, and all the meals he cooks to sustain us, I am grateful and blessed to have Axel in my life.

Lyrics from "I Want to Know What Love Is": Words and lyrics by Mick Jones from the *Agent Provocateur* album (1984).

Lyrics from "Dance Me to the End of Love": Music and lyrics by Leonard Cohen from the *Various Positions* album (1984).

Lyrics from "Why Worry": Music and lyrics by Mark Knopfler from the Dire Straits album *Brothers in Arms* (1985)

About the Author

A former travel media consultant, communications agency principal and penguin herder, Gina Roitman is the author of the collection, *Tell Me a Story, Tell Me the Truth* and co-author of a biography about a globetrotting Montreal businessman: *Midway to China and Beyond.* Gina's essays, short stories and poems have appeared in anthologies and magazines including *Poetica,* the *Forward, Moment,* and *carte-blanche,* and most recently in *Wherever I Find Myself, The New Spice Box,* and *Undead: A Poetry Anthology.* In 2013, the award-winning documentary film *My Mother, the Nazi Midwife and Me,* co-produced with Jane Hawtin, aired for two years on CBC's Doc Channel. She has also written and voiced two radio documentaries for CBC and was commissioned to write several biographies of Holocaust survivors as well as a poem to accompany original music for San Francisco's Pink Triangle Project. Since 2015, she has led numerous memoir-writing workshops for the Quebec Writers' Federation and The Generations After of Greater Washington, DC. *Don't Ask* is Gina's first novel. She lives among the dwindling forests of Quebec's Lower Laurentians.